T0146712

An Excerpt from...

Loves Me, Loves Me Not

He brushed a silken wisp of copper hair away from her face and realized instantly he hadn't forgotten the way it felt: smooth, soft, like liquid flowing through his fingers.

He hadn't forgotten the way it smelled either. He closed his eyes, took a deep breath, remembered vividly how it felt to bury his hands in her hair.

Bonny stirred and groaned.

His eyes flew open. "It's okay, sweetheart. I'm here."

"Timothy?"

Her voice was a low, husky murmur. His eyes dropped automatically to her lips, and he had a sudden urge to kiss her.

"Timothy!"

Too late. Bonny was struggling to sit up, her eyes spitting fire, her lips thinned to a grim line, no longer in the least inviting. She pushed aside the hand he'd reached to help her. "Get—out."

"Sweetheart, I didn't mean—"

"Don't call me sweetheart."

"But—"

"What part of 'get out' don't you understand?"

He hesitated. *Say what you came to say,* an inner voice urged him. Taking a deep breath, he did: "I meant it when I said I'm sorry, Bonny. I'm sorry for everything."

Her expression didn't change. His gaze didn't waver.

"I don't care if I have to crawl over broken glass, Bonny Fairley," he said, suddenly fierce. "I aim to win you back."

Loves Me, Loves Me Not

BARBARA JEAN HICKS

WATERBROOK
PRESS

LOVES ME, LOVES ME NOT
PUBLISHED BY WATERBROOK PRESS
5446 North Academy Boulevard, Suite 200
Colorado Springs, Colorado 80918
A division of Random House, Inc.

The characters and events in this book are fictional, and any resemblance
to actual persons or events is coincidental.

Scripture taken from the *Holy Bible, New International Version*®. NIV® Copyright
© 1973, 1978, 1984 by International Bible Society. Used by permission of Zondervan
Publishing House. All rights reserved. Also quoted, the *New King James Version.* Copyright © 1982 by Thomas Nelson, Inc. Used by permission. All rights reserved.

ISBN-13: 978-1-578-56124-7

Copyright © 2000 by Barbara Jean Hicks

Library of Congress Cataloging-in-Publication Data
Hicks, Barbara Jean.
    Loves me, loves me not / Barbara Jean Hicks.—1st ed.
        p.   cm.
    ISBN 1-57856-124-8
    1. Dating (Social customs)—Fiction. 2. Divorced women—Fiction.
3. Personals—Fiction. I. Title
PS3558.I22976 L68 2000
813'.54—dc21   99-053702

2000—First Edition

146620572

To Betty, Christine, and Daisy Mae—
You are my safe haven.

1

Valentine's Day was not one of Bonny Van Hooten Fairley's favorite holidays. At least not since the divorce.

Hearts and flowers? Bah!

Romance? Not for *her*.

Men? Who needed 'em?

Frowning ferociously, she closed the drawer to the antique cash register with a resounding bang.

"Boss-Lady?"

"What's wrong, Bon-Bon?"

"Wrong?" Bonny peered over the top of her reading glasses at Robin and Rosie, the nineteen-year-old twins who helped her out in the store part-time between their community-college classes. Her nieces now, she had to keep reminding herself. They hadn't been when she'd first hired them. Their mother, Cait—Bonny's best friend—had married her brother, Jack, six weeks ago.

Another reason romance was for the birds, she chafed: It changed people. It changed relationships. She hardly ever got to spend time alone with Cait anymore.

"Nothing's wrong," she snapped.

"Then why the frown?" Rosie pressed.

"Why the drawer banging?" Robin demanded.

Bonny consciously smoothed her expression. She even attempted a smile. No reason to take her foul mood out on the twins.

After a lifetime of looking like clones, Rosie and Robin were finally starting to express their individual personalities. Robin was into the WOB look—wears only black—while Rosie usually chose soft pastels and florals. And while Robin's close-cropped hair was dyed black in dramatic contrast to her naturally pale skin, Rosie had blonde streaks woven through her nutmeg-colored bob and regularly visited the tanning booth at the local beauty salon.

At the moment, however, the twins did wear identical expressions—a combination of concern and wide-eyed curiosity that was almost comical. Or would have been, if Bonny had been in a different frame of mind.

"Look, it's a big day. Okay?"

"Ah," said Robin with a knowing expression. "The day before Valentine's Day."

"And you don't have a date," said Rosie sadly.

Bonny's eyes widened. How did they *do* that?

"Not to worry, Bon-Bon," Rosie added. "We—"

"Spare me the sympathy," Bonny interrupted. "Since when do I worry about not having a date? Valentine's Day or *any* day?"

"But it would be nice—"

"What would be *nice*," she interrupted again, "would be to have employees who thought like professionals. Listen up, twins." She lifted a hand and started counting off on her fingers: "The Keebler-Krueger wedding is tonight. The ad in the *Daily News* came out last night. It's Saturday. And yes, tomorrow is Valentine's Day. All of which should mean floods of customers"—she switched hands and continued counting—"most of whom will need help making up their minds, and every one of whom will want their purchase gift-wrapped. It's a big day."

"Oh," said Robin.

"We're on it," said Rosie. "Or will be. As soon as you open the doors."

"Ka-ching, ka-ching," Robin agreed.

"Good." Bonny slid her spectacles off her nose, frowning at them for a moment before slipping them into the pocket of her slim wool skirt. They added an odd lump to her hip, but she was always losing track of the things, and she wasn't about to wear them around her neck on a chain. It was bad enough she had to *wear* reading glasses. She was only thirty-five, for pity's sake.

Only thirty-five? Pah! How in the world had she gotten to be thirty-five already?

"But about not having a date for Valentine's Day—"

"Enough already, Robin!" Bonny bounced the edge of her hand off her breastbone. "I'm up to *here* with Valentine's Day!"

As a woman who'd been disappointed in love, Bonny would just as soon forget about Valentine's Day. But as owner of the Blue Moon Gallery of Fine Crafts, she couldn't. Not when every February the good saint led a stream of paying customers through her door.

She hated to be so mercenary, but working in retail did that to a person. She had to watch herself at Christmas. The first year in the store she'd been so focused on holiday sales she'd almost forgotten the reason for the season—and the reason for the season was an important part of Bonny's life.

June was almost as big as December at the Blue Moon; the handcrafted items Bonny carried lent themselves to weddings. Mother's Day was always good for business too, and with a little coaxing—an ad in the *Bellingrath Daily News* as well as the *Pilchuck Post,* a loss leader or two, the promise of free gift-wrapping—Valentine's Day could be rewarding. In a financial sense, at least.

In fact, if the past two Februaries were any indication, romance was alive and kicking in the little town of Pilchuck, Washington. Even if it hadn't come anywhere near *Bonny's* door, let alone her heart, for a coon's age.

"We're just trying to say it's a good thing we placed the ad," Robin interrupted her musings.

"I hope so. I hope we give Buds 'n' Blossoms and the Sweet Shoppe a run for their money." Bonny sighed. "People are about as original as peanut butter and jelly about gifts for Valentine's Day. Flowers and candy! Candy and flowers! People need to be nudged, twins. Hence the ads in the *Daily News* and the *Post.*"

3

"Not those ads," said Rosie.

"The one in the *Tillicum Weekly*," Robin explained.

Bonny looked blankly from one twin to the other. She'd thought about placing an ad in the county alternative, but their rates were high. "I didn't advertise in the *Tillicum Weekly*."

"We did," said Rosie, looking extremely pleased with herself.

"In the personals," Robin said proudly. "Today's edition."

"Just in time for Valentine's Day," added Rosie.

"The personals!" And once again Bonny found herself frowning. "How's that supposed to help business?"

"We didn't do it for the business, silly auntie!"

Bonny took a deep breath. Rosie's cheerfulness was beginning to wear.

"Let me get this straight," she said. "The two of you took out a personal ad in the *Tillicum Weekly*. As in 'SWF seeks kindred spirit for moonlit walks,' blah-blah-blah ad nauseam?"

"As in *Loves Music, Loves to Dance*," said Rosie.

Bonny shuddered. She remembered the thriller from a few years back. "If I recall, the guy who placed the personal ad in that story was a serial killer. Tell me you're joking, twins."

"It was just a story, Boss-Lady!"

Bonny shook her head. Serial killer or not—the personal ads? Surely a pair as pretty and outgoing as the Reilly twins didn't need to resort to the personal ads to find dates. Neither had a steady boyfriend, but they had plenty of admirers. Bonny knew. Young men stacked up in the store like excess inventory every shift one or the other twin worked.

"Does your mother know about this?" she asked, rubbing the tip of her nose with her index finger in a habitual gesture that signified, to those in the know, that she was feeling unsettled.

"Mom *and* Uncle Jack," said Rosie.

"And they approve?" she asked.

"You know how much they want you to find a good man, Boss-Lady," Robin said irrelevantly.

Bonny blinked. "A good man? Me? What are you talking about?"

"A boyfriend," she answered patiently, as if her aunt were a little slow.

"Forget a boyfriend," said Rosie. "A *husband!*"

"A husband?" Bonny rubbed her nose with vigor. "You all should know by now I'm not the least bit interested in a husband!"

Old Chief Wooden Face—which was how she not-so-fondly referred in her mind to her ex-husband, Timothy—had pretty much soured her on marriage. In fact, he'd pretty much soured her on men, at least in the context of romance. Brothers, fathers, ex-fathers-in-law, colleagues, friends—sure. Boyfriends, sweethearts, husbands—not if the fate of the universe depended on it.

If she wanted a cigar-store Indian, she'd buy one, thank you. One with wooden legs instead of a wooden face and a wooden heart, so he couldn't make tracks out of town when he decided a wife and a job were just too much responsibility.

She shook her head emphatically. "Uh-uh. No way, twins. Been there, done that. Never again."

Robin and Rosie arched their brows in unison and exchanged a significant glance.

"Denial?" Robin suggested.

Rosie nodded sagely. "Denial. Fear. Probably unresolved anger."

"Excuse me?" Bonny said incredulously. "You've taken one semester of introductory psych, and you're *analyzing* me?"

"One semester of introductory psych and one year of working with you," said Robin.

Bonny winced. She did have a habit of picking people's psyches apart—but only in the interest of understanding them. And helping them out, of course, although they didn't always see it that way.

A student of human behavior—that's how she liked to think of herself. Since her divorce five years ago she'd stocked her personal library with almost as many pop-psychology and self-help tomes as the local bookstore carried. Plus, she read every issue of *Psychology for the New Century* cover to cover as soon as it came, whether she had time or not.

She might not be a professional in the field, but when it came to human behavior, Bonny knew what was what. And she didn't take to a couple of impudent teenagers co-opting her expertise either.

"Humph," she sniffed. "Be that as it may—and I'm not saying it is—I still don't think it's a good idea to go fishing for boyfriends in the personal ads. I can't imagine what Cait and Jack were thinking to encourage you."

"We *all* think you should have a good man," said Rosie.

Bonny threw her hands in the air. "Why does this conversation keep coming back to me?"

The twins looked identically puzzled.

"Because it *is* about you," said Robin.

"About…me?"

The light bulb suddenly flicked on in Bonny's brain. "Oh no."

"Oh, Bon-Bon!" Rosie said, wide-eyed. "You mean you thought we placed the ad for *us?*"

"We're not *that* desperate! We did it for *you,* Boss-Lady."

As if it was generally understood Bonny *was* "that desperate."

"We really do think you deserve a fantastic guy," Rosie added sweetly.

"Deserve—you think—fantastic guy!" Bonny sputtered. "You can't—the *personals?*"

Robin clapped her hands. "We knew you'd be excited!"

"It's gonna be so romantic," Rosie sighed.

Bonny dropped her head in her hands and groaned.

The twins apparently took her groan and her gesture as signs of profound and speechless gratitude.

"It's nothing, really," said Robin modestly.

"We think you're wonderful," Rosie gushed.

"Happy Valentine's Day!" they squealed in unison.

Timothy Fairley had never been so nervous in all his life. Or so certain he was doing the right thing. A lot more certain than he'd been five years ago, for instance, when he'd packed his bags and barreled out of town without a backward glance.

Five years! His palms were so wet they slid along the steering wheel as he exited the freeway. Five irretrievable years, only to come full circle back to Pilchuck, Washington. Back to "the bosom of his family," as his late Grandfather Fairley would have put it.

Back to Bonny. If she'd have him.

His deep sigh elicited a sloppy kiss from the large, tricolored dog of indeterminate parentage who shared the cab of the pickup with him. Ever since he'd announced they were crossing the Tillicum County line half an hour ago, she'd been leaning against his arm like a high-school sweetheart who couldn't get close enough.

"Cleo!" he scolded, swiping at his face with the back of his hand. "Control yourself!" But he really didn't mind. At this point, he'd take what he could get.

He grinned at the dog. "Bet you thought we'd never get here, mutt. Bet you thought I was making Pilchuck up, didn't you?"

She grinned back at him, making a distinctive gurgling sound in the back of her throat.

"That's right, I *wouldn't* lie to you." Timothy massaged Cleo's neck and nodded toward a bank of dense gray clouds to the east as they rounded the curve of the off-ramp. "Trust me on this one, too, girl. It's hard to believe when all you can see is clouds, but over there is the second highest peak in Washington. Mount Balder.

"We'll do some trail runs later in the season to get ready for the Balder-to-Bellingrath at the end of June." The annual relay from the ski lodge on Mount Balder to the ferry dock on Bellingrath Bay drew teams from all over the country. "I always love the mountain leg. Sound fun to you?"

Cleo gurgled happily. She liked to run almost as much as her master did.

Timothy wondered if he could get by Grummond's Easy-Off Easy-On Gas and Auto Doctor without Otto's spotting his old white pickup—the same 1989 Chevy short-cab he'd been driving for ten years, with the same white camper shell. Otto would know it was him.

He sighed. *Any* resident Pilchuckian would know it was him. He was Timothy Fairley, the third generation Fairley of Fairley's Drug and Fountain.

Timothy Fairley, *late* of Fairley's Drug and Fountain, he corrected himself.

He wondered if people would think he was back in town to take up his place in the family business again. He wondered if his father thought so.

He wondered if anyone would guess he was really here for Bonny.

They passed the Riverside Golf Course, its greens flooded as they always were this time of year, and a neat row of greenhouses on the other side of the road into town, new since he'd been here last, their windows reflecting the gray of the Northwest winter day.

It was comforting, somehow, the grayness of the day. He wouldn't even have minded a little drizzle. After the last three years in San Diego—where the natives joked there were only two kinds of days, beautiful and unusual—he missed real weather. Clouds, rain, occasional snow, even the frigid winter northeasters that blew off the Arctic across the Canadian plains and funneled down through the Ruby River valley.

His heart sped up when he saw the carved wooden sign that marked the Pilchuck city limits on the near side of the bridge that led over the river into town: WELCOME TO PILCHUCK.

Was he? Welcome, that is? Welcome to Pilchuck?

Most especially, would he be welcome to Bonny's heart?

Ha. The real question was whether or not his ex-wife would even bother to say hello before she showed him the door—with the toe of her boot, most likely.

Cleo, ever responsive to her master's mood, whined uneasily. Timothy slid a hand off the steering wheel and draped his arm over her back, burying his fingers in her silky fur. "You know what, Clee? You're about the best friend a guy could ask for."

Sighing, he scratched the sweet spot under her chin. "I haven't been totally honest with you, girl," he said as they crossed the bridge. "I don't know what kind of reception we're going to get. What kind of reception *I'm* going to get, I mean. You—everybody's going to love you."

Strictly speaking, he didn't even know if that was true. His parents had never had a dog. When he'd told his mother he was bringing Cleo, she'd seemed a tad reluctant, though she hadn't come right out and said no. Timothy figured she was worried about his father's reaction. There was already enough bad blood between the Fairley men without bringing a dog into the equation, even a dog as sweet-tempered as Cleo.

Bonny, on the other hand, was bound to adore his sweetheart— if he ever got a chance to introduce them. His ex-wife had an extra-tender heart toward animals, especially animals with sad histories like Cleo's. Once she heard that Timothy had found the dog limping, dirty, and half-starved in a parking lot, Bonny would pour out her love and affection on his baby.

Some of which Timothy hoped might slop over onto him. He was no dummy.

Not anymore.

All he needed was a chance to prove it.

2

"Please, Bon-Bon?" Rosie begged. "It's only a block away…"

"It" was the Kitsch 'n' Caboodle Café, the *Tillicum Weekly's* only Pilchuck drop-off point. The alternative paper hit the counter at the local diner every Saturday morning at ten—at least according to the twins, whose sister Cindy waited tables there part-time while she was getting her designer clothing business off the ground.

In truth, Bonny would have liked to be on hand at the Kitsch 'n' Caboodle herself—to snatch up the entire stack of *Tillicum Weekly*s and stuff them in the Dumpster behind the Blue Moon before anyone else could grab one. But the gallery opened for business at ten, and customers were already crowding around the front door.

Besides, it wouldn't have done a bit of good. A fact that made her feel…well, *grumpy*, to put it plainly. And who could blame her, when by the end of the day every last person in Pilchuck would have seen or at the very least heard about the twins' misguided scheme?

Like it or not, even without her name attached to the alleged ad, in this town Bonny would not be anonymous. Especially not with Rosie and Robin involved. At least they'd had the good grace to look sheepish when they told her they "might have mentioned" their brainstorm to "one or two" people: their mom and Jack, their sister Cindy, their best friend, Narcissa…

"And oh, yes! True Marie down at the Belle o' the Ball…"

That was the clincher. The Belle o' the Ball Beauty Salon was Pilchuck's gossip central and True Marie Weatherby its doyenne. Frankly, with True Marie in the know, Bonny didn't understand why she hadn't heard about the twins' project long before this morning.

So in answer to Rosie's pleading, she crossed her arms, glowered, and said in no uncertain terms, "No, no, and in case I haven't made myself clear, *no.*"

"But don't you want to see your ad?"

"*Your* ad," Bonny corrected her.

"But don't you?" Robin took over for Rosie.

Bonny sighed in frustration. "All right. I confess I'm curious. I do want to know how you've..." She paused, searching for the word. "How you've *characterized* me." Both twins claimed they "couldn't remember" exactly what the ad said. "But at the moment, ladies, my curiosity doesn't matter. What does matter"—she uncrossed her arms and pushed the sleeves of her ribbed, plum-colored turtleneck to her elbows—"is that we have a store to open and customers waiting at the door."

With one last look around the gallery while Rosie rolled the vacuum cleaner into the back room, Bonny pasted on her most gracious smile and headed for the door.

Timothy, meanwhile, was still trying to explain the situation to Cleo: "When I left...well, let's just say there were some hard feelings."

An understatement if he'd ever made one. His father had shouted at him in an unusual display of temper. His mother had wept—not at all unusual. And Bonny...

He could see his ex-wife in his mind the way she'd looked the last time he'd seen her: a pillar of fire, her flame-colored hair pouring like molten lava over her shoulders, her brown eyes flashing with fury, her skin practically radiating angry heat. She hadn't condescended to words—hadn't *needed* words—to tell him what she thought of him: *You've broken every promise you ever made me. You've betrayed me. I will never forgive you.*

Without warning Cleo slapped another kiss on Timothy's cheek.

He smiled forlornly. What would he do without Cleo?

She wriggled out from under his arm at the first red light over the bridge and paced the bench seat, her plumed tail wagging joyously. Her master, on the other hand, was having a hard time deciding what the queasy feeling in the pit of his stomach was: excitement, nerves, or just plain unadulterated dread. Whatever it was, joy didn't enter into it.

At this point, he told himself, it didn't really matter much how he was feeling. He was here. He knew what he had to do. All he had to do was do it.

He slowed as he approached the next block. According to Timothy's mother, Bonny's Blue Moon Gallery of Fine Crafts—a place he'd never been, as it hadn't existed until three years ago—was just ahead, on the ground floor of the old First National Bank building. Fairley's Drug and Fountain was another block farther on.

His parents were expecting him. Reese would be in the pharmacy, counting out pills, joking with some old woman who'd been coming to Fairley's since Timothy's grandfather opened the drugstore fifty years ago, reminding her to take her antibiotic with food and to call him at home if she had any trouble…

Donnabelle would be at a desk tucked into a crowded corner, not far from her husband—she never was far from Reese—going over the books or looking through gift catalogs or maybe ordering supplies for the fountain.

But he hadn't told his parents exactly when he'd arrive.

And as much as the idea made his palms sweat—

"I've got to see Bonny," he said to Cleo.

Timothy Fairley had made his peace with God. His mother, too, had forgiven him, and if his father hadn't yet, at least they were communicating again. Sort of.

But his ex-wife…

Up to now Timothy hadn't even tried. He'd been too darned scared. He still was.

He confessed as much to Cleo, who snuffled and looked at him adoringly. That was the wonderful thing about a dog, he thought, sighing. A dog didn't condemn a man for his failures.

"But isn't Bonny the reason I'm here?" he demanded.

Cleo whined.

"Well yes, I do have an interview next week. But I didn't come to Pilchuck for a job, Clee." If all he'd wanted was a job, there were jobs in San Diego. If all he'd wanted was a job, there were jobs in a hundred places in between.

There was, on the other hand, only one Bonny Fidelia Van Hooten Fairley.

With that thought Timothy swerved into the nearest parking space, which just so happened to be directly in front of the Buds 'n' Blossoms flower shop. Lace-trimmed hearts plastered the windows of the store, as they did the windows of the Sweet Shoppe next door.

"Valentine's Day!" he exclaimed. "What could be better?"

Cleo tilted her head and raised her eyebrows, as if asking him to clarify.

"Flowers and candy," he told her confidently. "What woman could resist?"

Bonny held the door wide and greeted her customers by name: "Good morning, Mrs. Pfefferkuchen. Mrs. Thigpen, Camilla, it's nice to see the two of you this morning. Suzie, how're you doing? My word, Lonetta!" And before she could stop herself: "You look like you're ready to pop!"

Lonetta Yates taught science at Pilchuck High School, where Bonny herself had taught before opening the gallery. At the moment, Lonetta looked about nine-and-a-half-months pregnant.

"Thank you so much, Bonny," she said wryly. "You do have a way with words."

"Open mouth—"

"—insert foot," Bonny heard from behind her, one twin finishing the other's quip without a pause between.

She pretended not to hear. "Any luck finding a sub for your classes yet?" she asked Lonetta conversationally. The new mom—the soon-to-be new mom—was planning on taking the rest of the school year and the entire summer to be with her baby full-time. Substitute teachers were easy enough to find, but long-term subs who could handle the science labs Lonetta taught were not.

"Simon's interviewing next week," Lonetta said—Simon Wyatt being the principal at Pilchuck High School. "And just in time, is my guess, even if Doc Ambrose says I have another three weeks to go."

Lonetta and most of the other customers disappeared down the aisles to browse, though the Thigpen mother-daughter duo went straight for the bridal registry table. And a lone young man who'd ventured into the store stood just inside the door, gazing vacantly around the gallery as if he'd wandered into a foreign country. Except for Robin and Rosie, the Blue Moon didn't have much to offer teenage boys.

The twins, of course, both made a beeline for the boy, whose wholesome good looks and air of sweet bewilderment obviously weren't lost on them. Bonny managed to head them off, directing Robin toward the Thigpens at the bridal registry and Rosie toward old pink-haired Mrs. Pfefferkuchen. Bonny herself took the teenage boy in hand. In his state, even one twin would have been overwhelming.

He was looking for a gift for his girlfriend, he told Bonny shyly.

She was wrapping up a pair of hammered-silver earrings she'd helped him pick out when a pretty blonde burst into the shop waving a tabloid. The twins' sister, Cindy, dressed in the pink Capris and white camp shirt that was the uniform at the Kitsch 'n' Caboodle Café.

Bonny's heart sank.

"Bonny! Have you seen it yet? The ad? Oh, isn't this *exciting?*"

"Aren't you supposed to be at work?" Bonny asked balefully.

"I've been working since six. I'm on my break. I knew you wouldn't get a chance to come by for a while, so *voilà!* Here I am!"

She opened the pages of the *Tillicum Weekly* and folded them back. "I've circled it for you. Oh, Bonny! I wonder how soon you'll start getting calls?"

"Calls?" That was Olga Pfefferkuchen, peering around Cindy's shoulder, her turquoise-shadowed eyes squinting at the paper. "Women Seeking Men," she read aloud. Her thin, frail hand flew to her equally thin and frail chest. "Oh my!" she said breathlessly. "Oh my!"

"Bonny! You've placed a personal ad?" That was Suzie Hunt, sounding delighted. "Good for you! Aren't you the brave one!"

"We did it," Rosie piped up. "Robin and me. We knew she'd never do it herself."

"You got that right," Bonny said darkly.

Lonetta Yates suddenly popped around a corner, her rounded belly leading the way. "Now why didn't I ever think of that?" she said. "I set her up on a blind date once," she told the twins, "but a personal ad? It never occurred to me!"

Bonny swallowed. Said blind date, her one and only ever, had been nothing short of excruciating.

"He's no Mel Gibson, but he's really an interesting fellow," Lonetta had told her. She'd been right about the Mel Gibson part, but her friend clearly had a different definition of *interesting* than Bonny did. The guy had shown up on her doorstep wearing a full-length mink coat, taken her by a hot dog stand for dinner, and then escorted her to a yodeling concert.

Excruciating. There was no other word for it.

"Oh, please hurry, Bon-Bon," urged Rosie. "I can't *wait* for you to see it!"

Bonny picked up a pair of scissors and snipped several feet of curling ribbon from a spool on the counter. "You seem to forget why we're here," she said to Rosie. "Now why don't you and Robin—"

"Bonny's busy," Cindy interrupted cheerfully. "I'll read it." She stepped back from the counter to get a better angle of light from the overhead spots, and Bonny missed her chance to grab the paper away.

"Really, I don't think that's necess—"

"The Boss-Lady," Cindy read aloud. She glanced up. "That's the headline."

The Boss-Lady! Bonny's scissors clattered to the counter. She groaned and dropped her head in her hands, curling ribbon forgotten.

"It's like a play on words," Robin explained seriously to the gathering crowd. "Like, you know how *boss* is another word for really cool? Bonny's a cool lady, plus she really is our literal boss."

"What do you think, Bon-Bon?"

Bonny shuddered. At least they hadn't used Rosie's nickname for her. "Really twins, I wish—"

"Listen up now," Cindy intervened. "Here's how it starts: 'Works too hard, would never have written this ad—'"

"You got that right," Bonny said again.

"So we wrote it for her!" the twins quoted in unison.

Bonny pressed her fingertips against her temples. Now, of course, they remembered their silly ad word for word!

"Spunky redhead—"

Bonny's head snapped up. "Spunky!" she wailed. *"Spunky?"*

"It's a word they use a lot in these ads," said Robin matter-of-factly.

"It seemed to fit better than *sweet*," Rosie added.

"And those were your only two choices?"

"Is she spunky or is she not?" Rosie appealed to the gallery customers, almost all of whom seemed to have migrated toward the front counter.

"She is," several voices chimed in together.

"Spunky's not a bad thing, Bonny," Suzie tossed in. "Harrison calls me spunky. It's one of the reasons he fell in love with me."

Rosie sent Bonny a triumphant look.

"Spunky redhead," Cindy tried again, "has head for business, eye for art, heart for God."

"Did you notice the parallel construction, Bonny?" Rosie asked brightly. "'Head for business, eye for art, heart for God.' We learned that in your sophomore English class!"

She groaned again. Something *else* she'd taught the twins only to have them use it against her! And to think she'd always worried she wasn't getting through.

"Good work, twins," Lonetta put in, her tone admiring. "Elegant and succinct. You packed a lot in that sentence and made it pretty."

"We only had thirty-five words to work with altogether," said Rosie.

"More than thirty-five words would have cost us extra," Robin explained.

"If Bonny wasn't such a technophobe, we could have got e-mail service added for free."

Bonny folded her arms over her chest. "I am not a technophobe!"

True, she didn't use a computerized cash register. She didn't even use a modern one. She loved the antique National she'd salvaged from the Shoe Tree when Mr. Pederson had gone out of business. Partly because Mr. Pederson had salvaged it from an earlier Apple Basket Market remodel.

Her cash register had a *history.* And was elegant to boot, unlike some ugly putty-colored box with half a dozen cords protruding out the back—though she did have one of those hidden away in her office for bookkeeping and inventory. She wasn't stupid.

But as for e-mail—

"I just prefer something a little more personal," she said. "And verifiable."

"How's snail mail more verifiable than e-mail?" Robin challenged.

"Postmarks. At least you know where your mail's coming from. Besides, I don't like all that misinformation floating around out there in cyberspace."

"What misinformation?"

"See? You don't know. Nobody knows. Anybody can say whatever they darn well please—true or false, right or wrong."

Robin must have decided that prolonging the argument would be about as effective as barking at the moon. "Anyhow—we ended up just doing the voice-mail part. A blind box for letters would have cost extra too."

LOVES ME, LOVES ME NOT

"Bonny doesn't pay us that much," Rosie added.

"Hint, hint," said Robin, arching an eyebrow at Bonny.

"It's a good thing you put in that part about having a heart for God," Suzie told the twins. "That should weed out some undesirables."

Undesirables! Bonny stared at Suzie in disbelief. Didn't she get it? Didn't *any* of them get it? She didn't *want* a boyfriend. They were *all* undesirables!

"Keep reading," Rosie pressed Cindy, her voice eager.

Cindy did, with feeling: "An all-American beauty."

Bonny groaned again.

"We thought of putting 'a real babe'—" Robin started.

"—but we decided it might attract a bad element," Rosie finished.

"All-American beauty's better," Suzie agreed.

Olga Pfefferkuchen reached over and laid a wrinkled hand on Bonny's smooth one. "And you *are* a beauty, young lady," she said. "Don't you let anyone tell you different either. Why, those freckles are hardly noticeable—really, dear, they blend right in."

Suddenly every freckle on Bonny's face—and there was more than a smattering—stood out like paprika on mashed potatoes. At least she imagined they did. Her hands flew involuntarily to her suddenly burning cheeks, as if to hide the hideous flaws.

"Especially when you're blushing," added Olga.

Cindy held up a hand. "One last line, everyone. You ready for this?" She grinned at Bonny. "'Needs a good man!' Exclamation point and all."

Bonny's mouth dropped open. And then snapped shut again.

Something else snapped too. She couldn't have stopped herself if she'd tried: "I DO NOT NEED A GOOD MAN!"

She knew instantly she really should have tried. For one thing, the twins exchanged that knowing look again. They'd never let her hear the end of it. For another, Camilla Thigpen, who was not one of Bonny's favorite teenagers, had a gleam in her eye that said no one in *Pilchuck* would ever hear the end of it.

Finally, the young man who'd been waiting patiently for his

girlfriend's earrings through Cindy's entire recital jumped like a bull-frog poked with a stick—and looked just about as bulbous-eyed. Poor kid. Bonny would be surprised if he ever set foot in the Blue Moon again. *You mean that place where the crazy redhead works?* she could almost hear him say. *No thanks! I'll take my chances at Wal-Mart!*

What he said now was, "Never mind the ribbon." And grabbing his purchase before Bonny could say "Thank you and please come again," he was out the door.

To the rest of her audience—and by this time every eye in the store was riveted on her—Bonny said firmly, "I apologize for losing it, ladies. But if any one of you thinks I plan to follow through with this crazy scheme, here's my final word: *no.* About as likely as—" She stopped, wanting the comparison to be a zinger. "About as likely as my ex-husband walking through that door!"

She pointed dramatically. Every head swiveled. Said door opened and a man walked in. Tall, athletic, mid-thirties—though he had a shock of silver hair Mrs. Pfefferkuchen would have died for. He carried a bouquet of multicolored daisies and a heart-shaped white satin box.

"Timothy!" Bonny gasped, and promptly fainted.

3

"Sweetheart!"

Timothy jumped into action the instant he saw Bonny's eyes glaze over, the endearment slipping out as naturally as if he'd been saying it every day since he'd walked out of her life.

He knew that look. She'd swooned on him before—most notably right in the middle of their wedding ceremony. At the very moment he'd slipped the gold band on her finger and told her, gazing into her beautiful eyes, "With this ring, I thee wed."

He'd teased her about it for years. Until he'd stopped teasing her at all. Practically stopped talking to her.

Fortunately for Bonny, one of her clerks was standing behind the counter with her when she keeled over. Unfortunately for the clerk, Bonny took the girl down with her. But Timothy could move like lightning, and he was squatting beside them almost before they hit the floor, the candy and flowers he'd been carrying biting the dust along the way.

The clerk untangled her limbs from Bonny's and sat up, looking dazed. The girl's skin looked unnaturally pale, but perhaps that was only because her close-cropped hair was unnaturally black. At least she was moving, which was more than could be said for her boss.

Timothy quickly checked Bonny's pulse and breathing, just to be sure. If she followed pattern, she'd come around shortly, none the worse for wear. He glanced at the waif who sat across from him, brushing dust from her loose tunic and the skinny leggings she had tucked into clunky work boots—black from head to foot. "You all right?" he asked.

"I think so..."

"What about Bonny?" a breathless, anxious voice came from behind him. "Should I call 911?"

Bonny groaned before Timothy could answer. He reached a hand to stroke her cheek as her eyes fluttered open. "It's okay, sweetheart," he soothed, tenderness welling up inside him.

She sighed and closed her eyes again, a smile playing at the corners of her mouth. Which meant either she was glad to see him or she wasn't completely conscious yet.

"She'll be all right," he said, glancing over his shoulder at the questioner. He started. The young woman hovering over him had the same dark eyes and the same winsome features as the clerk who still sat on the floor across from him, but her sun-streaked hair and flowing, pastel-flowered dress were at the opposite end of the fashion scale. Plus, her skin was a golden shade a resident Pilchuckian got only from a tanning booth or a month in the Bahamas.

"A glass of water should do it," he told her, barely missing a beat. They had to be the Reilly twins—all grown up since the last time he'd seen them but still cute as kittens.

Bonny let out another long sigh. Timothy took one of her hands between his own and lifted it to his cheek. "You'll be fine, sweetheart."

It wasn't exactly the reception he'd been hoping for—Bonny's fainting the moment she set eyes on him. Then again, it wasn't the reception he'd been dreading either. At least she hadn't booted him out, and his flowers and candy after him—something she was certainly capable of doing. She did have the temper to go with her hair.

Speaking of which, even if only to himself, he'd forgotten exactly how beautiful that hair was. Long, shiny, copper-penny hair that begged to be touched.

How could he not obey? He brushed a silken wisp away from her face and realized instantly he hadn't forgotten the way it felt: smooth, soft, like liquid flowing through his fingers.

He hadn't forgotten the way it smelled either; she was still using that tropical coconut-sandalwood shampoo he'd always loved. He

LOVES ME, LOVES ME NOT

closed his eyes and took a deep breath, remembering vividly how it felt to bury his hands in her hair.

Bonny stirred and groaned again.

His eyes flew open. "It's okay, sweetheart. I'm here."

"Timothy?"

Her voice was a low, husky murmur. His eyes dropped automatically to her lips, and he had a sudden urge to kiss her. She'd always had the softest, sweetest, most responsive lips...

"Timothy!"

Too late. Bonny was struggling to sit up, her eyes not only open but spitting fire, her lips thinned to a grim line, no longer in the least inviting.

"Bon-Bon! Are you okay?" It was the blonder, tanner twin, leaning over her with a paper cup filled to the brim with water. Timothy reached for it just as Bonny pulled herself into a sitting position and answered the question with an extremely snappish "I'm *fine!*"

An instant later the paper cup was rolling across the floor, and Bonny was dripping wet and howling: "Ahrgh, ahrrggh, *ahhrrggh!*"

Timothy, quick enough to have leaped to his feet when her arm knocked against his, bit his lip to keep from grinning. She was a sight. She was also the only person he knew outside the funny papers who said things like *ahrgh, bah, oof,* and even, on occasion, *oh, pshaw!*

But he knew better than to tease her at the moment. Bonny was in no mood. He swallowed his mirth and reached a hand to help her up. "Sweetheart! I'm so sorry!"

She shrugged off his hand as if it were some particularly repugnant insect and struggled to her feet on her own. Timothy stared down at her upturned face—she was tall, but he was a good head taller—and once again had to bite his lip to keep from laughing. Cliché or not, "mad as a wet hen" was the perfect description of his ex-wife. Mad as a wet Rhode Island Red, to get specific.

Bonny's eyes narrowed even further. "Get—out." Her voice was dangerously calm.

"Sweetheart, I didn't mean—"

"Don't call me sweetheart."

"But—"

"What part of 'get out' don't you understand?"

Timothy's silent mirth dissolved. It was the reception he'd been dreading after all.

Say what you came to say, an inner voice urged him.

"I meant it when I said I'm sorry, Bonny. I'm sorry for everything."

Her expression didn't change. His gaze didn't waver.

"I don't care if I have to crawl over broken glass, Bonny Fairley," he said, his voice edged with steel. "I aim to win you back."

The shop bell echoed eerily as Timothy walked through the door and closed it deliberately behind him. His final words hung in the air like heavy perfume. A *skunk's* perfume, Bonny told herself fiercely. The odious words had turned her lungs inside out and left her gasping. Thank goodness she had the excuse of her near-drowning as a cover.

For a moment no one said a word. Rosie handed Bonny a paper towel, in which she immediately buried her face. She didn't need to see Timothy Fairley's backside to know what it looked like, thank you. The jerk. The coward.

"Whoa." Someone finally broke the silence. Then everyone started talking at once.

It was all about Timothy too, Bonny thought resentfully. You'd think nobody had a clue in the world he was the guy who'd torn out her heart and drop-kicked it halfway across the county. Here she was, dripping wet, trembling, practically traumatized, for pity's sake, and no one even bothering to ask if she was all right. Not even the twins.

Rosie, in fact, was fanning herself with her hand as if it were mid-July in New Mexico. "Wow! And I do mean wow!" Her tongue might as well have been hanging out of her mouth, Bonny thought, disgusted.

"He's *gorgeous!* " Robin breathed.

"I'll say," Lonetta agreed. "Whoof! I'd forgotten, Bonny."

"It's that hair," said Suzie, sounding almost worshipful.

Bonny closed her eyes. As if that would help, when Timothy's image was imprinted on her brain. He'd started going gray—or silver, to be more accurate—at eighteen, like his mother. His hair was striking, she admitted grudgingly. Especially with his Southern California tan.

"And those eyes," Cindy added, her voice dreamy.

The silver-blue of moonlight, Bonny remembered unwillingly. That's how she'd always thought of Timothy's eyes. Romantic fool that she'd been…

"Handsome is as handsome does," she said darkly.

"He has such wonderful presence," Rosie enthused, ignoring Bonny's comment.

"Yeah, right. Like a cigar-store Indian has presence," she muttered. Although, come to think of it…

No. She didn't *want* to think of it. "Cindy, shouldn't you be getting back to work?" She tossed her soggy paper towel into the wastebasket behind the counter. "I know the twins and I need to."

"I guess you won't be answering any *Tillicum Weekly* personal ads," Cindy said instead of answering Bonny's question. She folded the tabloid in her hands and tucked it under one arm. "Not with your ex-husband back in town."

"Not with your ex-husband back in town and set on getting you back," said Lonetta.

"Even if he has to crawl over broken glass!" Suzie said, still sounding worshipful.

"I like a man who knows what he wants and isn't afraid to say it," Olga Pfefferkuchen put in.

"*I* like a man who brings his sweetheart flowers and candy," Suzie said.

"Unoriginal," Bonny muttered. And then more forcefully, "I am *not* his sweetheart."

Suzie laid an exquisite bouquet of rainbow-colored gerbera

daisies and a heart-shaped box of candy on the countertop and continued as if she hadn't heard: "He dropped these when you fainted, Bonny."

"You should have seen him leap to your rescue," said Cindy, sighing. "Like Superman."

Groaning, Bonny planted her elbows on the counter and dropped her head into her hands. Didn't they get it? Didn't one single solitary person in the entire place remember that Timothy Fairley had broken his vows, betrayed her trust, broken her heart?

"I'd better be getting back to the Kitsch 'n' Caboodle," Cindy said. Finally. "Biddy'll be wondering."

Cindy's boss wouldn't be wondering long, though, Bonny thought grimly. Not after Cindy got back to the diner with the scoop on Timothy Fairley. Timothy back in Pilchuck was even bigger news than the twins' taking out a personal ad for Bonny. It wouldn't be long before True Marie got hold of it too. By the end of the day, everyone in town would know that Timothy was home again.

Not to stay, of course. Not Timothy. Maybe he'd come home for his mother's birthday—though why now, when he'd missed the last five, Bonny couldn't imagine. It wasn't one of the big 0's or anything—not till next year. Donnabelle Fairley would turn fifty-nine next Saturday.

In the old days, Bonny and Timothy had always taken Donnabelle and Reese to dinner at the Inn at Lummi-Ah-Moo—Tillicum County's only four-star restaurant—for Donnabelle's birthday. For the last five years, in Timothy's absence, Reese had taken Donnabelle and Bonny. But if Timothy was going to tag along this year...

She'd just have to find another way to wish her ex-mother-in-law a happy birthday, Bonny told herself.

"What on earth is he *doing* here?" she muttered, not even aware she'd asked the question aloud till Rosie answered:

"Trying to win back your heart, Bon-Bon."

Bonny gave her a withering look.

"What? That's what he said."

Suzie nodded. "It is what he said. Maybe he's seen the error of his ways, Bonny. Maybe he *has* come back to reconcile. Wouldn't that be wonderful? Like the Prodigal Son."

"Like the prodigal *husband*," Robin said.

"The Almighty does work miracles," Olga Pfefferkuchen declared.

Bonny shook her head in despair. They didn't get it. Not one of them. Feeble-minded romantic fools, every one, like she herself had been once upon a time. From high school all the way through the first few years of their marriage, as a matter of fact.

Until Timothy unexpectedly contracted a virulent case of the seven-year itch.

Until he'd brought up the ugly *D* word…and then gone through with it.

She didn't know what in the world was going on in that tiny little pea brain of his that he'd tell her in front of a host of witnesses that he aimed to win back her heart. It wasn't true, of course. Timothy wasn't back in Pilchuck for her. Not after all this time.

Whatever his reasons, at least he wouldn't be staying long—thank the good Lord. He'd made it abundantly clear before he left town five years ago that he'd never live in a "backwater, backwoods town like Pilchuck" ever again. It was about the only thing he *had* said with respect to his leaving.

He must have a job somewhere, she told herself. He couldn't have more than a week or two of vacation…

The nerve of him—showing up in town. Showing up in her gallery!

"Wait!" she called after Cindy, who was on her way out the door.

She picked up the flowers, the warm yellows, apricots, roses, and scarlets vivid against the deep green leather fern. In the middle of all that color nestled a single white blossom. She felt a pang. Timothy still remembered that gerbera daisies were her favorites. And as always he'd included one white flower in the center of the bouquet. If she'd given him a chance, he'd have plucked it out and handed it to her, urged her to pull off the petals one by one: *He loves me, he loves me not…* And if she had, the last petal would have fallen with "He loves me."

At least it had in the past. Always. As if he'd arranged it.

But that was before he'd gone cigar-store Indian on her. "He loves me" no longer applied.

She thrust the daisies toward Cindy. "Here. Take these flowers back to the Kitsch 'n' Caboodle with you."

"The Kitsch 'n' Caboodle!"

Bonny raised her chin in a certain Van Hooten way that signaled to everyone who knew her she'd made up her mind about something and no one had better try to change it. "Somebody might as well enjoy them. If you don't take them, they're going in the trash."

"The trash!" Robin and Rosie cried in unison, their voices identically horrified.

"And Suzie, open that box of candy and pass it around. Pecan caramels, if I'm not mistaken. It would be a shame to waste pecan caramels. Oh, Cindy, by the way—where's that copy of the *Tillicum Weekly?*"

"Here," said Cindy, pulling it out from under her arm. "But Bonny—"

"The twins went to a lot of trouble for me. I think I owe it to them to give it the old college try. As a matter of fact"—she shook open the paper and glowered at her entire contingent of customers over the top of it—"I've decided that meeting a few good men through the personal ads might be just what the doctor ordered."

"But Bonny—"

"*Just* what the doctor ordered," she repeated emphatically, pretending to scan the blurry columns.

She wasn't about to ruin the effect of her newfound resolve by stopping to fish her glasses out of her pocket.

4

Cleo greeted her master with a whimper and a soulful look, as if she knew things hadn't gone well. Timothy ran his hand down the dog's silky back and plumed tail, drawing comfort from the contact, before he backed out of the parking slot and headed down the street toward the pharmacy.

They were parked in front of Fairley's Drug and Fountain, however, before he could bring himself to share the details. Cleo's sympathy was gratifying, if a little sloppy—she would have lapped him to death if he hadn't held her off.

Not that being lapped to death didn't have a certain appeal at the moment.

"I hate to keep you cooped up another minute, girl," he said, giving her a final scratch behind the ears. "But it can't be helped. I promise I'll make it up to you later." A good run ought to do it, he thought, and maybe a juicy bone from the butcher at the Apple Basket Market.

He reluctantly got out of the truck, wishing he could postpone the reunion with his parents at least until after a long, hard run and a long, hot shower to work out his tension. A man could take only so much emotion in one morning.

But if the news of his arrival in Pilchuck reached his parents before he did, he knew his mother would be hurt, which wouldn't do. And wouldn't help his case with his father either. Personally, he didn't see how after five years away another two hours could make much difference, but Reese and Donnabelle wouldn't see it that way.

When he pushed through the door of the pharmacy a moment later, on the other hand, the expression on his mother's face made him glad he hadn't waited. She wasn't just happy to see him; she was ecstatic—a welcome change after his encounter with Bonny. Donnabelle, like Cleo, had no agenda except to love him. Her hug didn't say "I love you even though you've hurt me." It said "I love you." Period.

In fact, he mused, his mother loved him as if he'd *never* hurt her. The way he'd finally come to understand that the God of the universe loved him.

Would Bonny ever be able to love him that way? Or would the hurt always stand between them, the way it still stood between Timothy and his father?

Reese wasn't outwardly hostile toward his son, but he wasn't exactly friendly either. He descended from his glass box at the back of the pharmacy briefly—long enough to ask Timothy how the trip had been, whether he'd had snow over the Siskiyous, how the dog had traveled. Then he shook Timothy's hand and retreated to his glass box to "take care of business."

His father just wasn't a touchy-feely sort of person, Timothy tried to console himself. And he'd never been easy to read.

The acorn doesn't fall far from the tree, does it? an inner voice taunted.

That had been Bonny's major complaint the last year of their marriage: that Timothy didn't talk to her, that she never had any idea what he was thinking or how he was feeling, that he hid behind his shrug and his carefully schooled expression just the way his father did. "You might as well be a cigar-store Indian," she fumed. "You show about as much feeling! *Talk* to me, Timothy!"

But he hadn't. He couldn't. And now that he finally wanted to...

How was he ever going to get her to listen?

His mother insisted on making him an ice-cream treat at the fountain. Timothy didn't often resort to banana splits anymore. But in earlier times a Fairley's Famous Banana Fudge Royale had been the remedy of choice for almost anything that ailed him—and right now, he could use a cure-all.

Donnabelle kept up a happy chatter while she worked, catching him up on local politics and gossip—much of which he already knew. He'd been telephoning his mother fairly regularly for the last year or so. Apparently she didn't remember what she had and hadn't told him.

There'd been a rash of weddings since he'd been gone, the latest being that of Bonny's brother, Jack, and the Reilly twins' widowed mother, Cait—Bonny's closest friend. Cait's oldest daughter Cindy was married now too, to the heir of the Strawbridge & Fitz department store chain. Quite the coup for a small-town girl, Timothy thought.

"How's the Kitsch 'n' Caboodle surviving without Cindy?" he asked.

"Oh, she's still there part-time," Donnabelle said as she added a scoop of rocky-road ice cream to the French vanilla already in the dish. "Franklin hasn't come into his inheritance yet. But when he does, the Kitsch 'n' Caboodle will have to get along without Cindy. She'll want to concentrate entirely on Glad Raggs."

"Glad Raggs?"

"Designer gowns. Miniver Macready won't wear anything *but* a Cindy Fitz original these days." Miniver was Tillicum County's resident celebrity, a world-class concert pianist who lived in Bellingrath when she wasn't touring. "Doesn't have anything to do with Miniver being Franklin's aunt either—she was wearing Cindy's designs before Cindy ever met Franklin. Cindy's a real talent, Timothy."

Suzie Wyatt had married another out-of-towner, Donnabelle told him, "though he does have Tillicum County roots. Harrison Hunt, his name is. A writer and a scholar. His grandmother was a Hokanvander." Hokanvanders, as Timothy knew, had been among the earliest settlers of the area.

"And tonight," she added as she sprinkled walnuts across the top of her ice-cream concoction, "our honest-to-goodness Tillicum

County tycoon, Garson Krueger, is marrying one of the Keebler girls. Her parents don't seem to mind, even though Garson's old enough to be her father."

Not to mention bald and potbellied, Timothy thought. But he was as rich as old Croesus. Garson Krueger was a coup for the entire Keebler family.

Thank goodness the marriage bug hadn't bitten Bonny, Timothy told himself. Yet. "Mom…"

"Hmm?" She set the sundae in front of him proudly, the way he used to set bouquets of dandelions and clover in front of her when he was a kid. He lifted his spoon but tapped it absently against his hand instead of digging in.

"Is Bonny seeing anyone special?"

"No. At least not that I know of. You get to be a certain age in Pilchuck—at least if you're a woman—and the pickings get mighty slim. Believe me, Bonny was *not* interested in Garson Krueger."

Timothy's heart tripped. "You mean he tried?"

"She's a very attractive woman, Timothy."

"I know she is." He sighed. "*Do* I know!"

Donnabelle smoothed back the silver hair that Timothy had inherited and settled her blue gaze on his face. "Just to warn you—I don't think she's going to see the pickings as any improved with you back in town."

He dropped his eyes to the ice-cream dish and dug in his spoon. "I know. I stopped by to see her on my way here."

"I take it she didn't roll out the red carpet."

"Ha."

A bell rang somewhere behind him in the store. His mother wiped her hands on a damp bar towel. "You've been away a long time, Timothy."

Not long enough for Bonny, he told himself ruefully.

"Kimberlee needs me at the register," she added, coming around from behind the counter. "You enjoy your ice cream, dear. I'll be back when I can."

"Thanks, Mom."

He twirled his seat around, the way he used to do, before lifting a spoonful of ice cream, banana, and hot fudge to his mouth. Then, spoon in hand, he picked up one of his father's crossword-puzzle magazines from the stack at the end of the counter and flipped through it as he ate. The logic puzzles—Reese's favorites—were all filled in, but the crosswords were available for anyone who wanted to while away a little time at the fountain.

He closed the magazine and pushed it aside, sighing. Time was such a funny thing, he thought. Sitting at the counter of Fairley's Fountain, eating a Banana Fudge Royale, he felt almost as if the clock had rolled backward and he was a child again.

But he wasn't a child. He was a man. He'd *become* a man since he'd left this town.

He'd been so unhappy those last few years he'd lived in Pilchuck—and so convinced his unhappiness had been everyone's fault but his own. If only he could get out! If only he could get away from the small-minded small-town people who were holding him down. If only he could escape their plans, their expectations, their *demands*—he'd be able to find the happiness he deserved.

He hadn't, of course. Not until he'd stopped blaming everyone else and started taking responsibility for his own choices. That was the distance he'd come.

Could he have learned the lessons he'd needed to learn some other way? Some way that would have been easier on his parents and Bonny? He didn't know. He only knew it was time to make things right again.

"Well?" His mother's voice broke into his ruminations. She sat down on the stool next to him and gestured toward the banana split. "As good as you used to make 'em?"

"Mmm..." He closed his eyes and rolled the ice cream around on his tongue for a moment, losing himself in the combination of flavors and then in the sudden flash of memories they evoked. He himself behind the counter, for one: a skinny, bespectacled, pimply-faced kid creating his own masterpiece Banana Fudge Royales for Fairley's customers. Starting out in the family business the same way his father had before him.

"Better," he said. He reached for his mother's hand and squeezed it lightly. "Because you made it for me, Mom."

Tears sprang to her eyes. Timothy shifted uncomfortably and dropped his gaze, giving her hand a final squeeze before letting it go. His heart felt enormously heavy as he carved out a piece of fudge-drizzled banana, dipped the edge of the spoon into the rocky road ice cream, and brought it to his mouth.

Funny—the Fairley's Famous Banana Fudge Royale was just as delicious as he remembered, but it didn't seem to be working the way it had when he was a kid.

Some things even hot fudge couldn't fix.

"Bye, now! Happy Valentine's Day! Be sure to come back for our Presidents' Day Sale next weekend, you hear?"

Bonny locked the door behind her last customer and fished her reading glasses out of her pocket as she retreated behind the counter to close the till. Thank goodness the store had been hopping with customers right up through closing. All those last-minute wedding and Valentine shoppers she'd been counting on had come through for her. She'd needed the business—and she'd needed to be too busy to think about Timothy Fairley.

The big question now was what she was going to do this *evening* not to think about Timothy Fairley. A year ago she would have invited herself across the street for dinner and a video, but she rarely did that anymore—not with Cait and Jack still practically newlyweds. Besides, Jack was taking Cait out tonight for Valentine's Day. What a fool for romance *he* was turning out to be!

Cait just wasn't available to Bonny in the way she had been pre-Jack, Bonny told herself, though she did try. Today, for instance, she'd come by the Blue Moon the minute she'd heard about Timothy, just to make sure Bonny was all right...

She sighed. Too bad the twins hadn't put her personal ad in *last* week's *Tillicum Weekly*. Maybe she'd have a date for tonight.

"What am I thinking?" she muttered to herself as she stacked and straightened the charge slips and laid them to one side.

"What *are* you thinking?"

Bonny started. "Oh! Robin, don't sneak up on me that way!"

"Sneak? In these clodhoppers?"

She had a point. It was hard not to hear Robin coming.

The twin shrugged into her jacket—black, of course—and eyed her aunt curiously. "So?"

"So what?"

"So what are you thinking?" she asked impatiently. "Really, Boss-Lady, sometimes you are so not there!"

"Well, *duh,* Robin! Who would be? After this morning?"

That was Rosie, who really had sneaked up behind them in her soft-soled ballet slippers. Ridiculous shoes to wear to work when she was on her feet all day, Bonny thought with unwarranted irritation. As ridiculous as Robin's heavy work boots.

"Not another word about this morning," she said darkly. "This morning didn't happen. And I am *not* thinking about *him.*"

"Who?" they asked in unison, pretending innocence.

Her lips thinned. "No one. Aren't you both supposed to be somewhere?"

"Nowhere so important we'd desert our favorite auntie in her hour of need," said Robin, dimpling.

"Want to talk about it?" Rosie said, oozing compassion.

Bonny crossed her arms and glared at them. "Very funny. If you want to play armchair therapist, practice on each other, twins. You might start out with why you both feel so compelled to run my life!"

"Aw, come on, Boss-Lady," Robin said cheerfully, undaunted by Bonny's irritation. "You know we only want you to be happy."

"And man! Does that ex-husband of yours look like he could make you happy!" Rosie sighed. "But if you want to go for it with the personal ad—"

"Go," Bonny interrupted, pointing at the front door. "Scram. Vamoose. Get outta here. Robin, I'll see you tomorrow."

They went, Rosie tossing over her shoulder, "By the way, you might want to check out the message we left on your *Tillicum Weekly* voice mail."

"Oh—I almost forgot," Robin added. "We used your birthday as your access code. Month and day. So you can get your messages, I mean. Have fun, Boss-Lady."

Bonny barely heard them. She was too busy thinking about that first glimpse of Timothy walking through her door this morning, and the way her heart had jumped, and the way all the blood had seemed to rush from her head.

She was thinking how much like that she'd felt on her wedding day when he'd gazed into her eyes and placed the gold band on her finger and tenderly said, "With this ring I thee wed."

She was thinking how unfair it was—and how infuriating—that he could still make her feel that way.

Timothy had supper ready for his parents when they arrived at their old farmhouse a mile outside of town. Nothing fancy—with lasagna from the freezer section, Caesar salad in a bag, and garlic bread already buttered, seasoned, and ready to warm, the Apple Basket Market made a home-cooked meal easy. A home-*assembled* meal, at least.

So easy that the delighted surprise that transformed his mother's tired face when she walked in the door almost made him feel like a fraud. Especially when she exclaimed, "Timothy! You've been slaving over a hot stove all afternoon, haven't you?"

"You should see the blisters," he teased. He helped her out of her coat and hung it on the hall tree.

His father cleared his throat. "Your mother and I planned on taking you out to dinner tonight."

Timothy felt his hackles rise. A simple statement, but somehow it felt like criticism.

"To welcome you home," his mother said soothingly, as if she could read his mind. She placed an arm around Timothy's waist and gave him a quick squeeze. "But we can do that another time."

"Where's the dog?" Reese asked, as if it related to anything. Timothy couldn't tell if he was really interested in Cleo or if he just couldn't think of anything else to say.

"Back porch. Chewing happily on a bone from the butcher at the Apple Basket." He hesitated. "Would you like to meet her before we sit down to supper?"

"You go ahead," his mother urged her husband. "I want to freshen up a bit."

When Timothy opened the door to the enclosed back porch, Cleo abandoned her bone and leaped to her feet, grinning from ear to ear, plumed tail wagging. "Arf!"

"Arf yourself," was Reese's surprising response. When he reached out his hand, Cleo bounded across the room, ears flopping and tongue hanging out of her mouth.

Watching Cleo run always startled Timothy. She was distinctly canted from left to right, which gave the impression she was aiming for some spot fifteen degrees off to the side of her target. At the moment, though she was racing toward Reese, she looked to be on a collision course with the washing machine.

"Hey, girl." Reese surprised Timothy by kneeling in front of her, accepting a blitz of wet kisses—bone-breath and all—and scratching Cleo under the chin in the exact spot she most liked to be scratched. She sighed and stared at him with the adoration she normally reserved for Timothy.

His mother appeared in the doorway. "What's that funny wheezing noise she's making?"

"A sigh of contentment, Mom. She has quite the vocabulary—it won't take you long to figure it out. At least not if you're as smart as she is," he teased.

Donnabelle didn't see the humor. "How are you going to find a place to live with a big dog like that?" she worried. "Landlords don't like pets, Timothy." And then, as if it mattered, "She isn't very pretty, is she?"

"Mom! You're going to hurt her feelings."

His mother snorted.

Reese looked up. "Don't laugh, Belle. Dogs know. Had a dog once knew more'n I did, seemed to me." He turned back to Cleo. "That was old Hambone, girl. Grinned the way you do."

Timothy stared at his father, dumbfounded. You lived with a person most of your life, you thought you knew him…

"There's a place by the stove you can lay out her blanket," his father said, giving Cleo one last scratch under the chin.

"Oh, Reese, are you sure?" Timothy's mother didn't sound happy.

"Back porch is cold in February. Let's eat."

Timothy grinned at Cleo. If she could charm a stubborn old coot like his father…

"You're meeting Bonny, Clee," he whispered. "As soon as possible!"

5

If there was one thing Bonny had learned from all the self-help books she'd read since Timothy had left her, it was that getting her needs met—including feeling loved and nurtured—was her own responsibility.

Which was why on her way home from work later that evening she stopped at the Apple Basket Market for a salmon steak, fresh asparagus—a pleasant surprise this time of year—a package of her favorite wild rice mix, and a bottle of imported sparkling water. And why once she was home, before she even thought about fixing dinner, she poured herself a glass of the effervescent beverage, drew a hot bath, lit candles around the rim of the tub, put a Leggett Lee jazz tape in her boom box, and sank into lavender-scented bubbles up to her neck.

Most of her life—predivorce, that is—the idea of nurturing herself had never crossed her mind. She hadn't had to think about such things. Hubbard and Mickey Van Hooten had lavished affection on their only daughter, born a dozen years after their only son. Bonny had missed them terribly since they'd retired to Arizona to relieve Mickey's debilitating allergies to Pilchuck's double scourge, mold and mildew. She'd missed them even more after Timothy left. Thank goodness she hadn't lost her in-laws along with her husband.

And of course there was Jack, although until recently their relationship had been mostly long-distance. According to Bonny's mother, Jack had adored his baby sister from the moment she wrapped a tiny hand around one of his fingers and hung on. It was a good thing he left home when she was five, her father used to tease, or she would have been spoiled rotten.

Bonny didn't know about that. Maybe if Jack had been around to look after her, she wouldn't have fallen in love with Timothy Fairley.

She sighed, knowing Jack couldn't have done a thing about her falling in love with Timothy Fairley. From the day he'd decked Simon Wyatt for calling her "Spreckle-Face" when she was a hypersensitive thirteen-year-old, Timothy had knocked Luke Skywalker right out of the running for her heart. And Simon—who she realized years later had been flirting with her in the only way he knew how—had never had a chance.

She didn't go *out* with Timothy, of course. For one thing, her conservative parents wouldn't have allowed it at her age. For another thing, in those days he was terminally shy, especially with girls. Especially with smart, funny, pretty girls—and Bonny, he'd finally gotten around to telling her, was the smartest, funniest, prettiest girl he'd ever known.

By that time he'd finished two years of his five-year pharmacy program, she'd graduated from high school and was on her way to the same university in the fall, and they'd worked together at Fairley's Drug and Fountain for two summers already—Timothy as his father's intern and Bonny as clerk and cashier.

How sweet and wonderful that third summer together had been!

For the duration of their long courtship—they didn't marry for another three years—Timothy had been as caring, attentive, and indulgent as she'd ever dreamed a man could be. And she, in response, had been caring, attentive, and indulgent in return. Most of their marriage had been more of the same. They'd taken responsibility for nurturing each other. For taking care of each other. The way partners in a happy marriage did.

Sitting at her kitchen table in a long T-shirt, warm leggings, and her fluffy, cream-colored robe, waiting for the fish to finish broiling, Bonny asked herself for probably the millionth time in the last five years why Timothy had stopped taking care of her. Stopped loving her.

Sometimes, especially after she'd just finished reading a self-help book or an issue of *Psychology for the New Century,* she had an answer. But on nights like tonight, after days like today, she knew her answers were nothing but shot-in-the-dark guesses. She really didn't know. She couldn't even imagine, when things between them had been so good for so long.

What was it that had broken the cycle of love?

Timothy's dinner was a smashing success—at least with his mother. He'd gone out of his way to dress up the table in the dining room the way she would have for a special occasion: a lace tablecloth, the best china, the silver plate, candles, and in the center of the table a white ceramic pot of miniature narcissus.

"My valentine to you," he'd told his parents.

"Your valentine to us is being here. This—" Donnabelle sneezed unexpectedly. "Excuse me!" She got up to get a tissue and blow her nose, finishing her thought on the way back to the table. "Dinner is above and beyond, dear." She beamed at her son. Cleo, at least for the moment, was clearly forgotten.

Reese said nothing, but his gaze did briefly meet his son's; Timothy thought he saw a sort of grudging acknowledgment that at least he was making his mother happy.

"How often do you see Bonny?" Timothy ventured as casually as he could manage while he served up slices of strawberry cheesecake at the end of the meal.

"We try for once a month or so. And we always do the holidays together." Donnabelle hesitated. "She usually joins us for my birthday dinner, but with you here…"

She didn't have to finish the sentence. "Mom, I know Bonny wasn't exactly happy to see me this morning. But she doesn't…well, *hate* me, does she?"

Donnabelle hesitated once again, then answered with another question. A completely irrelevant question, Timothy thought at first: "You know the flowers and candy you gave her this morning?"

"Yeah, but I didn't know you did." He sighed. The old Pilchuck pipeline must have been buzzing today: *Extra! Extra! Timothy Fairley Back in Town! Makes Peace Offering to Ex-Wife Bonny!* "What about them, Mom?"

"The daisies ended up in the Kitsch 'n' Caboodle Café. And the chocolates got passed around the Blue Moon Gallery like hors d'oeuvres at a wake."

He winced. Considering the circumstances, the metaphor was a little too appropriate. Especially if looks could kill. He laid down his fork, no longer hungry for his dessert. "Doesn't sound too hopeful, does it?"

Donnabelle sneezed. "Excuse me!" she said again, and Timothy couldn't help but wonder if getting up for another tissue was an excuse not to have to answer.

Unexpectedly, Reese cleared his throat and spoke up for the first time since his brief introduction to Cleo. "There's always hope, son. Even starting at less than zero."

Less than zero! Timothy leaned back in his chair with his arms across his chest, staring in disbelief at his father. "That's supposed to be encouraging?"

A flicker of surprise crossed his father's face before his expression settled into its familiar impassivity. "Yes. It is."

But it was hard to think about hope once he'd figured out Reese's meaning: Everything else being equal, a perfect stranger had more chance with Bonny than Timothy had—because Timothy was a notoriously *im*perfect ex-husband.

Would Bonny have ordered a stranger out of her store this morning? Of course not. Why would she?

Would she have rejected flowers and candy from a stranger? Well, maybe, if the stranger just walked in from out of the blue. But if he'd come with a recommendation from a friend, she might even have agreed to go out with the guy.

The thing was, a stranger would get to start at ground zero with Bonny. Any stranger—perfect or not. But because of his history with

Bonny, Timothy would, as his father said, be starting in the red.

Reese was right. In fact, he hadn't even gone far enough.

In Bonny's eyes, Timothy was willing to wager, he wasn't just starting at less than zero; he *was* less than zero.

Enough is enough, Bonny told herself peevishly. She'd been home from work for two hours now and thought about nothing else but Timothy. A perfect waste of a soothing bath and a delicious meal— her muscles were all tied up in knots again, and she'd barely tasted her dinner. A pox on Timothy Fairley! Did he know how *expensive* asparagus was this time of year?

It was time for drastic action. It was time for the *Tillicum Weekly* personal ads.

With the tabloid folded open to the personals section, a steno pad and pen, and her portable phone in hand, she nestled into her favorite overstuffed chair in the living room, long legs tucked beneath her. She was ready to take on the world—or at least Tillicum County.

She listened to her outgoing message first. To her surprise, it didn't give her a thing to complain about. In fact, it actually made her smile. It was complimentary, and fairly accurate concerning her interests, and kind of cute, really, when you thought about it—two earnest teenagers who thought so much of their "Boss-Lady" they'd go to all this trouble to find her a man.

Then she tapped in to her personal voice-mail box and discovered she had five messages. Five would-be suitors, just since ten o'clock this morning! She would never have guessed her reaction, but a little thrill of anticipation shivered up and down her spine when she heard the recording, in a sultry woman's voice: "You have five new messages. To listen to message number one…"

Thought you didn't want a boyfriend.

I don't. This is just a distraction.

On the other hand…

What if there really was someone out there who could turn her heart inside out the way Timothy used to? Someone as dependable and true-hearted as she used to think Timothy was?

She grabbed her paper and pen and for the next half-hour took notes like crazy.

The first call was promising. Pete was a painter who liked her "eye for art." "I wonder if you might be a closet artist yourself?" he suggested. Wouldn't he be surprised to find out she'd taught high-school art along with her English classes? He had a diverse background, he said, and no set schedule, which made sense for an artist. "Give me a call and let's talk!" he ended his message.

An artist could be interesting, Bonny told herself. His voice sounded vaguely familiar though, which worried her. What if he was someone she knew—someone from Pilchuck? The pool of so-called eligible bachelors in Pilchuck was small. She didn't know any she'd be interested in having a cup of coffee with, let alone dinner and a movie. But she didn't think any of Pilchuck's bachelors were artists either, so maybe he just had one of those familiar voices.

Next was Doug. Doug was thirty-eight, had two kids—a sixteen-year-old boy and a thirteen-year-old girl—and was a road-construction superintendent who wore his long brown hair in a ponytail. He loved beautiful women, especially redheads, and described himself as "playful and passionate."

Bonny hadn't considered children, though it was perfectly reasonable to expect most men in the right age group would have them. She hadn't considered long hair either. Or what to do if someone's idea of *passionate* meant something more…well, *personal* than a simple zest for life. What exactly did Doug mean about loving beautiful women? How many beautiful women had he loved?

Her third message was from Theo, who liked her "Boss-Lady" headline and said it was great her employees thought so highly of her they'd placed an ad. He lived in Bellingrath, worked as a private-practice therapist, and was "committed to family values."

His work and his commitment to family values perked her interest right up. She starred his name. Theo undoubtedly had it all together, and he'd be fascinating to talk to.

Next came Steve. Steve waxed eloquent about himself: He was honest, fun loving, caring, vibrant, independent, secure, happy, health conscious, intelligent, young at heart, tall, handsome. Or so he said. "In short, I am not a bad guy," he ended his message.

Bonny wished he'd stuck to "in short." Frankly, he tooted his own horn a little too much for her taste. She almost crossed his name off the list, but then decided he might have been nervous and rattled on without knowing how he was sounding.

The last message was from Jules, who left a veritable dissertation on her voice mail. He was forty-six—a year younger than her brother Jack—and looking for a one-on-one relationship. "One person to cherish for the rest of my life" was how he put it. He enjoyed the peace and quiet of his country property east of Schuyler, a small town in the foothills a dozen miles northeast of Pilchuck. He liked working with his hands, he said. He was a reader, a learner, and a traveler; he was open to new adventure, and he loved meeting new people.

She put a big star by his name. It was that word *cherish*, for one thing; it actually made her heart speed up. And she liked his self-description. He sounded intelligent and interesting—without having to say he was.

She read back over her notes a second time, thoughtfully, prioritizing this time. First Jules, then Theo, then Pete. Doug next and Steve last.

She couldn't believe it. Some of these guys actually sounded interesting! She'd always heard there were great men out there if you just knew where to look—but whoever would have thought to look in the personal ads?

You're not really going to go through with this.

Oh, probably not. But it's fun to think about. A whole lot more fun than thinking about Timothy.

Which, unfortunately, she was forced to do a moment later, when a sudden clatter against one of the living room windows practically had her heart jumping out of her skin. She leaped from her chair and ran to the window, pulling her thick terry robe more tightly around her.

It was *him*. His silver hair reflected the glow from the streetlight. A grinning mutt with large floppy ears, a black snout, and a white patch over one eye sat on its haunches next to him, as if waiting for a command.

Timothy with a dog? She frowned.

And he was carrying a ukulele, of all things, which he started to strum the minute he spotted her.

Oh no. He was going to serenade her. On the eve of Valentine's Day, with a ukulele, in his low, rumbling, always slightly off-key baritone. And the lights were still on next door where Nella Norland lived. Nella Norland, who was the community news reporter for the *Pilchuck Post*.

And *yes*, she made a mental note to herself; she *was* going to follow through with her personal ad. Timothy standing outside her window with a ukulele clinched it.

She ducked below the window sill, crawled back to her armchair, and reached up to switch off the lamp, plunging the room into darkness. *Go away*, she telegraphed through the walls, in case he didn't take the hint. *Don't do this to me!*

Do what to you? another part of her brain inquired.

Embarrass me. Humiliate me. Mortify me!

And?

The ukulele plinked. Where on earth had he come up with a ukulele? Where on earth had he learned to play?

And? her brain reiterated.

She could have retired to her bedroom on the other side of the house. She could have covered her ears. She could have turned on the radio. Loud. But she had to admit—she was curious. Her ex-husband didn't sing. He especially didn't sing in public. Timothy as a musician was an entirely unexpected concept.

So was his song:

My Bonny's a beautiful woman,
My Bonny's courageous and free.
I'm begging her now for forgiveness—

Oh come back, my Bonny, to me!

Bonny, her brain insisted, *what is it you're really afraid of?*
She dropped her head in her hands and groaned again. *Okay, okay. That he'll make my insides go all soft and mooshy! All right? Are you satisfied?!*

Come back, come back,
Oh come back, my Bonny, to me, to me...

Mournful words. A mournful tune. So mournful it actually set the dog to howling. And sent a pang through Bonny's heart.

Come back, come back,
Oh come back, my Bonny, to me!

That was all. When Bonny got up the nerve to peek back over the window sill, the yard was empty. She almost might have imagined the entire scene.

Except that the plunk of the ukulele, the dog's plaintive bay, and Timothy's surprisingly expressive baritone still resonated in her ears.

And her insides were without question all soft and mooshy.

6

Timothy slipped into the back row of the balcony at the Pilchuck Church of Saints and Sinners on Sunday morning just as Pastor Bob closed the offertory prayer with a hearty amen.

His eyes skipped over the minister's shoulder to the choir seated on the tiered platform. Bonny looked stunning even in a choir robe, her long hair falling over the forest green vestment like liquid copper.

The organist and the pianist launched into an up-tempo musical duel, and the ushers started down the aisles with the offering baskets. Timothy slunk down in his seat, not wanting Bonny to see him. Not wanting *anyone* to see him. Because late last night, lying in bed reviewing the day, he'd realized what a complete and utter fool he must have looked to both his ex-wife and the entire town.

Timothy was a private man, a man who kept his own counsel, a man who didn't air his laundry—clean *or* dirty—in front of the neighbors. But yesterday…

He sighed. He might as well have draped his shorts and T-shirts all over the Blue Moon Gallery. *I don't care if I have to crawl over broken glass,* for crying out loud! In front of Lonetta and Suzie and Cindy and Olga Pfefferkuchen! And then last night…

Nella Norland lived next door to Bonny. What had he been thinking?

He *hadn't* been thinking. That was the thing. The moment he'd caught sight of Bonny through the glass door of the Blue Moon Gallery, his brain had gone on vacation. When her eyes had met his and she'd gasped out his name and slumped against the counter, it had been instinct and not conscious thought that prompted him to leap to her rescue. After that, thinking hadn't entered into the picture for one single, solitary minute all day long.

It wasn't like him—not thinking. It wasn't like him, making a spectacle of himself.

Coming a little late to church to avoid being seen—now that was like him.

He hadn't purposely set out to be late this morning, of course. His parents' old farmhouse had only one bathroom, and Reese and Donnabelle weren't used to making time in their schedule for a third person. On top of which, his mother was coming down with a cold, slowing down her morning routine. She'd looked miserable with her puffy eyes and her red nose, and she had "all the energy of a slug" besides, she said.

Then, in his hurry to be on time, he'd knocked over his bottle of aftershave in the bathroom and had to take time to clean it up. And finally, just when he was ready to go, Cleo had gotten out the back door and run off in a huff when she realized Timothy was leaving without her, and he'd had to chase her down.

He'd have thought she'd be tired of tooling around in the pickup after a three-day road trip, but apparently not. When he finally left, he'd heard the howl from her back-porch prison all the way down the driveway. The sound was so heartrending he'd almost turned around. He was already late, and besides, he smelled like he'd bathed in cologne—not exactly the way to stay low-profile.

But here he was—and glad of it, even if he *was* hiding out in the balcony. It certainly wouldn't be the first time. In fact, it looked as if the balcony was still the high-school hangout. He was the only "old" guy there.

The woman seated next to Bonny on the platform, an attractive blonde in her forties, leaned toward Bonny and whispered something. Timothy ducked his head. Even the back row of the balcony wasn't that far away from the platform. And if Cait Reilly—no, Cait Van Hooten now, he reminded himself—if Cait spotted him, she'd be sure to point him out.

He didn't doubt for a minute that Cait knew he was back in town. She was Bonny's best friend, after all, and all three of her daughters had been present for the spectacle in the gallery yesterday morning.

He sighed. No doubt every last person in the congregation knew he was back in town—and knew Bonny had thrown him out of the Blue Moon. Good grief, half of them probably already knew about his and Cleo's serenade outside Bonny's window a mere twelve hours ago.

He had to ask himself: Was he really ready for small-town life again?

The choir rose. Timothy slumped down further in his seat.

Bonny didn't notice him though. She was focused on the choir director, which gave Timothy the space of the anthem to focus on her face.

A beautiful face. Not just the way it was put together either, but how it expressed her inner fire, her enthusiasm for life, her passionate nature. Bonny poured herself into whatever she did: singing, talking, teaching, loving…

Such passion! Such spirit, such humor, such grace.

And he'd left her. Talk about foolish!

Was there another woman in all the world who could move him the way his ex-wife moved him? If there was, he hadn't found her. And he didn't care to look. Bonny Van Hooten Fairley was the only woman he wanted.

And if the entire town of Pilchuck thought it had to poke its collective nose into the affair—

Then so be it.

If he had to go public to get her attention, to prove that he loved her, to show her he was a new man—

Then amen and amen.

Because Bonny Van Hooten Fairley was every bit worth his making a fool of himself.

Bonny normally didn't have a problem sitting.

Timothy, now—the man couldn't sit still to save the universe.

51

She'd once mistaken a minor earthquake for Timothy jiggling his leg under the table. If he hadn't had his running to siphon off some of his excess nervous energy, she swore he'd have brought the house down around their ears.

This morning, however, it was Bonny who couldn't sit still. Fortunately she sat directly behind the podium, so she could for the most part hide her agitation from everyone but Cait, who sat on one side of her, and Cindy, who sat on the other. Both were kind enough not to comment on the fact that for some reason her arms and legs seemed to have a life of their own—crossing and uncrossing, shifting to this side and that, one leg or the other jiggling, fingers tapping against her thigh.

She blamed it on the kids who trooped up on the platform after the choir anthem and milled about like bees on a honeycomb while the Sunday school superintendent tried to get them to say their lines.

More honestly, she blamed it on their lines—and the ridiculous two-foot, lace-trimmed hearts they carried, each bearing a Scripture reference. The jitters started immediately after the littlest girl, with a shy dip of her head, recited: "Love comes from God."

Her agitation continued through "Perfect love casts out fear" and "Love does no harm to its neighbor" and accelerated with "Love covers a multi-plitude of sins." And it wasn't because of the mispronunciation either.

"Hatred st-stirs up dissension," an owlish boy with a slight lisp quoted with great solemnity. "But love covers all wrongs."

The reinforcement of that last thought brought a frown along with the jitters. Why, exactly, should wrongs be covered? Especially a "multi-plitude" of wrongs? Whatever happened to exposing wrongs to the light?

Thank goodness for Gordie Wyatt, who could always be counted on for comic relief. Bonny suspected his misquote was deliberate; he was almost seven now, and he liked to play to the crowd. But she snickered along with everyone else when he offered, "Better a meal of veg'tables with love than a fat ol' cow with hatred!"

At least no one could accuse her of being a "fat ol' cow."

It was back to the frown on hearing the next verse, though. "Let no debt remain outstanding, except the continuing debt to love one another," Gordie's neighbor recited.

She didn't like that line. Not one little bit.

The next passage, delivered with dramatic flair by a young teenage girl, caught her so by surprise she actually *stopped* agitating for a moment: "Love is as strong as death, its jealousy unyielding as the grave. It burns like a blazing fire, like a mighty flame. Many waters cannot quench love; rivers cannot wash it away."

That was the way she'd felt about Timothy once. Like a blazing fire, like a mighty flame…

"Clothe yourselves with compassion, kindness, humility, gentleness and patience," a sweet-faced girl, the last in the group, recited. "Bear with each other and forgive whatever grievances you may have against one another. Forgive as the Lord forgave you. And over all these virtues put on love, which binds them all together in perfect unity."

Without even thinking about it, Bonny lifted her index finger and rubbed vigorously at her nose.

"Greater love has no one than this," the entire group finished loudly, "that he lay down his life for his friends."

Love, love, love! Bonny fumed as the kids left the platform. She was up to *here* with love! And personally, she thought Pastor Bob was pandering to commercial interests to dedicate the entire church service to love.

Commercial interests! another voice inside her head protested. *Those verses weren't written by some ad copywriter, doofus. They're the real thing!*

But she didn't want to hear the real thing. Which was why, after she had hung her choir robe on the rack in the foyer following the anthem, she walked out the door instead of following Cait back down the aisle into the fifth pew from the front on the left side where Jack always saved the two outside spots for them.

She knew better than to stick around for a sermon based on 1 Corinthians 13. She'd heard quite enough about love for one day, thank you. Love and Timothy.

Timothy hadn't been *specified*, of course, but she knew. All that stuff about her "continuing debt" to love him, and the charge to forgive whatever "grievances" she had against him. As if all she had to do was wave her hand and it would be done.

As for the sermon—she had no interest at all in listening to Pastor Bob talk about love being patient and kind, which she hadn't even attempted to be toward Timothy yesterday. And she especially didn't need to hear that love wasn't easily angered and kept no record of wrongs, when his mere presence in her store had brought her blood to boiling—not to mention calling up a catalog of old grievances longer than a spoiled kid's Christmas wish list.

Ten minutes later she was in her office at the back of the Blue Moon, where she buried herself in paperwork till just before she unlocked the door at noon. Robin and Rosie were waiting on the sidewalk, though only Robin was scheduled to work.

"Hey, Bon-Bon!" Rosie greeted her cheerfully as Robin disappeared into the stockroom to hang her jacket.

"Hey yourself. What are you doing here?"

"Can't a niece come by to say hello to her favorite aunt?"

Bonny eyed her suspiciously. "Didn't we say hello before church this morning?"

"Speaking of which—"

"—you sure were outta there like the devil was after you," Robin finished, reappearing from the stockroom, her dark eyes bright with speculation.

Hardly, Bonny thought wryly. It wasn't the devil who'd penned those Scripture verses.

"I wasn't feeling so great," she said, not untruthfully. "I didn't think I could sit through the sermon."

The twins were immediately solicitous, Rosie even offering to stay and work so Bonny could go home to bed. But she wouldn't have left the store in the twins' hands in any case, and she certainly didn't want to go home to bed, where she'd have all the time in the world to brood. "That's sweet of you, Rosie, but it might get busy today. I should be here."

Robin busied herself straightening the spools of curling ribbon on the wrapping table. "We thought maybe you left early because You-Know-Who was there."

"You-Know-Who?" Bonny's heart sank. They couldn't mean Timothy, could they? She'd checked out the congregation when the choir first settled into the chairs on the platform and had breathed a sigh of relief when she spotted Reese and Donnabelle Fairley in their regular spot—without their errant son. Donnabelle had looked a little under the weather though. No doubt Timothy had something to do with that.

"We heard him sing to you last night, Bon-Bon," Rosie said. "Him and that funny-looking dog. Did you notice how he walks sort of crooked?"

"Crooked?"

"Like if you look at him you think he's going one way," Robin clarified, "but really he's going a totally different direction. It's weird."

"Oh. The dog." She hadn't noticed, but then she'd only seen the creature sitting sedately by Timothy's side, and the light hadn't been that good. And frankly, for the brief seconds she'd allowed herself a peek through the window, her attention had been focused on her ex-husband.

"Of course the dog. Nothing crooked about the way Timothy Fairley walks," Rosie said, sighing.

Good grief, Bonny thought. The way she said his name you'd think he was a movie star or something.

"We saw you turn the lights out on him, by the way," she added.

"He *was* a little off-key," said Robin, "and the ukulele was out of tune and that dog could use some singing lessons—"

"—but turning the lights out on him seemed pretty harsh," Rosie concluded.

Bonny crossed her arms and glared at them. "Look," she said, "I know harsh. What Timothy did to me was harsh. Turning the lights out on him was nothing. Okay? *Nothing.*"

"Sheesh. Take a chill pill, Boss-Lady."

"I'm outta here," said Rosie. "Oh—I almost forgot, Bon-Bon. Mom wants you to give her a call. She's worried about you. Skipping out on church and all."

"I'm *fine.*"

Rosie raised an eyebrow. "I thought you were sick."

"I never said I was sick," Bonny snapped. "I said I wasn't feeling well."

Robin raised an identical eyebrow. "Your monthly moodies?"

"It is *not*—"

Fortunately a customer walked in the door just then. Otherwise Bonny might really have lost it.

Cleo, true to form, had greeted Timothy after church as if he hadn't wounded her feelings earlier in the day. Oh, sweet forgiveness! If only humans forgave so easily.

And if only all he had to do to make things up to Bonny was buy her a juicy bone and take her for a pickup ride! Dog love was so easy.

"Okay, Clee," he said as he approached downtown, where he'd promised to give her the fifteen-minute walking tour after he'd run his errands. "Help me out here. I tried flowers. I tried chocolates. I even tried a serenade. What can I give her for Valentine's Day she won't have the heart to turn away?"

"Arf!"

Grinning, he lifted his hand off the steering wheel and draped his arm over the dog. "Good idea, girl—but I'm afraid I can't do without you. She doesn't get *you* till she marries *me.*" He absently massaged the spot on Cleo's neck where his hand lay. "Then again, maybe if she fell in love with you…"

Maybe if she fell in love with you, she'd find her way around to loving me, he finished in his mind. He couldn't count on it, but it certainly couldn't do any harm. He knew already that Bonny and Cleo would adore each other. Considering Bonny's tender heart toward animals with sad stories and Cleo's profuse appreciation for anybody who paid her the slightest attention, how would either of them be able to resist?

Besides, Cleo was already an expert at this. The attention she got when they were out together—and the attention *he* got as a result of being attached to her leash—still caught him by surprise sometimes. The dog was a veritable "chick magnet."

As his mother had noted, Cleo wasn't especially pretty. Not that she didn't have attractive features, like the long silky "feathers" on her legs and her long plumed tail, plus about the happiest grin he'd ever seen on a dog. But her black snout was short and her brown ears were long and limp and her mud-colored eyes did have a nearsighted sort of look about them. And there was that oddly off-center walk, too.

No, you couldn't call Cleo a beautiful dog. Yet she carried herself with dignity and at the same time seemed eminently approachable. That smile, maybe, and the way her tail waved—like a long-lost friend across a crowded room. Whatever it was, it made Timothy approachable too. Cleo was the perfect icebreaker.

With that less-than-zero thing he had going with Bonny, it was probably going to take more than Cleo, of course. But an alliance between his ex-wife and his dog could only be good for Timothy— maybe just the thing to soften her up so he could start worming his way back into her heart.

And there was no better moment than the present, he told himself as he spotted the smiling Blue Moon sign over the gallery. It was high time Bonny Van Hooten Fairley and Cleo met.

He got as far as a parking slot directly in front of the Blue Moon, where a sign on the door blared, NO DOGS ALLOWED EXCEPT SEEING-EYE AND OTHER SERVICE DOGS.

"Okay, Clee. So how am I going to get around this one? There's no way I'm going to convince her you're a seeing-eye dog—let alone that I'm a blind man."

He stared at the sign, his brain whirring. Cleo nudged his arm with her snout, then made a sound between a snort and a snuffle, ending with a high-pitched whine. Her engine whine, he called it.

Timothy dropped his keys, he was so startled. "Say what?"

Cleo pawed at the seat excitedly and repeated her snort-snuffle-whine.

"That's what I *thought* you said." Timothy's smile, for once, was almost as wide as his dog's. He pulled her under his arm and gave her a hug.

"You're the better part of my brain, girl. I swear it!"

7

Bonny stared at the front door in disbelief, which rapidly transformed into indignation and then outrage. "You can't bring that mutt in here!"

"She's a—"

"Can't you read? *No—dogs—allowed.*" She emphasized and separated each word, as if she were talking to a toddler. Or an imbecile.

"Right. Except—"

"You're not going to tell me she's a seeing-eye dog, Timothy. What—you've gone suddenly blind? You seem to be tracking just fine to me. Your eyes seem to be tracking just fine, I should say. Your mind, on the other hand—"

"It says seeing-eye or *other service dogs,*" Timothy interrupted.

"What—she's a hearing-ear dog? I don't think your ears are the problem, Timothy, I think—"

"She's my feeling-heart dog," he said firmly.

Bonny's disbelieving gaze slid from her ex-husband to the dog at his side. The mutt gazed back nearsightedly, lifted a paw, and snorted. Or was it a snuffle?

"A feeling-heart dog!"

"They're the latest thing for cigar-store Indians."

She jerked her eyes back to Timothy's. So he remembered. "If you think—"

"I need cards for Mom and Dad. Valentines. You do sell cards?"

"Of course I sell—"

"Picking out the right card is *exactly* the sort of thing I need Cleo for."

Bonny crossed her arms. "I suppose she reads them for you?"

"She's very smart," Timothy said, his voice serious but his eyes sparkling with humor. "Not *that* smart though. I read them to her. She helps me choose."

"This I've got to see."

He looked pleased. "Your wish is my command. Come on, Cleo."

"Wait! You can't go back there—"

"You did say you wanted a demonstration, Boss-Lady," Robin cut in.

"I was being sarcastic!"

"But this could be a once-in-a-lifetime opportunity. A real, live feeling-heart dog! Right here in the Blue Moon!"

Bonny threw her hands in the air. "I can't believe this. Are you out of your mind, Robin? He's making it up! There's no such thing as a feeling-heart dog!"

"How do you know," Robin challenged, "unless you check it out for yourself?"

By this time Timothy was standing in front of the wire card rack with his feeling-heart dog sitting at attention next to him. He glanced over the display. "Wow. These aren't cards—they're works of art." He pulled one off the rack and opened it.

"Aren't they? I have several artists who—" Bonny stopped mid-sentence. How did he *do* that—distract her so completely that she forgot she had nothing to say to him? Nothing, now and forever, *amen.*

Timothy replaced the handmade card and removed another, then several more, opening each in turn. "But they don't *say* anything." He sounded puzzled.

"If that feeling-heart dog of yours was doing the job she's supposed to be doing," Bonny said shortly, arms folded once again, "she'd have told you that a personal note written in a lovely handmade card is much more meaningful than some sentimental claptrap you'd find in a card at—" She almost said "Fairley's," as the pharmacy carried a major line of mass-market greeting cards, but she didn't want to insult Reese and Donnabelle. "—the mall," she finished.

"Well of course!" said Timothy, slapping his hand against his forehead. "That's why Cleo brought me here instead of taking me to the mall!" He grinned at Bonny. "Told you she was smart, didn't I?"

"Bah! Sounds to me like an excuse to get out of having to prove she's really a feeling-heart dog."

At which the creature barked sharply.

"But I haven't introduced you," Timothy said, smacking his hand once again against his forehead. "Where are my manners?"

"A very good question. I—"

"Bonny, Cleo. Cleo, Bonny," Timothy interrupted, as if *interrupting* wasn't bad manners. "I know you're going to get along famously."

"Arf!" said Cleo, a grin spreading clear across her wide, homely face. Her tail thumped against the wooden floor.

Bonny's heart sank. Timothy must have known she wouldn't be able to resist a smiling, tail-thumping dog. The bum. The beast.

"Cleo, huh?" She addressed herself to the dog instead of Timothy. "How'd you ever get mixed up with a reprobate like this guy anyhow?"

Kneeling, Bonny reached to stroke the animal's head. Cleo's fine hair, tan and white on the top of her head, was soft and silky. She leaped to her feet, plumed tail waving, and tried to get at Bonny's face with her tongue.

"Sit, girl!" Timothy said sternly.

Cleo promptly sat. *What a good dog,* Bonny thought, scratching her under the chin, her heart softening. Stretching her neck as if to give better access, Cleo emitted a sound very much like a heartfelt sigh.

Bonny's heart softened even more. She loved animals; she'd have had a dog if she hadn't been working such impossible hours the last three years since she'd opened the store. Keeping a dog cooped up inside the house or chained in the backyard didn't seem fair somehow.

She'd had a cat for a while right after Timothy left, but he'd adopted the family across the street and down one, next to Cait and Jack's house. *That* hadn't done much for her already wounded self-esteem. She couldn't even keep a *cat's* interest, for pity's sake!

"What a sweet thing you are!" she cooed to Cleo. "But I have to say, you don't look much like a Cleopatra. Is that what Cleo is short for, girl? Cleopatra?"

Cleo snorted. A definite snort this time, not a snuffle.

It really was impossible to tell the creature's heritage, poor homely thing. She seemed to be made of spare parts, none of which really went together—like a Frankenstein creation. But she did have a certain dignity about her, and her happy grin was completely disarming.

Bonny glanced up at Timothy and said without thinking, an actual smile lifting the corners of her mouth, "A Prince Albert retriever, right?"

Timothy looked surprised. "A Prince Albert retriever! I haven't thought about Mutt in years." He grinned broadly. "You're right. She must be."

Bonny's smile faded. She looked away, upset with herself. Why that memory? Why now, when what she really, really needed to remember was what a beast Timothy was?

They were both readers, she and Timothy. In the first years of their marriage, the good years, they'd often read aloud to each other—favorite passages from whatever was on their nightstand.

It was Timothy who'd discovered Farley Mowat's classic about his boyhood dog, a homely mutt named Mutt for whom Mr. Mowat Sr., embarrassed by the mongrel's lack of pedigree and wanting to impress his friends, had invented the Prince Albert breed. What Mutt had lacked in pedigree he'd made up in personality. *More* than made up. Bonny and Timothy had howled together over the dog who refused to be held back by the conventions of doghood.

And Cleo looked as if she could have given Mutt a run for his money.

"I knew you'd love her once you met her, Bonny."

She kept her eyes downcast. What a cheap trick, bringing his dog in the store, trying to get at her through her love for animals. Claiming Cleo was a feeling-heart dog, of all things!

Not that a feeling-heart dog wasn't an excellent idea, she told herself, running her hands down Cleo's ears and neck, dodging her eager tongue. There were probably a lot of men out there who could benefit from a feeling-heart dog. A *lot.* Cold-hearted, hard-hearted, wooden-hearted men like Timothy Fairley.

Not that Cleo wasn't doing a good job as a feeling-heart dog either. Bonny's insides were once again heading toward soft and mooshy.

She gave Cleo one last scratch under her chin and stood, though she kept her eyes downcast. "How come a dog, Timothy? Now? You never wanted one when we were—" She stopped herself. "You never wanted one before."

"I couldn't help myself. She was half-starved when I found her. Looked like she'd tangled with the Abominable Snowman too—or *something* big and scary. Besides, when we—" He, too, stopped for an instant. "Back then I didn't know what I wanted."

She wasn't sure what made her lift her chin just then to meet his eyes with her own.

"Now I do," he said, his gaze unwavering. "I want lots of things. Mostly, I want you."

Two minutes later Timothy and Cleo were out on the sidewalk in front of the Blue Moon. Not on their behinds, though they might as well have been. Bonny had not taken Timothy's declaration well. And he'd been doing so splendidly! Or at least Cleo had. He'd been right about Bonny falling for his dog.

He opened the passenger door so Cleo could jump in the pickup. "I knew it wasn't going to be easy, girl—winning Bonny back." Slamming the door, he moved around the front to the driver's side and climbed in. "But I guess I'd hoped for a little less grief in the process."

"Aaroo," Cleo howled in sympathy.

"Thanks, Clee. But I want you to know I do think we're making inroads. She wasn't quite as furious today as she was yesterday when she threw me out." He started the engine and backed out on the street. "If I could just find her the right little something for Valentine's Day…"

He found a parking spot close to Fairley's Drug and Fountain. After flowers, candy, and a moonlight serenade, perfume seemed the next logical step. His mother didn't stock the most expensive brands, but she did carry the musk-scented Elysian Fields Bonny had always favored for special occasions. And he could pick up a new bottle of Whitewater aftershave for himself while he was at it.

"Be back in two shakes," he told Cleo, "and then I'll give you that walking tour I promised you."

His mother was happy to wrap the bottle of perfume. She looked better than she had this morning. She ought to, with so many cold remedies lining the shelves of the pharmacy and Reese to recommend the right one.

Maybe he'd walk Cleo over to Bonny's house on Mulberry Street, he thought, hurrying out to the truck with his bag of purchases. He could leave the bottle of perfume on her doorstep. Something told him it wouldn't be a good idea to drop by the Blue Moon again today.

"Ready, Clee?"

Cleo thumped her tail against the bench seat and gurgled joyously, but she stayed put till Timothy whistled. Then she leaped to the ground, settled on her haunches, tongue lolling, and waited patiently while he bent to attach a leash to her collar. Pilchuck had very strict leash laws now, his mother had warned him.

"Good girl! Let's do it!"

Cleo bounded to her feet, tail waving. But when Timothy tugged on the leash a moment later, she resisted.

He looked at her in surprise. "Clee?"

She was standing stock-still, gazing into the window of the Shoe Tree next door to the pharmacy, her neck stretched out, her tail stretched out, her nose quivering. She was, in fact, doing her "point-ing thing," as Timothy called it.

Although it was hard to tell much about Cleo's ancestry from her appearance, some kind of bird dog—Prince Albert retriever or not—had to be in there somewhere. She had pointing down to a science. Maybe someone in her past had trained her; maybe she was just a natural. In any case, when Cleo stood the way she was standing now, Timothy paid attention.

He followed her gaze. There weren't any shoes in the Shoe Tree's window, he noticed with surprise. Instead there were dolls and tea sets and stuffed animals. And what must have caught Cleo's eye—a kite in the form of a flying mallard duck suspended from the ceiling. He glanced at the sign above the door and saw that it no longer read THE SHOE TREE, but TEDDY BEAR PICNIC. He glanced back at the window display—

And there it was. The perfect gift for Bonny. *Better* than Elysian Fields. Elysian Fields could wait.

"Cleo, you are a wonder." He quickly tied the dog's leash to a NO PARKING 9 TO 5 MON. THRU FRI. sign and squatted next to her for a moment, smoothing his hands over her long ears and down her neck.

She gazed at him with an injured expression.

"I know. But I promise I'll be right out, Clee, and then you can help me make a very special delivery."

"Arf!" And Cleo got in a lick to his chin before he could get away.

Bonny usually closed the store on Sundays just in time to add up the day's receipts, fill out a bank-deposit slip, and drop the cash in the night-deposit box at the First National Bank on her way to the evening service, which she rarely missed. On Sunday evenings the old plaster walls of Saints and Sinners practically vibrated with celebra-tion: singing, special music, interpretive readings, drama, sometimes even interpretive dance.

Tonight would be no exception.

And she wasn't in the mood to celebrate.

Particularly because the service would probably be a rehash of this morning's, or at least a variation on the theme. She didn't need the gift of prophecy to figure *that* out.

Thank goodness Valentine's Day came only once a year. Because frankly, Bonny couldn't bear the thought of hearing one more word about love.

Especially not if Timothy planned on coming to the service, which she had a good idea he'd do. The rat. It wouldn't be as easy throwing him out of church as it had been kicking him out of her store. In fact, it hadn't really been all that easy kicking him out of the store this afternoon. But only because of Cleo, she tried to assure herself.

The phone rang just as she was locking the door behind Robin. It was Cait, concerned that Bonny hadn't called.

"Didn't Rosie tell you I was fine?"

"I needed to hear it from the horse's mouth."

Bonny snorted, threw back her head, and let out a loud "Nei-gh-gh-gh!"

Cait laughed. "You sound pretty healthy all right."

"Physically at least. Emotionally..." She sighed. "I'm sure you'll hear all about Timothy coming by as soon as Robin gets home."

"He came by the store again? Today? The man just doesn't give up, does he?"

Bonny narrowed her lips. "He will. That's what Timothy's famous for—giving up."

"Well, forget about Timothy then. Think about dessert."

"Much better food for thought! What kind of dessert?"

"Biddy's apple betty. At the Kitsch 'n' Caboodle. You and me and Jack, tonight after church."

But being with a couple of lovebirds on Valentine's Day had no appeal at all. "Thanks Cait—that's sweet. But you and Jack don't need me hanging around tonight." Besides, she told herself firmly, she had phone calls to make. Five at least. Maybe more.

Once again, at the thought, a little thrill of anticipation shivered up and down her spine.

Changing your mind about finding a boyfriend?

No boyfriend. Just a few dates. Distraction till Timothy's gone.

"We *like* it when you hang around," Cait said.

"I'll take a rain check," Bonny said.

"All right. Save you a seat at church?"

"Nope. I'm not about to sit through another tribute to love."

But when she climbed the steps to her front porch twenty minutes later and saw who was waiting for her, she wished with all her heart that Cait had worked harder to persuade her.

Cupid himself was propped up in the corner of her willow swing like an old man propped against a park bench, gazing at Bonny as if to say, "Yup. It's me. Aren't you happy to see me?"

Yes, *Cupid.* In the form of a large silver-gray teddy bear—complete with a pair of silver wings, a bow and quiver of arrows, and a red satin heart appliquéd on his furry chest.

8

Bonny's heart sank. Even in the dusk she recognized the sweet-faced bear; he'd been living in the window at Teddy Bear Picnic on the other side of Fairley's Drug and Fountain for at least a month. His silver-tipped fur was the exact same color as Timothy Fairley's hair, and his blue glass eyes the exact same color as Timothy Fairley's eyes. In fact, she'd avoided the display window at the toy store for that very reason.

Maybe the teddy bear was from the twins, she told herself as she slowly climbed the stairs and picked him up by one plush paw.

But the twins had paid for her personal ad. They wouldn't have bought her a bear.

She tucked him under her arm as she dug in her purse for her keys. He was deliciously soft and squeezable.

Maybe he was from Cait and Jack?

Nah. Cait wouldn't be so insensitive as to get her a cupid-bear. Especially one with Timothy's eyes and hair.

Maybe he was from her ex-in-laws, who'd always loved her like a daughter…

He wore a heart-shaped tag around his neck, tied on with a length of red satin ribbon. She could have opened it.

The bear was big enough to sit in one of her kitchen chairs and still see over the top of the table, which he did, quietly watching Bonny while she brewed herself a pot of Tension Tamer tea.

She sat across from him as the tea water boiled, staring into his pale moonlight-blue glass eyes, and flashed suddenly to Timothy, gazing down at her as she lay on her back on the floor in the Blue Moon

Gallery.

Not an image she cared to prolong. Her eyes slid hurriedly away from the bear's to focus instead on the tiny silver wings that sprouted from his shoulders. They didn't look as if they'd be able even to get him off the ground if he really wanted to flit around the planet shooting arrows at people's hearts. Cupid-bear was one well-upholstered bear.

Now *there* was a way this pale-eyed, silver-haired animal and Timothy Fairley were as unlike as any two creatures could be, she told herself. Timothy had never had an extra ounce of stuffing in him. He was tall and lean and strong, hard-muscled and sharp-featured—all planes and angles to cupid-bear's soft curves.

All planes and angles to her *own* curves...

She jumped as the whistle on the teakettle shrieked. Just in time too. Her mind had been on the verge of wandering into territory too dangerous to contemplate—territory she'd been avoiding like the proverbial plague since the moment she set eyes on Timothy standing in the doorway of the Blue Moon Gallery yesterday. Good grief, his physical presence had been so overwhelming she'd actually fainted.

Fainted! He must have gotten a sense of satisfaction out of *that*.

He hardly looked self-satisfied when you came to, Bonny, she chided herself as she poured the hot water from the kettle into her bright green teapot. And there was the image again: Timothy leaning over her at the gallery, his expression concerned and sympathetic.

He'd called her sweetheart, she remembered. He'd brushed her hair away from her face with such a tender touch...

Stop that! she told herself fiercely, banging the kettle down on the stove. Thinking of Timothy as sweet and tender was as dangerous as thinking about how strong and masculine he was. *More* dangerous.

"All right," she said over her shoulder as she returned the kettle to the stove. "Give it up. Who are you really? Where did you come from? What do you want?"

The bear didn't answer, so she reluctantly walked around the table and opened the heart-shaped card hanging from the ribbon around his neck. There was no mistaking her ex-husband's bold hand:

Bearley needs a home. So does my heart. Please give us a chance.

"I knew it." She glared at the teddy bear. "You're a spy. An intruder. The enemy. Why did I even let you in my house?"

I'm not your enemy, the innocent glass eyes seemed to say. *I'm just a stray bear looking for a home...*

"Yeah, right. Like the Trojan Horse was looking for a home. What does the man think? That after what he's put me through, all it takes to get me back is a teddy bear? *You're* supposed to open the gates of my heart?"

Bearley looked hurt.

"Don't give me that injured expression," she said crossly, waving a finger at him. "He's probably waiting outside right now, isn't he? He probably thinks you've lulled me into thinking he's not such a bad guy after all. He probably thinks I'm going to go right out there and holler for him from the front porch." Her voice turned sugary: "Come on in, honey, I've just been waiting for you to come back home."

The idea made her blood boil. Without another thought she grabbed Bearley in one hand and a chair in the other and marched back out to the front porch.

"Over my dead body!" she yelled into the night, just in case Timothy was hovering about somewhere. Then she climbed up on the chair and did what she had to do.

There. *That* ought to tell her ex-husband exactly how she felt.

Two minutes later she was dialing in to her *Tillicum Weekly* voice mail. She needed distraction, and she needed it now.

"You have eleven new messages..."

Eleven new messages! Whoa! That made sixteen altogether now! She wouldn't have believed there were sixteen eligible single men in Tillicum County, let alone sixteen who would actually answer a *Tillicum Weekly* personal ad. *Her* personal ad.

She grabbed her pad and pen and started writing, Timothy Fairley and Bearley forgotten just like that. Whoever would have guessed the personal ads could be so much *fun?*

Her first call was from Steve—a different Steve from the one who'd left a message yesterday. He talked so fast she had to play him back three times before she finally got everything down. Talk about high energy! He sounded fascinating, if exhausting.

She played Kendall back three times too—but only because his *basso profundo* voice sent shivers up and down her spine. He sounded interesting; he was an instructor at the community college, he said, and a music buff and theatergoer. But with that voice he could have been a garbage collector and read to her out of the phone book and she'd have been enthralled. She drew a star by his name.

The guy who did his entire spiel in a Donald Duck voice she didn't even bother with after the second sentence. What kind of a guy left a message for a stranger—a woman he might want to date, for pity's sake—in a *duck* voice? A very odd duck, that was certain.

Al made her laugh; that seemed promising. She liked a sense of humor. "I can't believe I'm doing this—again!" he lamented. "Hope springs eternal..." Another star.

Ivan, on the other hand, apparently had no sense of humor. He was also exceptionally long-winded. He wanted this, that, and the other thing in a relationship, and if she didn't, she could just forget about calling him back. Then he concluded with a tirade about what was wrong with women in this day and age. A lot, in his opinion. Bonny didn't even bother to write his number down.

In contrast to Ivan's tirade, Guy, Charlie, and Sam left messages so short she couldn't tell a thing about them. She wrote down their numbers with question marks beside them.

A smaller star went next to Norman's name. Norman was a tax attorney, which sounded a little dull, but he was interested in personal growth and loved the outdoors. He skied, sailed, and hiked. And gardened—flowers in the spring and vegetables in the summer.

The reference to personal growth was intriguing, and Bonny liked the outdoors too, especially hiking. She didn't garden, but she liked the *idea* of gardening. Norman was a definite possibility.

Tomm and Melvin both forgot to leave a phone number. In the case of "Tomm-with-two-m's," she wasn't entirely sorry. His message was somewhat startling as an introduction: "I'm in a funk, could use some spunk, especially the red-haired variety. I'm quite a hunk, I was a drunk, but now I'm into sobriety."

Melvin, on the other hand, sounded nice. He was a high-school history teacher and had a big black Labrador named Mambo. Bonny wondered if she might have met him sometime in the past, at an in-service or a teacher's conference. Maybe he'd realize he'd forgotten to leave his number and call back later. She placed a star by his name too and then spent a few minutes going back through her notes and reprioritizing.

Then, with a deep breath for fortification, she picked up the phone.

Timothy decided to cruise by the house on Mulberry Street after church just to make sure Bonny had found Bearley. He'd been a bit surprised when she didn't show up at the service. She'd always loved Sunday nights at Saints and Sinners.

Maybe he should have propped the teddy bear right up against the door, he thought as he turned the corner. Even if she'd gone straight home after work, the front porch would have been dark—

It wasn't now. The porch light blazed like the midday sun.

Timothy slowed the truck, staring in disbelief.

Bearley was swinging from the rafters, a red satin noose around his neck.

Bonny was more than a little distracted when she answered the doorbell at nine. In fact, she was feeling a bit delirious. She'd never expected to have such a good time answering calls from the personals!

Amazing, though, how quickly a mood could change.

Bearley was at her door. With an arm wrapped around his middle.

"Bonny!" Cait's head popped out from behind the teddy bear's.

Her voice was breathless. "There's been an attempted suicide on your front porch!"

"It wasn't a suicide," Bonny answered darkly. She stepped back so Cait could come in.

"Murder?" Cait cried, feigning shock.

"It wasn't murder either," Bonny said. "It was self-defense, plain and simple."

Cait held the bear at arm's length and studied him. She shook her head. "A noose doesn't look good for self-defense, girlfriend. Besides, look at that sweet expression. You're saying this bear attacked you? You're going to have a tough time convincing a jury of *that.*"

"Yeah? Read the card around his neck."

"I don't think I have to. Timothy, right?"

"Read what he said."

She did, quickly, then raised her eyes to Bonny's. "Yikes."

"Yikes is right. What would *you* have done?"

"I'm not sure." Cait grinned. "I probably wouldn't have hanged Bearley though. Want to talk about it?"

"No. And I don't want that bear in here either."

"Aw, come on. Bearley's just an innocent pawn," Cait teased, following Bonny into the kitchen with the teddy bear under her arm. "Give him a chance."

Bonny shot her a startled glance. "I hope you don't mean Timothy."

Cait dropped into a chair at the table and settled Bearley on her lap as if he were a child. "You know I'd never tell you what to do with Timothy."

That was true, Bonny thought as she put on the kettle for tea. It wasn't in Cait's nature to give unsolicited advice. It was hardly in her nature to give advice even when someone asked for it. Unlike Bonny, who usually had a pretty good idea what people needed to do and didn't mind telling them. Cait and Jack, for instance, would still be pussyfooting around, pretending they weren't attracted to each other, if Bonny hadn't intervened.

People had their gifts. Bonny's was—to put it bluntly—butting in. Cait's was listening.

Which meant that more often than not, even when Bonny said she didn't want to talk, she ended up doing it anyhow. Just by being there, Cait invited full disclosure.

"So he made your insides go all soft and mooshy *again,*" she said with awe when Bonny was finished.

Bonny poured tea from the pot into a pair of apple-green mugs and handed one to her friend. "I tried to convince myself it was Cleo doing it to me today—and she is sweet, Cait—but it's Timothy who came up with the whole feeling-heart-dog thing, which, as much as I hate to say it, is even sweeter…"

"He sounds like a different person than the one you were married to."

"At least for the last year or two. On the other hand, in some ways he's like the person I married in the beginning. Before things turned bad." She sighed. "You can't imagine how scary that is."

"Because what's to keep things from turning bad again," suggested Cait.

"Exactly. Who is Timothy Fairley, really? The sweet guy I married? The cigar-store Indian? The running fool?"

"Or someone else altogether?" Cait added.

"Or someone else altogether," Bonny agreed. She sighed. "You can see how I might have overreacted with Bearley."

"Thank goodness he's still alive," said Cait, turning the teddy bear around on her lap to look at his face. "Though I do think, if he hadn't made it, the jury would have taken into account your state of mind."

Bonny wrapped her hands around her mug of tea, sighing again. "I suppose I've got to take him in now."

Cait nodded. "That would be the Christian thing to do."

Bonny wondered if Cait thought taking Timothy in was the Christian thing to do too. She probably wouldn't say, even if Bonny asked.

"All right then." Bonny sighed. "But I'm telling you right now,

Cait—he's sleeping on the living-room couch."

"Perfectly understandable," Cait soothed. "I'm sure he'll be very happy there."

"He'll have to be."

"What did you do tonight, by the way?" Cait asked over the bear's silver head. "Besides taking out your frustrations on Bearley, I mean?"

Bonny brightened. "Oh! Cait, I've been having such fun with the personal ads!"

"You have?" Cait planted her elbows on the table and rested her chin on her hands. "Do tell!"

She told. It was like lifting a gray pall from her heart. Talking to Cait about Timothy had probably been good for her, but it certainly hadn't been fun. Telling her friend that out of sixteen callers, six actually sounded intriguing, telling her she actually already had two dates set up—now *that* was fun.

"Two dates? Already?" Cait sounded as astonished as Bonny felt about the whole thing.

"Tomorrow and Wednesday. With my two top picks!" Her twenty-minute conversation with Jules had been delightful. He'd traveled all over the world, but his heart was on the small farm outside Schuyler where he lived now. He'd told her wry stories about the Jersey cow and the leghorn chickens and the calico cat who'd just had a litter of kittens. He had an appointment in Bellingrath tomorrow afternoon, and she'd agreed to meet him at a nice Italian restaurant in Oldtown for dinner.

"Dutch treat, or is he taking you out?" Cait asked.

"Hmm. Good question. I wonder what the protocol is for blind dates you make through the personals?"

"Guess you'll find out. Who's your other date?"

"Kendall. Basso-Profundo Kendall, I call him."

"Is he the professor who called yesterday? The James Earl Jones sound-alike?"

"That's him." She hardly remembered what they'd talked about, she'd been so mesmerized by his voice.

She'd also had short conversations with Steve number one, who had company and asked if he could call her back at ten, and Steve number two, who was on his way out the door to Seattle to catch an early morning flight to Montreal. He wouldn't be back till the first of March, he said. Why he'd bothered to leave a message when he was going out of town she didn't quite understand.

Al, Pete, Norman, and Theo had all been out, but she'd left messages—with her work phone number, for safety's sake. Tomorrow was the one day of the week the gallery was closed, but she'd be in her office for several hours at least. There was always plenty to do on her day off.

"I tried to reach the guy with the ponytail three times," she told Cait, "but his phone's been busy. Probably those kids of his." She was surprised Doug didn't have call waiting. She herself didn't, but then she didn't have teenagers around to hog the phone either.

Sam's phone had been busy too. Charlie's phone had rung and rung—no answer and no answering machine. Guy did have call waiting, but he was on another line and said he'd call her back when he was through. He might have tried; she'd had the line tied up till Cait rang the doorbell.

"Except for the two guys who forgot to leave their numbers, Donald Duck and Ivan the Terrible," Bonny finished, "that's everyone."

"Wow," said Cait.

"I know."

"The twins will be thrilled, of course. They've got you engaged within six months, you know."

"Get out!"

"It's possible, Bonny. Who knows what might happen?"

"Not that," Bonny said emphatically. "This is all about fun, Cait. Nothing more."

"Not romance?"

"Romance? Pah! I barely *believe* in romance anymore. Fun. Distraction. That's all I'm looking for."

"I see…" said Cait.

"And only till Timothy segues out of town."

"You're sure he's *going* to segue out of town?"

"Positive. And the sooner he's gone, the happier I'll be."

Cait was strangely quiet for a moment. Quiet in a way that made Bonny a little uneasy.

"What?" she asked, frowning.

Cait shook her head. "I just want to see you happy, Bonny. That's all. Whatever it takes."

"Timothy crawling back under his rock," Bonny said shortly.

"Like I said," Cait soothed. "Whatever it takes."

9

Timothy rubbed the sleep from his eyes early Monday morning and headed down the hallway to start a pot of coffee. Maybe he'd whip up a batch of pancakes for his folks this morning. His father worked the late shift on Sundays and the early shift on Mondays, and his mother, though her hours could have been more flexible, tended to work when Reese did. And Donnabelle had been so pleased with his dinner Saturday.

But Donnabelle was already up.

"Mom! What's wrong? You look horrible!"

She was sitting at the kitchen table in her fleece robe, nursing a cup of steaming, pale yellow liquid. Her eyes, red and watering, were narrow slits in her puffy face. She looked as if she'd been crying for hours.

She looked at him miserably. "Tibothy. We hab to talk." He'd never heard her sound so plugged up. Good grief, she must have been crying all night.

"What? What's happened? It's not Dad—"

The door from the back porch opened. "Nothing's happened," Reese said, closing the door behind him. Timothy caught a glimpse of Cleo before it banged shut. "But from all indications, your mother's highly allergic to dogs."

"Allergic to dogs!" Timothy dropped into the chair next to Donnabelle. "You never knew before?"

"It's been so long since I'b been around a dog, I just...hoped it had gone away. I'b so sorry..."

"No, no," his father said, "I'm the one who's sorry, Belle."

Cleo keened mournfully from the other side of the door, and a flicker of some unidentifiable emotion crossed Reese's face. "Shouldn't have brought her in the house. Knew you weren't happy about it."

"But dot that I was allergic," Donnabelle soothed.

Cleo howled again. She must be wondering why she'd been banished to Siberia after two lovely nights in the Bahamas, Timothy thought.

"I'm so sorry, Mom!" He peered at her brew. "Dad's got you on an antihistamine?"

She nodded. "Needs something stronger," his father said. "We already left a message with Doc Ambrose's answering service. He can authorize a prescription over the phone and refer Belle to a specialist."

"You'll have to go to Bellingrath for an allergist. See if you can get in today, Mom. I'll take you."

"Oh, Tibothy, you don't hab to do that. Don't you hab an appointment today?"

"It's early. Eight-thirty. And I know I don't have to do it. I want to."

"More important you find the dog another place to stay," Reese said, his face impassive. "And vacuum the house good when she's gone."

Cleo! Another place to stay! Timothy's heart sank, as much for himself as Cleo. What was he going to do without her?

"I'b so sorry," Donnabelle said again, sadly. Timothy wondered if she was feeling sad for him, Cleo, or Reese. She couldn't have helped but notice how much Reese had been enjoying having a dog around the house.

"We'll spend the day apartment hunting," he said. But he wasn't going to find an apartment ready for move-in tonight—if he found one at all. Pilchuck wasn't big on apartments; he'd probably have to go into Bellingrath. And dog-friendly apartments, he knew from experience, were few and far between.

He'd been living in a no-pets complex when he first took Cleo in, and his landlady—when some snoopy, stingy-hearted neighbor had let her in on the secret—had not been happy. He'd had a time of it finding another place to live where dogs were welcome. And San Diego had a hundred times the rental units available that Tillicum County did.

"She can't stay here another night, Timothy. Not with Belle so miserable."

"I know. Maybe I can kennel her." He hated the idea. Cleo had already been abandoned once in her past. How was she going to feel when he turned her over to strangers? Let them lock her up in a cage?

"Give Critter Keepers in North Bellingrath a call," his father said. "Kimberlee's folks use them when they go on their cruises." Kimberlee had been a clerk at Fairley's since Timothy was in high school. "The Collinses say it's the best in the county."

"Baybe Bonny'd take Cleo in for a few days," his mother suggested.

He brightened for a moment. Bonny! That would be perfect. A house instead of a cage, near downtown, and if she let him have a key, he could pick Cleo up and drop her off anytime during the day.

Yeah, right. When water runs uphill, another part of his brain kicked in. *Bonny won't even take in a teddy bear if it comes from me.*

"Don't worry about it, Mom," he said. "You get to the doctor. I'll find a place for Cleo."

Once in a while Bonny actually took a day off on her alleged day off, but not often. Though in some ways her job was tied to the clock— she did have to be at the gallery when the doors were open—her work didn't stop when she switched the sign on the door from OPEN to CLOSED, any more than it had stopped when the bell rang at the end of a day in the classroom when she was teaching. There was always work to do: competitors to research, artists to contact, commissions to calculate, ad campaigns to implement, displays to design, book-keeping to catch up, *mountains* of papers to file...

Cait and Jack worried that Bonny worked too hard, but the fact was—and she'd told them so a dozen times if she'd told them once—when you were basically a one-woman business, you put in long hours and you wore a hundred hats. Seven days a week was understood.

Which was going to make the Dating Game a challenge, she told herself Monday morning, pulling a yellow rain slicker over her slim blue jeans and apple green sweater. The rain had held off all weekend, but this morning it was pouring buckets.

She stowed her steno notebook—the one with her notes from her personal ad voice mail—in an outside pocket of her handbag, even though she was having second thoughts about the whole idea. Things looked different in the light of day—even a gray and rainy day—than they had last night, when she'd been caught up in the thrill of possibility and anticipation.

What could you tell from a voice-mail message really, or even from a telephone conversation? She doubted she was going to run into any *Loves Music, Loves to Dance* psychos. But she doubted she was going to run into the love of her life either.

Not that she was looking.

It was ridiculous really, when she thought about it. What kind of guys would look for a woman in the personal ads? If it weren't for trying to get Timothy off her mind...

She snorted. A pox on Timothy! A pox on Timothy for even showing up in town. A pox on Timothy *especially* for announcing to the whole world that he aimed to win her back. And in a way no one could possibly forget: flowers, candy, a vow to crawl over broken glass, for pity's sake!

Tired clichés, but used effectively—she had to give him that. He'd had every woman in the gallery practically swooning.

He had you *swooning!*

All the more reason to resist him.

What choice did she have? She sure as rain in Pilchuck wasn't going to give him the satisfaction of thinking all he had to do was play the part of Mr. Romance to have her falling at his feet, she told herself as she made a dash to her car.

All that romantic stuff might work on some women, but it wasn't what she was looking for. Or *would* be looking for if she was looking—which she was not.

So she'd answered a few phone calls. So she'd even made a couple of dates. All in the service of getting Timothy out of her hair. As she'd told Cait, she was in this for fun. For the short term. She definitely wasn't interested in romance.

But if she *were*...

It wouldn't be good looks and romantic gestures that would win her heart. It would be solid qualities like loyalty, dependability, trustworthiness. In a word, integrity.

Give Timothy a chance? Bah! He didn't *stand* a chance.

She pulled up in front of the Kitsch 'n' Caboodle Café and jerked to a stop.

A *pox* on Timothy Fairley.

"Morning, Bonny!" Cindy Fitz greeted her cheerfully when she slipped out of her raincoat and slid into an empty booth a minute later.

"Morning," Bonny returned, trying not to sound snappish. Timothy's flowers were staring her right in the face from the counter next to the cash register. She'd forgotten all about them, or she'd have had a bowl of Cheerios at home and been done with it.

Fortunately the diner was so crowded with Biddy Barton's stunning collection of kitsch—stunning in the sense either of "splendid" or of "stupefying," depending on one's point of view—the bouquet blended into the background and was hardly noticeable. How could a simple bunch of daisies possibly compete with the garish velvet Elvis on the wall opposite the front door? Or the deer-antler chandelier, or the gaudy lamps and salt and pepper shakers, or even the plastic-covered, red cut-velvet upholstery on the booths?

Nevertheless, she went to the trouble of moving to the other side of her table so her back was to the offending floral arrangement. She could just see herself mentally plucking the petals off that center white daisy while she had her breakfast. *He loves me, he loves me not...*

With an effort, she put the flowers out of her mind. She did not want to think about Timothy.

Cindy handed her a menu. "You're up early on your day off."

"Lots to do today. I'm off to La Conner this morning."

"What fun!" Cindy thrust her hands in the pockets of her pink Capris. "Need some coffee to get you going?"

Bonny nodded again, and Cindy scooted away.

The trip *would* be fun, though fun wasn't reason enough to make it. Practically every second store in the little town of La Conner, an hour down the freeway, carried pieces by local artists and craftsmen. Bonny was always on the lookout for new artists who might be interested in showing at the Blue Moon.

Not that the shop owners, even as far away from Pilchuck as they were, would necessarily be willing to give her any information; she planned to spend the morning sleuthing. If she got there when the stores opened, she could be back in Pilchuck in time to get some work done at the office before her dinner date with Jules.

"How ya doin', Bonny?" an old-timer at the counter asked around his toothpick. Alf Mayer owned the local feed-and-seed. His son Tony had been Pilchuck's mayor for a dozen years before he'd won a seat on the Tillicum County Board of Supervisors.

"I mean with Timothy back in town and all," Alf added before Bonny could even say "Fine, thank you."

She sighed. Now she *really* wished she'd opted for a bowl of Cheerios. She should have known better. After all, Cindy Fitz had witnessed the prodigal-husband-come-home incident in its entirety. She almost certainly would have reported the details to Biddy Barton, who along with her husband, Buster, owned the diner. People couldn't have helped but overhear.

"Heard you objurgated your ex but good," said Biddy from behind the counter. She adjusted her cat's-eye glasses and gave her bouffant hairdo a pat. "He's had it comin', is my opinion."

Buster stuck his head out the pass-through window from the kitchen. "*Objurgated*, Biddy?"

Cindy had given her boss a Learn-a-Word-a-Day Calendar for Christmas, and Biddy had been driving everyone crazy with her new vocabulary. Especially Buster.

"Castigated," Biddy clarified.

"*Castigated?*"

"For goodness' sake, Buster! She gave him a good dressin' down!"

"Why don't you just *say* so?" Buster grumbled.

"Why don't you just serve macaroni and cheese from a blue box?" Biddy retorted.

Buster shuddered and withdrew. He knew when to quit.

"Timothy's had it comin', all right," said Alf as if the exchange between Biddy and Buster hadn't happened.

"Now wait a minute," another old-timer protested from the stool next to Alf's. Packard Pruitt was a big berry farmer in the county. Rather, he *had* been—his two sons ran the farm now. "See them flowers down there?" Pack demanded. "From young Fairley to his wife."

"*Ex*-wife," Biddy corrected.

"He brought 'er candy, too, is what I heard," Packard went on, ignoring Biddy, "and she threw the man out on 'is ear. Don't candy and flowers count for nothin' these days?"

"Not when the man walked out of her life without so much as a by-your-leave," Jonas Muncey put in. Jonas owned Strip Joint Furniture Refinishing and Drive-Through Espresso on the edge of town. Bonny had worked with him on several projects for the Downtown Association. They'd always gotten along well. "The man had his nerve barging into the Blue Moon like some Romeo," he added, "after five years away and not a word from him."

"Yup," the old farmer agreed, but with a hint of admiration in his voice. "*Some* nerve. Gotta give 'im credit for it, I say."

"Heard he brought his mutt right into the store yesterday," Harley Burns said to Bonny from his regular seat at the counter.

Harley, a retired county extension agent, practically lived at the Kitsch 'n' Caboodle. "That true?"

"It's true," Cindy answered for Bonny, setting a cup of coffee and a creamer on her table. "My sister was there and saw the whole thing. He marched right in with the dog on a leash and claimed that she could read! Right, Bonny?"

"Not *read*, exactly..."

"You shouldn't have to put up with tomfoolery like that, Bonny," Jonas said, his voice sympathetic. "Timothy deserved to be out on his ear for that one. Good for you for standing your ground."

"All that squawkin' don't mean nothin'," Packard scoffed. He shook a finger in the air. "I'll give the little lady as long as I give them flowers from young Fairley. She'll be beggin' him back—you mark my words—before the last o' them blooms give up the ghost. *Beggin'* him back."

"Beggin'!" said Biddy. "Bonny Fairley beggin'? Now that's just plain derisible, Packard Pruitt, and you know it." Over her shoulder, before her husband could poke his head through the pass-through and ask, she added, "Laughable, Buster." She shook a plump finger at Packard. "You think Bonny Fairley's the beggin' kind, old man, you don't know Bonny Fairley!"

Bonny, meanwhile, could have fried an egg on her face, she was so mortified. The way they talked about her as if she weren't even there! And Packard Pruitt could give her till the last petal fell off the last daisy in the last days before kingdom come, and she still wouldn't beg Timothy to come back to her. The idea! At least Biddy had *that* right.

"Mom says you've had some calls on the personal ad," Cindy said in a lower voice, her eyes bright with curiosity.

"I have," Bonny answered cautiously, not sure she wanted to expound with Tillicum County's biggest ears and loudest mouths lined up along the counter.

"Mebbe young Fairley finally figgered out what it is he wants," Pack nettled from his spot next to Alf Mayer. "Some folks just take longer'n others. The Christian thing t' do—"

"Yes, I've had some *very* interesting calls on the personal ad," Bonny said loudly, not wanting to hear the rest of the old farmer's diatribe. She still wasn't ready to ponder "the Christian thing to do" regarding Timothy, and she *especially* wasn't ready to hear Packard Pruitt's take on the matter. The old goat!

"Sixteen, in fact," she said brightly. "An artist, for one. And a private-practice psychologist. And then there's the college professor with the voice like James Earl Jones."

"Really!"

"Really. And I have a date with a very nice man from Schuyler this evening. He's traveled all over the world." Then, without missing a beat, she added, "What do you recommend this morning, Cindy?"

"Buster's roast-beef hash."

"Fine. With eggs over medium, whole wheat toast."

"Sure picked a bad-weather day for drivin', Bonny," Harley said from the counter.

"If I waited for a good-weather day, I wouldn't get out of Pilchuck till mid-July," she said wryly, grateful for the change of subject. She didn't care what anybody said—when it came to gossip, the Kitsch 'n' Caboodle breakfast crowd was worse than True Marie Weatherby at the beauty salon.

"You got me there." Harley held up his coffee cup, and Cindy, seeing that Biddy had momentarily disappeared into the kitchen, hurried around the counter to fill it. Harley wouldn't put up with an empty coffee cup for long.

"You be careful out there," Otto Grummond cautioned from the stool next to Harley's. "You changed your wiper blades on the Civic lately?"

"Thanks for asking, Otto. Jack took care of it for me just last week." Pilchuck might have its share of busybodies—might, shmight, it *did* have its share of busybodies—but it had its share of good folk watching out for each other too. Bonny had no doubt that if she'd answered Otto's question with a "No, I've been meaning to do that, but I just haven't gotten around to it," he would have borrowed the keys, taken her car to his shop—Grummond's Gas and Auto Doctor near the freeway—and installed a new set of blades himself while she was having her breakfast.

"I hear tell Timothy Fairley got hisself hung in effigy over on Mulberry Street last night," Pack Pruitt said loudly. "Ain't that where you live, Bonny?"

"Can it, Pruitt!" Buster Barton growled through the pass-through from the kitchen. "Or I'm havin' the girls cut off your caffeine!"

Bonny didn't know if it was the threat to the old man's bottomless cup of coffee or something else, but Pack kept quiet after that. She knew the gruff-voiced, scruffy-bearded Buster was a real sweetheart when it came down to it, but even she wouldn't want to run into him in a dark alley. He looked like the kind of guy who'd be happy to cut off a whole lot more than caffeine.

Cindy, savvy enough to see Bonny wasn't in the mood for chitchat, brought her a copy of the *Bellingrath Daily News* someone had left behind. Everyone else seemed to take the hint as well, leaving Bonny to occupy herself with the paper while she waited for her meal.

Buster's roast-beef hash was worth waiting for too—enough to sweeten anyone's temper. Unfortunately, just as Bonny was pulling away from the diner after breakfast, Timothy Fairley pulled up, his mutt in tow.

Buster's hash turned instantly sour in her stomach.

10

"Hey, Timothy," Cindy Reilly—Cindy *Fitz*—greeted him when he walked in the door. "You just missed Bonny."

"Hi, Cindy. I saw her leave." She hadn't looked any too happy to see him either, not even just in passing. No way could he ask her to take in Cleo—not after she'd hanged Bearley by the neck on her front porch.

"She musta seen you comin'," a voice gloated from the counter. A nasty sort of gloating, Timothy thought. The hair on the back of his neck stood on end.

Maybe this hadn't been such a good idea, showing up at the Kitsch 'n' Caboodle Café on a Monday morning. But his parents hadn't been interested in more than a bowl of cold cereal this morning, and he hadn't felt like cooking just for himself.

At least Cindy seemed pleasant enough, and Harley Burns nodded a friendly greeting instead of adding his own dig when Timothy took the seat next to him. Frankly, he needed all the help he could get if he was going to win Bonny back; maybe he could enlist an ally or two this morning. Hiding under a rock certainly wasn't going to help his cause. Nor was picking fights with his neighbors—like the smug old farmer at the other end of the counter. Packard Pruitt.

"She hasn't exactly put out the welcome mat for me," Timothy agreed ruefully with Pack. Out of the corner of his eye he caught the bouquet of colorful gerbera daisies next to the cash register. *Hardly,* they seemed to mock him.

He turned his back on the flowers and glanced down the line of

89

curious faces turned toward him. Otto Grummond sat next to Harley, then Jonas Muncey and Alf Mayer, both small-business owners in town, then old man Pruitt, who never had been the most pleasant of fellows.

"Not unless hangin' a man in effigy's some new way of showin' affection," the old farmer crowed, as if to prove the point.

Hanging a man in effigy! Had that been Bonny's meaning?

Buster Barton stuck his head through the pass-through window from the kitchen and glared at Packard. "Maybe it's time you got on back to the farm, Pruitt."

Packard's face flushed. "Maybe it's time you—"

"More coffee?" Biddy interrupted him loudly, splashing hot coffee into his mug with such enthusiasm it sloshed over the sides.

Which didn't make the old farmer any more pleasant, but at least redirected his indignation. Timothy mentally checked the Bartons as possible allies.

"Bonny had the roast-beef hash," Cindy said in the midst of the commotion, handing him a menu with one hand and pouring him coffee with the other. "I recommend it."

"Fine," he said, handing the menu back. "Eggs over medium—"

"Whole-wheat toast," Cindy finished for him.

"You sure been puttin' the moves on that ex-wife o' yours, Fairley," Alf Mayer called down the counter.

Timothy's jaw tensed. "I don't know if I'd call it that."

"What *would* you call it?"

"The boy's courting her, Alf," Harley Burns answered for him. "That's plain to see. And a lot more heartfelt and respectful than 'puttin' the moves on her,' as you call it."

Harley definitely had the makings of an ally.

"Call it what you will," said Jonas Muncey, sounding belligerent. "Seems to me Bonny's making it pretty clear she isn't interested."

Timothy's palms began to sweat. Unlike old man Pruitt, Jonas usually *was* a pleasant fellow.

"Unless she's just playin' hard to get," Alf suggested.

Now *there* was an idea, Timothy thought, brightening. But the notion and the feeling died quick deaths. Bonny had never been one to play games.

"Says she's got a date tonight. Some world traveler lives in Schuyler," Alf went on.

Timothy's heartbeat quickened. So she *was* dating someone. "Schuyler?" he asked casually. "Someone she's been seeing for a while?"

"Not so far as I know," said Harley.

"Prob'ly someone from the personals," said Otto.

"The personals?"

"You know, them ads people put in the paper lookin' for husbands and wives."

"Bonny's answering personal ads?" Otto must be mistaken. That didn't sound like Bonny at all!

"T'other way 'round," said Otto. "There's guys out there right this minute answerin' Bonny's ad."

"You can't be serious." Timothy shook his head. No way. Not Bonny. Placing a personal ad smacked of desperation. *More* than smacked. Bonny didn't do desperation.

"Oh yes he is," Cindy said cheerfully, dropping a copy of Saturday's *Tillicum Weekly* on the counter in front of Timothy. The county's alternative paper was known for its daring exposés, its movie and restaurant guides, and its personal ads. "The twins put it in," she explained.

"The twins?"

Cindy opened the paper and leafed through it for him. "A surprise for Valentine's Day. Here. See if you can find her."

"Find her?" He shook his head, still not quite believing it.

WOMEN SEEKING MEN, a black box blared up at him. His eyes widened. An entire page of women seeking men!

"People really *do* this?"

"The twins' friend Narcissa got thirty-two responses to her ad," Cindy said.

Timothy almost fell off his stool. "Thirty-two!"

"Yup, and Bonny's had sixteen calls so far. Are you going to look for her ad or aren't you?"

Harley apparently decided Timothy needed help. He leaned over, squinting so he could see, and read, "'Fortyish and Fabulish.' Can't be the one. Bonny might be fabulish, but she's only thirtyish, if I'm not mistaken."

"You're not," Timothy managed, though he still felt as if he'd been smacked broadside with a two-by-four.

"Bimbo Blonde," Harley went on. "Nope. Bonny's neither." His eyes skipped over the page. "Gorgeous Gram..."

"Can't be a gram without bein' a mam," said Otto from the other side of Harley.

Timothy picked up the paper in a daze. His eyes skimmed down a column and jerked to a stop. "Let Me Fly You to the Moon," he read.

"*Blue* Moon, maybe?" Jonas asked.

"No," said Timothy, scanning the ad. "The rest of it doesn't fit." Let Me Fly was a curly blonde with blue eyes and definite New Age leanings. Not Bonny.

"Pretty Witty Wise," he tried again, warming to the task. "I'd say that fits Bonny."

Pretty Witty liked poetry and music and moonlit walks on the beach like Bonny did. But then, what woman didn't? Besides, Witty was forty-seven, not thirty-five.

He didn't even bother with Sweet as Sugar or Rubenesque. No one could accuse his ex of being either.

Taurean Redhead was an art and animal lover who wanted a man who could communicate, all of which was true of Bonny except that she was an Aquarian who didn't give a fig about astrology. The twins wouldn't have written her up that way, would they? And made a mistake about her sign? Nah.

A lot of women were looking for a soul mate, he saw, or if not a soul mate at least a kindred spirit. And one came right out and said she was looking for a sugar daddy! There were lusty women, lonely women, lovely women—or at least they said they were. So many women! And only one, somewhere in the maze, in which he had the slightest interest.

"The Boss-Lady," he read aloud.

One glance through the text and he knew he'd found his ex-wife, even before Cindy confirmed it. Bonny must be having fits over "needs a good man." That and "spunky."

"Read it, Timothy," Biddy urged. Out loud, she meant.

"You do it," he said to Harley, pushing the paper toward the man next to him. He didn't trust his own voice to hold out.

Harley adjusted his spectacles. "The Boss-Lady," he read. "Works too hard, would never have written this ad, so we wrote it for her. Spunky redhead has head for business, eye for art, heart for God. An all-American beauty. Needs a good man."

There was a moment of silence, then from Otto, respectfully, "That's a real nice ad, Cindy. You tell the twins. Real nice."

It *was* nice, Timothy thought unhappily. Too nice. No wonder Bonny had already had sixteen responses. He looked at Cindy, trying to ignore the pinch of jealousy at his heart. "So guys have been calling her. And she's been calling them back."

"Has a date tonight," Harley reminded him as Cindy nodded.

"Said she's heard from some interesting fellas," Alf offered from down the way. "An artist for one, and a psychoanalyzer..."

"A professor, too," Jonas put in.

"With a voice like James Earl Jones," added Harley.

Timothy's heart sank. Bonny would have a lot in common with an artist. She'd probably find a psychoanalyst fascinating. Likewise a professor, especially if he had a voice like James Earl Jones. Bonny had always been partial to the deep-voiced actor.

Preposterous as the whole idea was, what if she really did meet a *good man* through the personal ads? An attractive man? A man she had no reason to push away?

She wouldn't choose a perfect stranger over Timothy, would she?

Why wouldn't she? he answered himself glumly. *When as far as she's concerned I'm lower than gum on a shoe?*

Why couldn't she think back to the good times in their marriage? The loving times? The fun times? The close times? If only he could get her to listen to *everything* in her heart, instead of just the hurt and the anger. If only he could get her to listen to *him*.

He closed the paper, folded it in half, and pushed it toward Cindy. "It is a nice ad," he said morosely.

She pushed the paper back toward him. "You keep it, Timothy."

"Best movie reviews in the county," said Jonas.

Timothy ran his fingers through his hair. "Yeah, right." As if he'd be taking anyone to the movies anytime soon.

"I gotta be gettin' on back to the farm," said old man Pruitt, swinging his stool around. "See how them boys o' mine are mindin' things." He slapped Timothy on the back on his way to the cash register. "That ex-wife o' yers might be an all-American beauty, but she's a real spitfire, too, Fairley. I don't give you longer'n that bouquet of flowers she cold-shouldered."

Timothy stiffened. "Give me? Before what?"

"Before she runs you outta here." He cackled. "It's fittin' folks call you a runnin' fool, ain't it?"

The silence at the counter was sudden and suffocating. Timothy's face burned hot as a chimney fire. Not even Buster poked his head through the pass-through to challenge the old farmer. Biddy, taking Pruitt's money, at least gave him a good glare.

Finally Alf Mayer cleared his throat, breaking the thick silence. "Speakin' of runnin', Timothy," he said as old man Pruitt pocketed his change, "you plannin' on doin' the Balder-to-Bellingrath this year?" He paused. "Or you goin' to be around that long?"

Timothy set his chin. "Oh, I'll be around," he said. But he wasn't talking to Alf. He was talking to Packard Pruitt. "I'll be around for as many Balder-to-Bellingraths as I have breath for. And a *million* bouquets of daisies, old man."

"Hear, hear!" Biddy cried.

Taking a deep breath, Timothy turned his back on the farmer and asked mildly, "Know anybody who might be looking for an old guy to round out a team?"

The men at the counter released a collective sigh, as if every last one of them had been holding his breath.

"You ain't so old, Fairley," said Otto. "Harrison Hunt ran last year. He's forty-somethin'."

"Suzie Wyatt's husband," Cindy reminded him. "So you *are* still a running fool, huh, Timothy?"

He gave her a quick glance. Cindy, too? But her expression was ingenuous.

"I still love to run," he acknowledged. He'd been called a running fool from the time he was a kid. No reason to think it meant anything different now than it meant back then. *No reason but old man Pruitt and the way nobody looked at you when he said what he said...*

But the talk turned to last year's Balder-to-Bellingrath and this year's track team at the high school and the school levy coming up next month. Bonny's name didn't come up in the discussion again.

Timothy started to relax. He savored his roast-beef hash and listened to the conversation ricochet around him. This was the way he remembered the Kitsch 'n' Caboodle. As a community center, a public forum, the place of choice for Pilchuckians to express their opinions, discuss the state of the universe—the most important piece of the universe being their town—and argue about the best way to improve things.

By the time he finished his breakfast, he was getting back his feel for small-town life and politics. He'd never much cared for everyone's knowing his business, the way everybody knew everyone's business in a small town, but there were trade-offs. After five anonymous years of city life, it felt good to be known again. To be included—if not by Bonny yet, at least here at the counter of the Kitsch 'n' Caboodle Café.

"You could answer that ad yourself, you know," said Cindy confidentially when she slid his check under the edge of his plate.

"She'd fast-forward right through me as soon as she recognized my voice."

Biddy came up behind Cindy with the coffeepot. "Bonny's got good reason for feelin' how she feels toward you, Timothy," she said as she refilled his cup. "But she can't stay disapprobated forever."

He decided she must mean *angry*. As far as forever—Biddy was probably right. But she didn't know his ex-wife like he did. Bonny might not stay mad forever, but it sure could *feel* like forever when she was.

"You still love her, then go after her," Biddy added. "No reason why you shouldn't have the same chance as any o' those fellas answerin' her ad."

No reason at all.

Except for his sub-zero standing.

He didn't tell Cleo the story till later, on the way to Critter Keepers Kennels after his job interview, which had gone much more smoothly than breakfast at the Kitsch 'n' Caboodle Café, thank goodness.

Cleo's response was a gratifying howl.

"You got *that* right," Timothy said, grinning. "I would have punched his lights out except that he's an old man. A *mean* old man, but an old man still. Somehow I don't think laying him out would have helped my cause. Besides, I haven't decked anyone since I was fifteen."

Through the rain he saw the sign he was looking for and pulled into a long gravel driveway leading to a ranch-style house. Cleo sat up, her nose quivering and her long, limp ears as cocked as they ever got. She started to whimper long before Timothy heard the distant barks, bays, and howls.

He sighed. He'd been avoiding this moment since six o'clock this morning: the moment of truth. "I'm afraid I have some bad news, girl…"

11

Bonny didn't know exactly what "chemistry"—the kind that happened between two people—was all about. But she did know she and Jules didn't have it. He knew too. They'd had a pleasant meal together, enjoyed each other's company, and agreed at the end of a very early evening there wasn't any spark between them.

Bonny wouldn't have minded seeing him again on friendly terms, since she wasn't really interested in romance anyhow. But Jules was in serious search mode for a partner; he didn't want to "waste his time" with someone who clearly wasn't his one-and-only. She'd been a little miffed about being thought of as a waste of time, even though she understood.

It wasn't that there was anything *wrong* with Jules, Bonny told herself on her drive home through the wind and rain. He was a delightful conversationalist, sophisticated without being phony, and certainly not an eyesore—though his receding hairline made him quite a bit older-looking than Jack, who was her standard for guys in their mid-forties. Either Jules looked old for his age or Jack looked especially young.

He'd also insisted on buying dinner, and as it was one of those restaurants where the napkins were real linen and everything on the plate was priced separately and early-bird specials were unheard of, she'd let him. Having a man buy dinner for her felt very nice indeed.

It was so unfair, having chemistry with a rat like Timothy and not with an interesting, attractive man like Jules. Bonny didn't like to admit it, the way she and Timothy sparked off each other, but there it was.

Those brief, bemuddled moments when she'd first come out of her faint at the Blue Moon and found him kneeling beside her, looking at her so tenderly, brushing the hair away from her face so gently, calling her "sweetheart" in the same tone of voice he'd used in a former life when she'd known with absolute certainty that he loved her...

Another few seconds and she might have kissed him, for pity's sake!

Thank the Lord she'd snapped out of her stupor in time to stop herself.

Thank the Lord—though she hadn't done so at the time—for that splash of cold water to her face.

What had gotten into him anyhow? After all those years away? Why couldn't he just leave her *alone?*

She was almost afraid to go home. Afraid she'd find a teddy bear on her porch swing or flowers on her doorstep or a balladeer in her front yard. Or who-knew-what-all Timothy might have come up with while she'd been gone.

The problem was, as much as she wanted to deny it, good looks and romance did affect her heart. *Timothy's* good looks. Timothy's sweet romantic efforts. Not just any flowers and candy, but gerbera daisies and pecan caramels. And a duet with his dog, for pity's sake! The song echoed in her head, along with Cleo's mournful keening: *Oh come back, my Bonny, to me...*

And then last night, the blue-eyed, silver-haired, huggable, squeezable cupid-bear on her porch, with that note around his neck she didn't want to think about...

Maybe Timothy's trip back to the old hometown was over, she thought hopefully as she exited the freeway. Maybe when he'd pulled up in front of the Kitsch 'n' Caboodle this morning as she was backing out he'd been on his way out of town.

She was tempted to stop by the diner for a cup of decaf, a dish of Biddy's apple betty with vanilla-bean ice cream, and any relevant gossip she'd missed out on since this morning. Maybe, for instance, Timothy had left a hint as to why he'd dropped back into town. What his plans were. How long he was staying...

Maybe he's here forever. Maybe he means what he said. Maybe he really does want to win back your heart.

No, he didn't mean it. He couldn't mean it. If he meant it, he wouldn't have taken five years to let her know. If he meant it, he would have called or written or—

Right. Like you wouldn't have hung up on him and ripped his letters to shreds.

That wasn't the point. The point was that he hadn't even *tried* to communicate.

He's trying now.

"Shut up already!" she said aloud, and zoomed past the diner a good ten miles over the speed limit, which wasn't like Bonny at all.

It was early yet. She hadn't finished restocking the shelves this afternoon after her trip to La Conner. Maybe she'd stop by the gallery and put in another hour or two of work.

It was just too bad about Jules, she told herself as she let herself in the back door. And Steve Talks-About-Himself-Unendingly and Shy Guy, too, for that matter, both of whom she'd connected with after Cait had left last night. Steve, as feared, seemed egotistical and self-absorbed. She'd hardly got a word in edgewise. Guy, on the other hand, couldn't seem to think of a thing to say.

She'd said no to Steve, and Guy hadn't asked.

But she did have dinner with Basso-Profundo Kendall to look forward to on Wednesday. And breakfast with Painter Pete tomorrow morning. She hadn't actually spoken to Pete yet, but he'd left a message on her machine at work this morning suggesting breakfast at the Kitsch 'n' Caboodle, and she'd left a message on *his* machine this afternoon that breakfast was fine; she'd meet him at eight.

She'd have preferred to talk to him first. She knew nothing about him except what he'd left on her voice mail. That and the fact that his voice was familiar. But she had a feeling it was going to be easier just to meet him than to try to catch him on the phone.

Besides, as she'd discovered with Jules, some things you couldn't tell over the phone anyhow.

Which was why, when she found a message on her office machine from Norman suggesting dinner the following evening, she called him immediately and said yes. Even though he *was* a tax attorney and their conversation was less than scintillating. Who knew?

"It'll have to be a late dinner," she said. "I'll be tied up at work till seven or seven-thirty tomorrow." Jack and Cait were bringing a delivery by after the gallery closed. "Is that all right?"

"Why don't I come into Pilchuck to save you time?" he suggested. He lived in Bellingrath. "There's that café I've heard so much about—the Kitschy Something?"

"The Kitsch 'n' Caboodle," Bonny said. "You don't mind?"

"Not at all. And I don't mean to cut our conversation short, Bonny, but I'm expecting another call. So I'll see you tomorrow?"

"Fine. How about eight o'clock?"

There was a message from Cait too, which Bonny answered on her portable phone, wedged between her ear and her shoulder, as she worked on restocking the shelves.

"Too bad," Cait commiserated when Bonny told her about her disappointing date with Jules. "That chemistry thing is really a mystery, isn't it?"

When she heard about Bonny's breakfast and dinner dates the next day, she responded with uncertainty. "The Kitsch 'n' Caboodle Café? Do you really want to do that?"

"I wasn't sure at first. But number one, it's practical—especially with my schedule. Number two, it's safe—just in case I *do* run into some *Loves Music, Loves to Dance* psycho."

"Good point. I hadn't thought of that."

"And number three, Packard Pruitt threw down a glove in the Kitsch 'n' Caboodle this morning, and I've *got* to pick it up. It's a matter of pride."

"Huh?"

"Old Pack doesn't think I'll last as long as those daisies Timothy gave me before I'm begging him back," Bonny said indignantly. "And he said so to everyone there! Can you imagine? The idea!"

"So meeting your dates at the Kitsch 'n' Caboodle is rubbing it in Pack's face?"

"Meeting my dates at the Kitsch 'n' Caboodle is saving *my* face," Bonny said stubbornly. "Besides, I want to be there to see those petals fall."

Cait was silent for a moment. "Well, if public is what you want, the Kitsch 'n' Caboodle is it, all right."

Bonny was exhausted by the time she locked the door of the gallery just before ten and headed home. Restocking shelves took a lot of energy. So did prospecting trips. So did driving in this crazy northwest Washington weather, when you couldn't tell from one minute to the next if it was going to rain, snow, hail, blow, or even break into sunshine.

So did disappointment. Even with more dates to look forward to.

But what was more exhausting than anything, she told herself as she pulled into her driveway, was Timothy Fairley. Thinking about Timothy. *Not* thinking about Timothy. Which was almost as difficult as not thinking about an elephant in a pink tutu.

She stretched the tired muscles of her back and neck as she climbed the stairs to her front porch. In the old days, Timothy had given her wonderful backrubs when she'd been tense and tired…

The first thing she saw when she flipped on the light in the entryway was Bearley, sitting in the corner of her sofa in the dimly lit living room just like he belonged there.

She frowned at the teddy bear, as if he could see. As if a frown would prompt him to jump up, apologize for intruding, and beat a hasty retreat.

But her frown seemed to have the opposite effect. In fact, Bearley seemed intensely interested in her every movement as she hung her purse and jacket on the hall tree, exchanged her leather ankle boots for fleece-lined slippers, and crossed the living room toward the kitchen.

He was like those paintings in the Haunted House at Disneyland, she thought, the ones with the eyes that followed you wherever you went. The ones that had scared the stuffing out of her as a little girl.

Don't be silly, she told herself as an involuntary shiver crawled up her spine. And just to prove she wasn't afraid of ghosts or teddy bears, she changed direction, stepped around the coffee table, and plucked Bearley from the pile of pillows on the sofa, hugging him close in an embrace more fierce than affectionate, burying her face in his furry neck.

Oh no, she thought fleetingly as the faint scent of forest glens and fresh mountain air enveloped her. Whitewater aftershave. Timothy's scent. It was so subtle at first she wondered if she was imagining it. She hadn't smelled it last night when she'd brought the teddy bear in—but then she hadn't buried her face in his soft fur last night either.

Without thinking she drew in a long, deep breath, inhaling the crisp, clean scent—and then thinking wasn't an option. The flood of feelings that swept through her was so intense she could hardly bear it: joy, sorrow, anger, hurt, love, hate…

She must have cried for half an hour, curled up on the sofa with Bearley in her arms and an afghan pulled around her, before she fell asleep.

When she woke again, sometime in the middle of the night, it was to a nasty headache and an ugly crick in her neck. For a moment she was disoriented. But one look at the teddy bear she still clutched in her arms and she knew exactly where she was. And why.

She sat up abruptly, dropping Bearley as if he smelled of skunk rather than the fresh, inviting scent of Timothy's aftershave.

How dare he! Timothy, that is. Bearley, as Cait had pointed out, was merely an innocent pawn. Timothy, on the other hand—

Timothy must know very well as a student of the sciences—as Bonny knew from a recent and extremely fascinating article in *Psychology for the New Century*—that the sense of smell had remarkable powers to evoke emotional memories. Dabbing his Whitewater aftershave on Bearley had been anything but innocent.

Leaving the teddy bear on the floor where she'd dropped

him—innocent pawn or not, Bearley was wearing that after-shave—Bonny stalked into the kitchen with the afghan draped over her shoulders and pulled open the door to the freezer, where a pint of mint–chocolate-chip ice cream was calling her name loudly, drowning out the soft whisper from another recent and fascinating *Psychology for the New Century* article: "Food is not love."

Bonny knew food wasn't love. She knew a pint of mint–chocolate-chip ice cream couldn't fill the hole her ex-husband had left in her heart—the hole she'd thought, until he walked into the Blue Moon Gallery on Saturday, had healed over. Who would have guessed the wound had merely been patched? And when it came right down to it, not very well?

Ice cream was only a stopgap measure, she told herself—a temporary fix, a Band-Aid. But at the moment, it was all she had.

She sat down at the kitchen table, ice cream in one hand and spoon in the other, and was just about to dip in when she noticed that the message light on her answering machine was blinking. She hadn't made it as far as the kitchen when she'd come in earlier.

One message, she saw as she hit the rewind button.

The tape whirred on and on. She frowned at the machine, wondering if it was broken. One message should have rewound in about ten seconds. Unless it was Cait, who did sometimes tend to ramble on.

The tape finally clicked twice and started to play.

No message. Just music.

Music?

Saxophone music. Leggett Lee saxophone music. Frail and tinny through the tiny speakers on the answering machine, but unmistakably Leggett. She loved Leggett Lee; she'd been a fan for years before the world at large had discovered him. In fact, Timothy had introduced her to the jazz artist's music at an intimate harborside summer evening concert in Bellingrath when they were both still college students.

She closed her eyes, remembering as if she had been there yesterday the sailboat masts silhouetted against a glorious salmon-colored sunset, and Timothy's arm around her shoulders, warm against her night-cooled skin, and Leggett hopping off the stage, sauntering down the aisle with his saxophone, stopping right in front of them to play, swaying to the music he was making...

Timothy!

Her eyes flew open as the tape clicked off abruptly, in the middle of a tune.

"Lots of people like Leggett Lee," she reasoned aloud, trying to convince herself. But on top of Bearley's smelling of Whitewater aftershave—

The message was from Timothy, all right. Counting on the music to conjure up that concert by the bay. Counting on Leggett the way he'd counted on his aftershave. The man was no idiot.

And neither was Bonny. She knew exactly what he was doing with his cheap psychological tricks. And if he thought for a minute his sleazy stunts were going to get her to welcome him back with open arms, he had another think coming.

She dug into her mint–chocolate-chip in a fury. Why was he doing this to her? The creep. The jerk. The *skunk*.

Tomorrow, she told herself. Tomorrow she'd take her voice-mail notes to work with her. Tomorrow she'd start making dates in earnest. Tomorrow, if she had to, she'd even call back Steve Talks-About-Himself-Unendingly and Shy Guy.

Tomorrow would see the beginning of a whole new era in the life of Bonny Van Hooten Fairley.

"Boyfriend, here I come!" she declared, jabbing her spoon in the air. Forget fun. Forget distraction. This was *war.*

A full pint of ice cream later, still fuming, Bonny changed into her nightclothes and crawled between the sheets on her bed, where she promptly realized she'd failed to check her *Tillicum Weekly* voice mail. She crawled back out, dug her notebook out of her handbag, and dialed in.

She was glad she did. The seven new messages from seven new possible boyfriends flushed Timothy Fairley right out of her brain.

And after she hung up, she even got an hour or two of sleep before her alarm went off.

Bearley, on the other hand, got no sleep at all. He spent the night and most of the next day lying facedown on the living room rug between the sofa and the coffee table.

Right where Bonny had dumped him.

12

Bonny knew the minute she walked into the Kitsch 'n' Caboodle Café on Tuesday morning why Painter Pete's voice had sounded so familiar over the phone.

And also why so many *Tillicum Weekly* personal ads included the age of the advertiser.

Painter Pete was Pete Pickle Sr., whose last official act as president and CEO of the First National Bank of Pilchuck before he retired had been granting Bonny a loan to open the Blue Moon Gallery. Pete Pickle Jr. had taken his place, and Pete Pickle Jr. was at least fifty.

That made Pete Pickle Sr., who'd been widowed for six or seven years, a good seventy at least, though he declined to state his age when Cindy, who as usual was working the early shift at the diner, asked him. Cindy would ask anybody anything. It was just her way.

And *tell* anybody anything too. She made sure to tell Bonny, for instance, that Timothy Fairley had already been by for coffee this morning.

"On his way out of town?" Bonny asked hopefully.

"Nope. In fact, he was asking around about rental units."

"Rentals?" The information didn't compute. Why would Timothy be looking for a rental?

She didn't want to think about it. "Never mind. What are you having for breakfast, Pete?"

"Cindy says the German apple pancakes won Buster first prize in the *Bellingrath Daily News* Breakfast Cookoff," Pete said.

"Heavenly," said Cindy.

"Sold."

It wasn't that Bonny didn't enjoy her breakfast with Pete, despite the interested looks they got from around the diner. She could almost hear the news rumbling along the old Pilchuck pipeline already: "Bonny Fairley and Pete Pickle Sr.!" "Can you imagine?" "Whoever would have thought the old man would be answering personal ads?"

Pete was sweet and amusing and genuinely interested in how Bonny was doing with the gallery. But the fact that he was twice her age put him out of the running as a serious boyfriend candidate. Some thirty-five-year-old women might not have seen it that way, especially as Pete owned half the town, but the idea just didn't work for Bonny.

Oh well. There was still Norman tonight. And Kendall tomorrow night. And a good dozen guys she hadn't even connected with yet. And maybe even more calls to come. Who knew?

"So you've taken up painting since your retirement," she said to Pete as she finished up her pancakes. "What's your medium?" Since the Blue Moon was a gallery of fine crafts—items both beautiful and functional—she'd never shown paintings there. But it was a thought. Especially since Pilchuck didn't have a fine-art gallery of its own.

"Oils," he said, beaming.

"Really! Are you showing anywhere?"

"He's showing right here in the Kitsch 'n' Caboodle," Cindy answered for Pete as she topped off their coffee.

"Biddy bought my very first painting," Pete said modestly. "And two others since."

"Really," Bonny said again, her interest and enthusiasm waning.

"Look around, Bonny," said Cindy. "See if you can guess which paintings are Pete's."

Looking around the Kitsch 'n' Caboodle Café was something Bonny normally tried to avoid. Quite frankly, for someone who had "an eye for art," as the twins had put it, looking around the Kitsch 'n' Caboodle Café could be downright painful. That Biddy had bought Pete's paintings to hang in the diner was not an auspicious sign.

She glanced quickly around the restaurant—too quickly to catch any details—and then back at Pete. "I give," she said. "Where are they, Pete?"

"I'll give you a hint—"

"I'm no good with hints," she said, shaking her head. Oh dear! She could feel a bubble of mirth beginning to form in her stomach…

"Well then," he demurred. "It's the Van Gogh next to the Mickey Mouse clock—"

The bubble rose. Bonny rubbed vigorously at the tip of her nose with her index finger.

"—the Gauguin over there by Marilyn Monroe—"

It was in her throat. She bit her lip to keep from snorting.

"—and the Matisse under the exit sign. Paint-by-number," Pete finished proudly.

Short of divine intervention, Bonny was going to explode in about three seconds. *Please, please, please, please, please, God!*

The explosion came, but in the form of a mighty sneeze instead of a belly laugh—for which Bonny later thanked the good Lord profusely. Pete might have misinterpreted—or even worse, interpreted *exactly*. She had no desire to hurt his feelings. Or Biddy's, for that matter.

A chorus of gesundheits from all over the diner hit her in surround sound.

"Excuse me!" she said, her eyes watering, when she recovered herself.

"That was a powerful sneeze," Pete said, sounding awed.

"Lily Johansen says there's a bug going 'round," said Cindy. Lily Johansen was Pilchuck's resident nurse.

Bonny shook her head and dabbed at her eyes with her napkin. "I don't think it's a bug," she said. "I think I'm allergic to—"

Once again, divine intervention. She'd almost said "bad art."

"—mornings," she said instead, and dissolved into hysterical giggles.

Which everyone in the restaurant took as embarrassment and forgave her for.

Business at the Blue Moon on Tuesday morning was slow as an old dog in a heat wave, and Bonny had about as much energy. Breakfast might have been funny, but it had been disappointing, too. Disappointment was wearisome. She ought to know.

So she pulled a stool up to the wall phone behind the counter and started making phone calls. She tried Cait first, just to give her a quick report on her breakfast with Pete Pickle, but nobody answered.

Business first, she told herself, and then she'd return some of those *Tillicum Weekly* calls she hadn't gotten around to.

Yesterday on her prospecting trip she'd located several artisans whose work would be excellent fits for the gallery. Her first call was to the fine furniture maker whose "dancing furniture" had kept her in La Conner longer than she'd planned while she tracked down his address and telephone number. The his-and-hers maple burl dressers she'd found in one of the fine craft stores, leaning against each other with their curved legs playfully intertwined, had delighted her no end.

Yes, he'd be interested in showing in Pilchuck, he told her. Yes, he could send photos of his work and a price list. Yes, he'd be happy to show her around his workshop. Monday? He'd be out of town next Monday, but the following week would be fine.

She'd also made contact with a talented weaver who spun and dyed her own yarns and a glassblower who'd studied with Seattle's world-renowned Dale Chihuly, and she left messages for a millefiori beadmaker and an ingenious welder who created playful garden-tool sculpture. All in all, she was pleased and excited about her prospects.

And she was just as excited about her personal prospects, even after the disappointment of her first two *Tillicum Weekly* dates. After all, how many people found their prince after kissing a single frog? Or even *two* single frogs?

Prince? the little voice niggled inside her head. *Three days ago you were protesting all over Pilchuck you weren't the least bit interested in romance—and now you're looking for your* prince?

Only to get Timothy out of her hair, she assured herself.

Out of her hair? Pah! More like out of her *life*. There were plenty of frogs in the pond, and if none of them happened to be a prince in disguise, she didn't care. The whole idea was to prove to her unreliable, irresponsible, indefensible ex-husband that she was doing just fine without him, thank you, and he might as well throw his suitcase back in his pickup and move on.

But if there happened to *be* a prince out there somewhere, and if she happened to run into him…well, so much the better. Surely there was nothing wrong with keeping an eye out for possible princes.

Like Basso-Profundo Kendall maybe, who somehow managed to catch her between phone calls just to say he was looking forward to dinner tomorrow. "I wish I could take you somewhere more romantic than the Kitsch 'n' Caboodle Café," he said in his impossibly deep voice, "but if you don't get off work till after six and have to be at choir practice by seven-thirty…"

To tell the truth, she wished he could take her somewhere more *private* than the Kitsch 'n' Caboodle Café—especially after her breakfast date with Pete this morning—but Kendall taught evening classes, and Wednesday was his earliest window of opportunity.

"Would you rather reschedule?" she asked.

"Oh no. I've been looking forward to meeting you ever since our phone call Sunday night."

That gave her a buzz. So did her call to Therapist Theo. He didn't have much time to talk, but he'd love to take her to dinner on Friday if she was free.

She'd just hung up with Theo when Agnes Schlichenmeier pushed her way through the door of the Blue Moon. Agnes was an extremely high-maintenance customer, but Bonny never minded paying her the attention she required; sometimes she thought it was the only attention the poor woman ever got. Mrs. Schlichenmeier's family all lived out of town and didn't visit often, even though most of what she bought in the Blue Moon was for them. You'd think, especially with her weak heart, that her children would make the effort to see her once in a while.

"Something for my son. I just have no idea," Mrs. Schlichenmeier fretted now, fluttering her hand. "He has everything he could possibly need."

"We'll find him something," Bonny soothed. "Now tell me about him again, Agnes…"

"She isn't going to let you in the door, man," Timothy mumbled to himself as he pulled up in front of the Blue Moon Gallery mid-morning on Tuesday.

"She will if she knows I'm here for a gift for Mom," he argued back. Bonny had always adored her mother-in-law. And Reese, too, for that matter. Even before Reese and Donnabelle Fairley were her in-laws, she'd adored them.

Besides, he wanted to share his good news with somebody. No—not just with somebody. With Bonny.

He sat in the car for a moment, staring at the old ivy-covered building that had housed the First National Bank of Pilchuck for eighty years before it was deemed unfit for the image of a progressive, forward-moving financial institution. Too bad—the turn-of-the-century brick building fit the historic character of Pilchuck a whole lot better than the modern monstrosity the city fathers had felt obliged to allow around the corner and down the street.

On the other hand, the old bank building was a perfect site for Bonny's Blue Moon Gallery of Fine Crafts. It was as good a site as any in Pilchuck—close enough to the Kitsch 'n' Caboodle Café and the Apple Basket Market and Fairley's Drug and Fountain that it was an easy stop for locals. And if a traveler made it off the interstate, past the golf course, and over the bridge into town—well, it would be hard to resist a detour into the Blue Moon.

Even without the whimsical, hand-carved sign that hung out front—a smiling, winking, full-face moon stained pale blue—the aging brick building had a warm and gracious ambience that invited one inside. And so did the well-designed window displays to each side of the entryway—especially on a dreary day like today. Timothy took a moment to study them through the drizzle, something he hadn't taken the time to do on his two previous visits to the gallery.

Bonny loved to decorate, and he'd always admired her artistic flair. She must be thrilled having window and floor displays she could change every week if she wanted to.

To the left of the door, the arched brick window framed a parlor scene, backed by folding wooden screens painted antique red. A writing desk in the Stickley style Bonny had always loved sat at an angle to the window, and a fuzzy forest-green afghan was casually draped across the back of the matching chair. A wicker tray on the desktop held a teapot shaped and painted like a purple cabbage head and a matching cabbage-leaf teacup and saucer.

Next to the tray a blue glass paperweight and a twig pen held down several sheets of stationery. A wrought-iron floor lamp stood to one side of the desk, its handmade paper shade embedded with leaves and flowers, and a tall reed basket filled with dried cattails stood to the other side. Underfoot a multicolored, flower-strewn rug tied the "room" together. The display looked ready for someone to move in.

You are *looking for a place of your own...*

He grinned at the thought. Just what he needed—living in a display window. As if dining at the Kitsch 'n' Caboodle wasn't public enough. As if simply living in Pilchuck wasn't public enough.

The window to the right of the door was made up like a bedroom, with a truncated four-poster dressed in lavender-lined white eyelet, the covers turned down, a mound of quilted and appliquéd pillows in lavender, yellow, and white pristine against the cherry headboard. A bit too frilly for Timothy's taste, but he could appreciate the appeal. A geometric leaded-glass table lamp sat on the nightstand next to the bed, along with a collection of brilliant cut- and blown-glass perfume flasks. A rag rug in purple, yellow, and grass green added another splash of bright color.

Bonny did know how to put a room together, Timothy thought. He wondered what she'd done with the house on Mulberry since he'd been gone.

And how long it would take to get her to invite him over to see.

Never, if you don't get inside right now and try once more to wriggle your way back into her affections. He got out of the car and hurried across the sidewalk to the gallery door before he could change his mind. Once that shop bell rang and Bonny saw him, there would be no turning back.

She was helping another customer when he walked in but turned her head at the sound of the bell.

Wow. Was she ever beautiful!

He liked the way she was dressing for work these days, in brightly colored rib-knits tucked into dark, slim skirts with matching tights, showing her willowy figure to advantage. Her sweater today was a rich red-orange turtleneck that turned the shiny copper hair cascading over her shoulders just a shade darker.

But once again, if looks could kill—

"Excuse me," she said to her customer—Agnes Schlichenmeier, he saw. He wondered if the elderly woman was still taking placebos "for her heart." "I can't take any excitement, you know," she used to flutter to Timothy's father when he filled her prescription for the sugar pills.

Reese had always been so patient with her too, patting her on the arm as he issued instructions. "You just keep taking your pills and you'll be fine, Agnes." He was good with his elderly customers. He knew how to put them at ease—a skill Timothy had never fully developed, maybe because he'd been so ill at ease with himself.

His ex-wife was walking toward him with the slight sway to her hips that had never failed to move him. And wasn't failing to move him now. He swallowed. How could he have been such a fool?

She stopped in front of him, arms crossed over her chest, and demanded in a low voice, "What are you doing here?"

He swallowed again. What *was* he doing here? She was never going to forgive him. Never going to accept him. Never going to love him…

"Mom's birthday," he managed in a fairly calm voice, thrusting his hands in the pockets of his slacks. "I thought I might find something here she'd like."

Bonny eyed him warily. "Where's your dog? You don't need her to help you pick out a gift for your mother?"

"I thought I'd let you help this time." He didn't want to tell her Cleo was in a kennel.

"I don't want a scene, Timothy," she warned. "No presents, no music, no anything."

"No anything," he agreed, pulling his pockets inside out to show her. He tucked them back in before adding, "But I did want to tell you—"

She raised a hand. "Save your breath, Timothy. No *anything*. Including whatever it is you think you have to say. I don't want to hear it."

"But—"

"You might want to consider a lamp in the Arts and Crafts style," she interrupted again, turning to gesture toward a table lamp like the one he'd seen in the window.

"Bonny—"

"Or perhaps a lap quilt." She pointed to a small crazy quilt draped over a hickory chair. "An Olga Pfefferkuchen original." Her tone was surprisingly pleasant—for Mrs. Schlichenmeier's benefit, no doubt. The old woman was staring at Bonny and Timothy, eyes wide, her hands clutched together over her heart.

"I just want to—"

"Donnabelle admired the lamps the last time she was in," Bonny went on smoothly. "And I have a feeling she'd like Olga's handiwork too. Why don't you look around while I finish helping Agnes?"

She turned her back on him. He watched her walk away, the subtle sway of her hips seeming to mock him, and suddenly he couldn't bear to be in the same room with her. Not feeling the way he was feeling— angry and hurt and so blasted frustrated he could hardly think. If he didn't get out of here now, he was going to do something he'd regret for a long time. Like throw something. *Anything.* Not a good idea when the handiest piece was a blown-glass bowl with a two-hundred-dollar price tag.

Besides, with his luck, Mrs. Schlichenmeier would surprise them all and *have* a heart attack, and he'd have that on his conscience too.

He turned on his heel and whipped the shop door open. The intense satisfaction he felt at the violent jangle of the bell and then the loud slam of the door behind him took him by surprise—and made him doubly glad he'd walked away from the two-hundred-dollar bowl.

He slammed the door of the truck so hard the windows shook. She was so infuriating! How could they ever work things out if she wouldn't even talk to him?

That's what she used to say to you.

Timothy slumped at the steering wheel for a moment, remembering. Over the last two years of their marriage, Bonny must have asked him that same question a hundred times. Pleading with him. Trying in every way she knew to engage him, to get some kind of response from him. Any response at all.

How can we ever work things out, she used to say, *if you won't even talk to me?*

116

13

She'd got rid of *him,* Bonny thought triumphantly as she rang up Mrs. Schlichenmeier's purchase. And without resorting to being mean and nasty.

Got rid of him? an inner voice scoffed. *You didn't get rid of him. He ran away. Just like always.*

"Surprise, surprise," she muttered under her breath, her sense of triumph fading.

He *had* slammed the door quite soundly on the way out, however, she told herself thoughtfully. That part wasn't just like always…

She bagged the hinged wooden chessboard and the exquisitely carved birch and cherry pieces hidden inside. "As always it was a pleasure, Agnes," she said, sliding the bag across the counter. "Your son's going to love that chess set."

"I do hope so. You have such lovely things, dear," the older woman fluttered.

Bonny walked her to the door and opened it for her. "You take care of that heart now, hear?"

"I do try," she said, still fluttering. "I can't take any excitement, you know."

Mrs. Schlichenmeier reminded people about her bad heart on a regular basis, which was partly the reason Bonny had handled Timothy's intrusion with such dispatch. Her own fainting spell on Saturday had been quite enough excitement for the Blue Moon for the rest of the year, thank you.

After Agnes left, between the few customers who drifted in and out of the store without buying anything, Bonny made a few more calls on the personal ad. She didn't reach anyone—no surprise for midday on a Tuesday. She tried to call Cait again too, but this time the line was busy.

She stifled a yawn. Last night's interrupted sleep was catching up with her. Another reason to be furious with Timothy, she thought, not even trying to stifle her second yawn. But somehow, she didn't seem to have enough energy to get worked up about him.

"You feeling all right?" Lavinie Howell asked when she stopped in with the mail a few minutes later.

"Just one of those low-energy days, Lavinie."

"Low blood sugar, I'll bet," the letter carrier said as she laid a stack of correspondence on the counter. "An apple a day, Bonny. Works wonders."

She didn't happen to have an apple available, but she did start a pot of coffee in the stockroom where the machine was plugged in.

Then Priscilla Wyatt blew into the Blue Moon on her midday break from the preschool around the corner, and Bonny discovered she didn't need a shot of caffeine, or even an apple. Priscilla woke her up but good.

Timothy, meanwhile, was sorting through his feelings the way he knew best—by stretching his legs out over the road, Cleo at his heels, both of them oblivious to the rain. Nothing in God's creation had ever kept Timothy Fairley from running when he wanted to run—rain, snow, or blistering sun.

As a child, he'd worn through sneakers "faster than any kid this side of the Ruby River," according to Mr. Pederson at the Shoe Tree. "Only kid I know who wears 'em out before he grows out of 'em," Mr. Pederson would say, shaking his head, when Donnabelle took her son in for a new pair of shoes. "Your boy keeps me in business, Miz Fairley." Then he'd tousle Timothy's dark hair, which Timothy had always hated, and say, "You just keep runnin', boy. You just keep on runnin'."

He had, despite Mr. Pederson's hair tousling. He'd run and run, faster and farther the older he got, and by the time he graduated from Pilchuck High School he'd broken every track and cross-country record in district history. As far as he knew, he still held the record for the two-mile—unless some other running fool had stolen it from him in the last five years. He'd have to check the next time he went by the high school.

Athletic scholarships and a part-time track-and-field coaching job had helped pay Timothy's way through pharmacy school. In fact, running had made his studies not only possible, but *bearable*.

He rounded the corner from the macadam road into his parents' long gravel driveway, splashing through a large puddle with abandon. He'd forgotten how therapeutic puddles could be. Cleo splashed right along beside him. Timothy hadn't wasted a minute driving out to Critter Keepers to pick her up after leaving the Blue Moon.

"Don't know how—I would've made it—through school—without running," he panted to his companion.

Or without Bonny either, he added to himself.

Bonny, too, had attended Duwamish University in Seattle, though she'd been two years behind him and across campus in the school of education. If only he'd signed up for her program instead of his! How much grief could he have spared everyone?

Even back then, Bonny had been as stubborn and prickly as the wild Northwest blackberry vines that could swallow a backyard in the space of a season. Stubborn, prickly, and as hotheaded as redheads come.

At least that was one way to look at it. Tenacious, courageous, and passionate was another. Bonny lived her truth, she spoke her mind—and she loved without reservation. At least she had in the past. He'd been crazy in love with her. He still was. His unhappiness had just confused him for a while.

Cleo raced for the doorstep leading to the porch as soon as they rounded the corner into the backyard. Timothy whistled her back.

"Sorry, girl. I rub you down in there and Mom'll be crying her eyes out."

He opened the back of the camper shell, grabbed a towel, and got most of the mud off Cleo before hoisting her over the tailgate and rubbing her down with a second towel. Not an easy task when he was standing outside in the rain and she kept lunging for his face with her tongue.

He didn't think anyone had ever been as happy to see him as Cleo had been when he picked her up at the kennel today. Not even his mom. And certainly not Bonny, unless he went way back to the early days...

"Okay, Clee." He gave her ears a final rub. "Give me an hour to get cleaned up and give the house a good vacuuming, and we'll go for a ride into town. You up for that?"

Cleo gurgled joyously and tried to jump out of the truck.

"Stay, girl!"

She did, but she didn't look any too happy about it. Timothy wasn't too happy himself; this arrangement was going to get old fast. He really had to find a place to live.

Ten minutes later he turned off the water in the shower and reached around the curtain for a warm towel. He'd always loved that heating vent in the floor beneath the towel rack in the bathroom— so much so that it was the first improvement he'd made to the house on Mulberry Street after he and Bonny moved in.

He missed that house. He missed the way he and Bonny, together, had made it a home. Did she remember—*could* she remember—how happy they'd been those first few years, before he'd ruined everything by running away?

And speaking of running away...

He'd been kicking himself all over the place for the way he'd stormed out of the Blue Moon this morning—and not because he'd slammed the door on his way out. For a cigar-store Indian, slamming doors had to be progress.

Leaving, however, was not. Leaving was what Bonny expected of him.

And the expected, Timothy realized as he toweled himself dry, was something he could no longer afford to do.

Of course he hadn't *really* run away. Bonny had made it exceedingly clear she didn't want him around.

She didn't kick you out. She invited you to look around the store.

"Yeah, right—in a tone of voice that invited me to jump in the nearest lake," he muttered.

She was waiting on another customer. You're taking this all too personally.

On the other hand—how else could one *take* such a blatant snub?

Maybe it wasn't a snub. Maybe...maybe she was just looking out for Mrs. Schlichenmeier's heart.

Hmm. Possible. Not many people except for old Doc Ambrose and Reese and Timothy knew that Agnes Schlichenmeier's heart was perfectly healthy. Oh, and probably the other pharmacist by now, the one his father had hired when he finally realized Timothy wasn't coming back...

Bonny would be careful about a thing like Mrs. Schlichenmeier's heart.

Maybe she's looking out for her own *heart.*

He winced. Of course she was. And with good reason. He'd tromped all over it once already. Why wouldn't she expect him to do it again?

If only she'd listen to him! If only she'd let him say he knew how much he'd hurt her. Not just with the divorce either. He knew now the divorce was only the final step in his abandonment. In those last few years, confused and unhappy, he'd progressively shut her out of his thoughts, out of his dreams and fears, out of his *heart*—until she wasn't even a consideration by the time he decided to make his leaving official.

That was the betrayal. That was what he needed Bonny's forgiveness for.

If only she'd let him ask for it!

He ran the towel over his still-damp hair. Would Bonny have understood how trapped his life had made him feel? If he'd ever been able to tell her?

Would it have made a difference?

It was Timothy's opinion—or at least it *had* been Timothy's opinion, Bonny corrected herself—that Simon Wyatt married Priscilla because Bonny was already taken. Of course, back then, Timothy had always said that any man who wasn't crazy about Bonny Van Hooten Fairley was just plain crazy.

But Simon was still with his wife. Unlike Timothy.

Pris was a redhead too, though her hair was short, curly, and a shade darker than Bonny's straight fall of copper. In Bonny's opinion, the similarity ended with their red hair. She could never hope to be as patient, even-tempered, and mellow as Priscilla was. She and Simon had two boys, the older of whom Bonny knew without a doubt would have driven her to the brink by now.

Bonny sometimes wondered—though she banished the thought as soon as she realized it had entered her head—how a child with her and Timothy's genes might have turned out...

"So I guess your ex is going to be around for a while, huh?" Priscilla commented, stepping to the counter with several greeting cards in hand.

Bonny's head jerked up from her stack of mail. She frowned at the other redhead over the top of her reading glasses. "Be around for a while? What do you mean?"

Pris handed Bonny the cards and pulled her wallet from her purse. "He got the job."

"Job? What job?"

Priscilla looked as puzzled as Bonny felt. "At the high school. You mean you didn't know he was back in town to interview with Simon?"

Bonny was too shocked to try to hide it. "I had no idea!"

Pris gave her a sidelong look. "Of course he has other reasons, too, I hear…"

Bonny ignored the prompt. "What kind of work could Timothy do at the high school?" she wondered aloud, mystified at the news. Surely Pris must be mistaken…

"He's taking Lonetta's classes while she's on pregnancy leave. And helping out with the cross-country team, which Simon's ecstatic about."

"What? Timothy?" She shook her head in denial. The coaching maybe, but… "Timothy's not a teacher."

"He's not?" Priscilla looked even more puzzled. "But he has to be, Bonny. Simon couldn't hire someone who didn't have the proper credentials."

"True," another voice broke in. "Timothy's fully certified, Bonny."

Bonny looked over Pris's shoulder to find Lonetta herself, shaking the rain off her coat and puffing from the effort of carrying her large belly around. Bonny hadn't even heard the bell on the door.

What was she doing here midafternoon on a school day, anyhow?

"Doctor's appointment," Lonetta said, as if she could read Bonny's mind—or at least as if she knew an ex-teacher would wonder. "I talked to your ex this morning, Bonny. Seems he went back to school for his teaching certificate a couple of years ago. Secondary, with math and science endorsements."

"B-b-but…"

"I know," Lonetta said. "Surprised me, too."

Surprised was hardly a strong enough word for what Bonny was feeling. *Floored,* maybe. Totally *flabbergasted.*

And to tell the truth, a little sick to her stomach at the implications. Timothy? With not only teaching credentials but a job at Pilchuck High?

So there was a reason he'd been asking around about rentals.

She remembered suddenly that he'd wanted to tell her something this morning. Something she'd refused to hear. Something that might have spared her the shock of hearing it the way she was hearing it now—

"What's the total on those cards, Bonny?" Priscilla pressed, as if she didn't realize she'd rendered the Blue Moon's proprietor virtually speechless. "Gotta get back to work or Suzie'll have my hide."

Bonny completed Pris's transaction in a daze while Lonetta prattled on: "He has glowing references, Bonny. And with his pharmacy degree, a solid math and science background. Perfect for my labs."

"B-b-but—"

"Thanks, Bonny," Pris said, slinging her handbag over her shoulder. "Bye now. Good luck."

Good luck? Bonny stared after Priscilla. What was *that* supposed to mean?

"Did you know about this?" she asked Lonetta bluntly when she finally found her voice. "Before today, I mean."

"Like I told you Saturday, I knew Simon was interviewing this week. He didn't pull me in on the process till this morning, after he'd done a first interview with Timothy yesterday. He wanted to get my feedback."

"Which was positive, I take it."

"He's perfect," Lonetta said again.

"Perfect." Bonny's voice was flat. "That's certainly the word *I'd* use to describe him."

"I know he hurt you, Bonny," Lonetta said, her voice gentle. Lonetta did know. Bonny had still been teaching at Pilchuck High when Timothy left, and Lonetta had helped hold her together.

"But people do change," Lonetta continued. "I have a good feeling about Timothy taking over my classes. And—"

She stopped, as if unsure whether or not to go on.

Bonny rubbed vigorously at her nose as the pause stretched out. "And?" she finally asked, dropping her hand to the counter.

"I probably shouldn't say it, but I have a good feeling about him, *period.* Maybe you should give him a—"

"Stop right there," Bonny interrupted. "You're right. You shouldn't have said it." Then, with a gargantuan effort to sound cheerful: "What can I help you with today, Lonetta?"

She didn't have any problem staying awake after that. Not with a pit in her stomach the size of Bellingrath Bay.

14

"I'm glad you're feeling better, Mom," Timothy said between bites of ice cream. "Cleo says to tell you she's very sorry."

Donnabelle looked skeptical. "You talk like she really says these things to you, Timothy."

He grinned. "I guess you'll never know now, will you? What did the allergist say this morning, by the way?"

"That if I'm going to insist on having a dog in my life, I'd better start getting weekly shots. He's going to inject dog dander right into my bloodstream—can you imagine?"

"You told him you had a dog in your life?"

"Well, don't I? She's part of your life, your father's already attached to her—I guess she's part of my life, too. So maybe I *will* find out if she really does talk to you or if you're making the whole thing up."

"You won't understand her unless you believe," Timothy warned.

"But how can I believe unless I understand her?"

"Sounds like a question for Pastor Bob," he teased.

It was hard to tell how Reese felt about his son's good news—talk about your cigar-store Indian, Timothy told himself—but his mother was thrilled.

Of course it was possible she was happy just knowing for certain her son was sticking around for a while. Whatever the reason, she'd insisted on making him a celebratory Banana Fudge Royale at the fountain.

This time the cure-all worked. He sighed with satisfaction as he pushed the empty bowl aside.

After all, despite his less-than-satisfactory encounters with Bonny so far, despite the setback with Cleo—he did have something to celebrate. Hadn't he just been hired for his first full-time teaching job? And wasn't he back in the place he'd come to think of as God's country, even while he was racing along a sunny beach in San Diego in midwinter?

The natives were proving friendlier than he'd expected—even his father. He and Reese still hadn't had a heart-to-heart, but he thought they might be warming to it. Last night they'd even worked on a logic puzzle together, which had pleased his mother to no end.

He wasn't completely home yet, but he did seem to be finding his way.

"Your father and I are so happy about the job, dear." His mother's voice interrupted his thoughts as she came around the counter with a cup of coffee for each of them and took a seat at the fountain next to him.

He glanced across the store at Reese, head bent over some unseen task in the glass cage where he worked all day. "I know *you* are, Mom—but Dad? Is he really?"

Donnabelle poured cream in her coffee and stirred it in. "Of course he is."

"He isn't disappointed that I haven't come back to work in the pharmacy?"

"Of course he is," she said again. She hesitated, then added, "He wants you to be happy, Timothy. But you have to understand—you're the last of the Fairley line."

"The last—for crying out loud! I'm only thirty-seven, Mom. It's not like I can't still be a father, if that's what he's worried about."

"He's worried about dying, is what he's worried about."

"What? He's—" Timothy's breath caught in his throat. "Dad's sick?"

"Your dad is as healthy as an astronaut. So am I. Well—except for this silly allergy thing. Doesn't mean we don't think about death. Just wait till you get to be our ages. When you hit fifty, you realize time is winding down instead of revving up. Every year after that is one year closer to the end. You can't help but think about dying."

"You're being morbid."

"I'm being realistic. And so is your father." She paused. "He's talking about putting the business up for sale, Timothy."

He fought the feelings of guilt that surfaced at the news. "I can't live his life, Mom," he said quietly.

"I know. I don't expect you to. And neither does he."

"But he doesn't really understand, does he?"

"You never gave him a chance to try."

"Meaning?"

"Did you ever tell him you didn't want to be a pharmacist?"

"I didn't know. I wanted to please him. I wanted to please you."

"You were a dear, sweet child who wanted to please everyone," Donnabelle said. "But what would have pleased us all the most—what pleases us now—is to see you happy. If teaching is the work God has for you, then do it, Timothy. Do it with your whole heart."

"Maybe he won't have to sell the pharmacy. Maybe I'll have a kid who wants to take it over…"

"And in the meantime? Your father's pushing sixty, dear."

"But if we started right away…"

"Not even if you sire a genius. And by the way, if you're thinking Bonny Van Hooten Fairley's the one who's going to provide you with an heir, you'd better get a move on, dear. She isn't waiting around."

The personal ad! How could he have forgotten? "Her date last night?"

"Her date last night, her date this morning…"

He spun his stool around and grabbed his hooded Gore-Tex jacket from the coat tree against the wall. "Thanks for the sundae, Mom. I'll see you later."

"I'll be praying," Donnabelle called after him as he hit the door.

Bonny had just got through to Cait on the phone when Timothy strode into the Blue Moon Gallery for the second time that day.

"I'll call you back," she said, and hung up without even saying good-bye. She barely paused for breath before she launched into her ex-husband:

"I don't know what you think—"

"Wait!"

She didn't know if it was his raised hand, the uncharacteristically commanding tone of his voice, or the glint of steel in his silver blue eyes that startled her into silence, but she didn't finish her sentence.

"Before you say another word, Bonny—I'm sorry for storming out of here this morning." He placed his hands on the edge of the counter and leaned toward her, holding her gaze. "I promise never to do that again, no matter how angry I am."

Like your promises mean anything, the thought flashed through her mind. "Angry! What right have *you* got to be angry?"

His eyes glinted again. His lips narrowed.

Much less the cigar-store Indian than she remembered, she noticed with interest. Maybe—

She jumped when he smacked his hand on the counter. That wasn't like Timothy either.

"You won't *listen* to me. I should have insisted. I should have made you listen!"

"Should have—look, bucko, you can't make me do anything!"

She watched in fascination as his expression changed from stormy to self-conscious to downright sheepish. "I know I can't. I didn't mean that the way it sounded, sweetheart."

"How many times do I have to tell you I'm not your sweetheart?"

"Cut me some slack, Bonny."

He was getting upset again. This was interesting. On his way out this morning he'd slammed the door. Now he was slapping his hand on the counter and raising his voice to her.

Not at *all* a cigar-store Indian. Her heartbeat quickened. *Very* interesting.

"Why should I?" she challenged.

"Because…because…" He took a deep breath and let it out slowly. She could almost hear him counting to ten in that little pea brain of his. "You're right. I shouldn't expect you to give me any breaks at all. But honestly, Bonny, all I wanted to do this morning was tell you—"

"You had Lonetta's job."

"So you've heard."

"Oh, yes. I've heard."

"As soon as I found out—" He stopped and ran his fingers through his hair, leaving it slightly rumpled. "You were the first person I wanted to tell, Bonny."

She had a sudden impulse to reach over and smooth his hair back into place. She clenched her fists and frowned fiercely. "Why on earth would you want to tell *me?*"

"Because I—"

"Never mind." She folded her arms across her chest and glared at him, spoiling for an argument. "I don't care why."

His lips thinned, and she could practically hear the retort forming in his brain. But all he said was, "Fine. Forget it. Now about those items you thought my mother might like for her birthday..."

She hesitated. She didn't especially want Timothy Fairley's business, but she certainly could use it. She hadn't sold more than a handful of gifts and cards today. Besides, to tell the truth, she did want him to have a good look around the store. She wanted him to know how perfectly fine she'd been doing without him. She wanted him to see just how successful she'd been. What sweeter revenge?

"All right then." Taking a deep breath, she smoothed the frayed edges of her temper and took her ex-husband in hand like a tour guide leading an unschooled patron through a museum. "Like I said this morning, Donnabelle admired Rowe Barnhart's lamps the last time she was in. Rowe models her work after examples from the Arts and Crafts Movement of the early twentieth century..."

She went on to show him jewel-toned glass bowls and perfume flasks, luxurious afghans and colorful quilts, bold jewelry and elegant evening bags, rustic willow porch swings and satin-finished fine furniture, whimsical teapots and stylish dinnerware. She told him about the artists who'd created them and how she'd discovered them and whose work she believed might increase in value over time. For a while she was having such a good time waxing enthusiastic about her artists and their work, she even forgot she was angry.

"I didn't know Jack was a craftsman," Timothy commented, sounding surprised, when she told him the willow lawn furniture was her brother's.

"Neither did he. Cait inspired him," she said.

Jack had been widowed three years and Cait a good ten when they'd bumped into each other last summer right here at the Blue Moon. Since then, Cait had inspired her brother to a whole lot more than furniture-making.

"Mom told me they just got married." Timothy picked up a hand-carved letter box from the shelf in front of him, testing its weight in his hand, staring at it but not really *looking* at it, she noticed. "I was sorry to hear about Helen's death after I—"

He stopped, but Bonny finished his sentence in her head: *"left."*

An unexpected wave of loneliness swept over her. Timothy hadn't been there for her when her sister-in-law was diagnosed with cancer. He hadn't been there when she died. And although she and Helen hadn't been close—Jack and his wife had always lived far away from Pilchuck—the loss had still been very real.

She could have used some support. Some comfort.

For some reason though, at the moment she couldn't seem to muster up any anger toward her ex-husband. "It was very sad," she said around the lump in her throat, not knowing whether she was grieving the loss of Helen or of Timothy. "She was very ill for a year before she died. Jack took care of her."

Timothy gazed at Bonny over the box in his hands. "I'm sorry," he said again, his voice so tender that tears sprang to her eyes. She turned away so he wouldn't see. Did he mean only "I'm sorry for your loss"? Or did he mean "I'm sorry I wasn't there for you when you needed me"?

Why was she even wondering?

"I'm glad he found Cait," Timothy added quietly. And after a moment of silence that Bonny found incredibly awkward and he seemed perfectly comfortable with: "Didn't they date in high school?"

She nodded, then shook her head no, then managed to murmur, "They were just friends." Then, with a wan smile, "I shouldn't say *just* friends. Cait and Jack were *best* friends. From the nursery all the way through high school. Until Jack went away to college and Cait married Joe-Joe and they just sort of drifted apart."

Like you and I drifted apart, she added to herself. Except that she and Timothy had managed to drift apart while living under the same roof as husband and wife. Without the reasons Jack and Cait could count. She wondered if the strain in her relationship with Timothy might not have been easier to understand—and to accept—if there had been reasons.

What was she talking about? There *were* reasons, she told herself, her anger reasserting itself. She just didn't know what they were. Timothy had refused to tell her.

Or *couldn't* tell her, another, more charitable part of her mind suggested.

"How did they get together?" Timothy interrupted her musings.

"Hmm?"

"Jack and Cait. How did they find each other again?"

"Jack dropped by the store while Cait was here. It was obvious to me the minute they set eyes on each other that there was something special between them. Neither one would admit it till after I pointed it out, of course."

"You played *Cupid?"*

"You don't have to sound so skeptical," she snapped. "Just because I made a lousy choice when I married you doesn't mean I'm anti-romance."

He winced. She almost felt sorry for him, until he opened his mouth again.

"Obviously. After all, you did take out a personal ad."

She glared at him. The beast! She wasn't surprised he knew—not in a town like Pilchuck—but bringing it up to her was downright ungentlemanly. "I did *not* take out that ad. The twins did."

He muttered something under his breath she couldn't quite catch, but she had an idea it wasn't complimentary.

"What did you say?"

"Noth—" He stopped. "No, I'm not going to do that anymore. I'll answer any question you ask me, Bonny."

"Right. Mr. Forthcoming himself. Why don't I believe that one?"

"Any question about myself," he amended. "Though I could probably take a good stab at that one."

"Never mind. So what did you say?"

"Busybodies. I called the Reilly twins busybodies."

She couldn't disagree with that. "That's all you said?"

"That's all I said. Any other questions?" He sounded almost eager.

But it was too late for the question she really wanted to ask: *Why did you leave me, Timothy Fairley?*

"What's the verdict on your mother's birthday present?" she asked instead.

He looked away, but not before she saw the disappointment on his face.

"One of the table lamps," he said evenly. "The one you thought she'd like. I think you're right."

About what? she almost asked him.

But she was afraid he'd answer.

15

"Careful now, Clee." Timothy settled his mother's birthday gift on the passenger-side cab floor. "Bonny packed it good, but it is breakable."

Cleo made her engine-whine noise and wriggled her head under her master's arm.

"A lamp," Timothy answered, scrunching his shoulder so Cleo couldn't get at his face with her tongue. "Bonny says Mom admired it last time she was in."

He pushed the package as far as he could under the dashboard, trying not to crush the cluster of white curling ribbon on top. Bonny had wrapped the gift for him using the Blue Moon's whimsical signature gift-wrap—smiling, fat-cheeked, ice-blue moons on a midnight blue background. It was patterned after a sixteenth-century German woodblock print, she'd told him, as delighted with the paper as she was with every piece in the gallery.

She had reason to be delighted. And proud—of the store and of herself.

"Okay, girl," he said a moment later as he slipped behind the wheel. "A stop at the Apple Basket for the *Daily News,* and you and I are going apartment hunting."

Cleo gurgled happily as Timothy, whistling tunelessly, backed into the street. He wasn't exultant about his progress with Bonny, exactly, but he was pleased. After all, she'd managed to put her anger aside and shown him a friendly face for half an hour at least. It was certainly progress from Saturday morning, not to mention

Sunday night. He was definitely inching up toward zero.

He'd actually meant to ask her out to dinner when he went back to the Blue Moon, but the opportunity just hadn't seemed to pop up...

Cleo snuffled and sidled over to sit next to him again.

He sighed. "You're right, Clee. It's not good enough to wait for an opportunity—I've got to *make* one." He laid a hand on her neck and dug his fingers into her silky hair. "You're my best hope, girl. Maybe we'll have to serenade her again sometime soon. Maybe she'll invite us in this time instead of turning the lights out on us."

"Aaroo," said Cleo, practicing.

"Aaroo," Timothy agreed.

He wondered if Bonny was doing well with the store. She looked as if she was, which was half the battle when it came to retail, his father had always said. "Look successful and you'll be successful." If that was true, the Blue Moon was doing very nicely indeed.

But then his ex-wife had always had a knack for looking prosperous even when she was scrimping and saving behind the scenes. He didn't know how she'd done it, but their house on Mulberry Street had been a showcase even when there'd been no money to furnish it, and she'd always dressed like a million dollars, even when all they'd had were pennies.

It wasn't just that Bonny was pretty and smart and hard-working —so were a lot of other people. It was the way she carried it off. She was clever. Creative. Quirky, even. Her sense of style—part whimsy, part elegance, and part just plain audacity—was refreshingly unique. And with her flaming copper hair and a personality as far from a shrinking violet as a woman could get—well, she got attention. As did anything she put her hand to.

With Bonny running the show, how could the Blue Moon be anything but successful?

"You know what else?" Timothy demanded as he pulled into the parking lot behind the Apple Basket Market. "Bonny is just plain having fun with that gallery. What a concept, huh? Having fun at your job?"

"Arf!"

Bonny could have taught him a thing or two about how to enjoy himself if he hadn't been so wrapped up in his unhappiness, he told himself as he made a dash for the grocery store through the rain. It was one of the ironies of his life—that he'd been married to the one person who could have taught him what he needed to know, and he hadn't learned it till after he'd left her. Bonny had always known who she was, which made it easy for her to make choices that were right for her. A key to happiness, he now knew.

And the Blue Moon was clearly right for Bonny, just as teaching was right for him. Not that she hadn't enjoyed teaching too, but she could bring even more of herself to the work she was doing now than she had to her classroom. How was it the twins had put it in her personal ad? "A head for business and an eye for art." A rare combination. A gallery was the perfect outlet for Bonny's talents and passions—especially a gallery of fine crafts, as she'd always loved what she called the "beautifully functional."

"Like you, sweet Timothy," she used to tell him, a long, long time ago...

As a matter of fact, Bonny loved her work so much that when she'd shown him around the store, talking a mile a minute about her accomplishments and her plans—she'd completely forgotten she was mad at him. That told Timothy more than anything.

Otto Grummond's apple-cheeked wife, Gilda, was working the register at the market. "Hey, Timothy," she said cheerfully as he placed a box of beef-flavored doggy biscuits, a can of mixed nuts—fortification for apartment hunting—and a copy of the *Bellingrath Daily News* on the counter. "Heard you were back in town."

"You heard right."

"Find everything you need?"

"I think so..."

He glanced at a display of books next to the cash register while Gilda rang up his purchases. Leftovers from Valentine's Day, it looked like, marked down forty percent. A title caught his eye—*Love Notes:*

Love Advice from the Kids. He picked up the thin volume and leafed through it.

"That one'll tickle your funny bone," Gilda said.

"Yeah? 'Don't kiss a girl unless you have enough bucks to buy her a VCR,'" he read aloud. "'She'll want to have videos of the wedding.'" He grinned. "I'll take it. My funny bone could use some tickling."

"So I hear," said Gilda.

Timothy pretended his face wasn't suddenly as hot as a fried tomato. He couldn't let a little embarrassment keep him from ferreting out potentially useful information. "Oh? What else do you hear?"

She told him. And she enjoyed every minute of it too—Timothy could tell. A few minutes later, back in the pickup, the classifieds spread open over the steering wheel, he passed the latest on to Cleo.

"Pete Pickle Sr.!" He chortled. "She must have been mortified!"

Cleo's gurgling sounded almost like a chuckle.

"On the other hand…" He sobered. "She's having dinner tomorrow night with that professor who sounds like James Earl Jones."

Cleo nudged his arm and did her snort-snuffle-whine.

He looked at her, startled. "You're right, girl. Apartment hunting can wait a few more minutes." He closed up the paper and tossed it on the dashboard. "It's time to make an opportunity."

"Arf!" Cleo barked enthusiastically as Timothy turned the key and the engine roared to life.

"Hey, twins." Bonny looked up from the mail she'd been sorting through and slid her reading glasses off her nose. "You forget you both have the day off today?"

Rosie dimpled. "We wanted to hear about breakfast with Pete Pickle."

She set her jaw. "Sounds to me as if you already heard."

"What we really want to hear about is your date last night," said Robin, waggling her eyebrows. "We saw you didn't get in till after ten."

Were they ever going to give it up? "The date was over by seven-thirty, ladies. I went back to work afterward."

"Seven-thirty! What was wrong with him?"

Bonny winced and put a finger to her lips. "Hey, Rosie, we're not alone in here, okay?"

"Well?" she repeated impatiently, her voice at half-volume.

"Nothing was wrong with him. We just didn't click."

"Oh. No chemistry," Robin said with a knowing expression.

"What would you know about chemistry?" Bonny snapped. And how in the world did they know her so well?

"We *are* nineteen," said Robin, sounding offended.

"We did go see *Titanic* seven times," said Rosie.

"And it wasn't for the special effects, believe me," Robin added. She sighed. "If I could meet a guy like Leo..."

"You'd have to share him with me," said Rosie. Then to Bonny: "So? Robin's right, right?"

"Okay, okay," Bonny conceded reluctantly. "There wasn't any chemistry."

"Less than with Pete Pickle?"

"Can it, Robin."

"We're sorry we didn't think to put your age in the ad, Bon-Bon," Rosie said. "I hope you don't get a bunch of old geezers like Pete."

"But," added Robin, "if you happen to run into a couple of cute guys like twenty or so—"

"—maybe you could pass our number on," Rosie finished.

"You wish. If you want cute guys, take out your own ads."

"We would, but Mom doesn't think it's a good idea."

"And she thinks it's a good idea for me?"

"You have the wisdom of age," said Rosie.

"You have perspective," said Robin.

"If that's another way to say I've been around the block a few times—"

"Only once," said Robin.

"But what a block it must have been!" Rosie sighed.

Bonny shook her head in despair. If it wasn't the personal ads, it was Timothy. When had the tomboy twins turned into such hopeless romantics?

"Anything else on your minds, twins?"

"Our schedules," said Robin.

"Oh. Right. There's the Presidents' Day Sale this weekend—I did give you both some extra hours. Now what did I do with that schedule?" She replaced her glasses on her nose and started checking drawers.

"Your desk, maybe?" Robin asked. "Want us to look for it in the office?"

She shook her head. "One wrong move and you'd start an avalanche. I'd better go find it. Watch the register for a sec?"

"You got it."

Bonny emerged from the stockroom a few minutes later with a sheet of paper in her hands. "Okay. Rosie, I've got you—"

"Timothy alert!" Robin interrupted in a low murmur.

"Crooked dog alert!" Rosie added, her murmur not quite as low.

"Not again!"

"Forget Pete Pickle," the twins said in unison, and sighed identical sighs.

"*Now* what?" Bonny demanded, arms folded, as Timothy and Cleo stopped in front of her.

Timothy gulped. She could see his Adam's apple rise and fall when he did. He didn't say anything for a moment. Then the dog snuffled, Timothy jumped, and the words tumbled out of his mouth like rabbits out of a cage.

"Have dinner with me tonight."

"Dinner!" She stared at him, dumbfounded. She blinked. She shook her head. "Dinner!"

He gave her a crooked smile. "Sure. You know…you, me, candlelight, food…I thought maybe the Inn at Lummi-Ah-Moo."

"Dinner!" Bonny said again.

"It's not like he's asking you to jump off a bridge, Boss-Lady," Robin said.

"Or take a stroll down the aisle," Rosie added.

She barely heard the twins. She was still too astounded at Timothy's audacity. How could he think—

"No."

"Just to talk about—"

"No."

She should have known. Give the man an inch, he took a mile.

She should have told him to buy his mother a birthday present somewhere else. She should *not* have given him a guided tour of the gallery, no matter how much she'd wanted to impress him. She shouldn't have talked to him *period*, even about something as innocuous as her work. And certainly not about something as personal as Jack and Helen and Cait.

"Aaroo," came a wail from the floor at her feet.

Bonny refused to look down. She was not going to be manipulated by that mutt again! How could Timothy just walk in here, after all the ways she'd made it clear she wasn't interested, and ask her out? As if she'd somehow encouraged him. *Invited* him, even.

"Why on earth would you think I'd go out with you?"

Timothy did that thing with his hair again, running his fingers through it and leaving it rumpled. Only this time she didn't want to smooth it back into place—she wanted to yank it out by the roots.

The violence of the thought brought her up short. Did she really want to hurt Timothy?

The answer to that question brought her up even shorter.

She did.

And she had. Timothy's pained expression said more than she'd ever believed his expression could say.

So why wasn't she feeling triumphant?

Because you know what it feels like to hurt the way he's hurting.

You bet I do. And he's the reason why!

No one should hurt that way if it's in your power to make it better.

She dropped her gaze. "Look, I'm sorry," she said, knowing she didn't sound the least bit penitent. "I could have said no more nicely. But however I said it, the answer would still have been no."

He was silent for a moment. "I don't suppose I can blame you," he finally said. "But I wish you'd reconsider, Bonny. I really want to talk to you—"

"*No.*"

"—about us."

She stared at him incredulously. How many ways did she have to say it? "*There—is—no—us,*" she said through her teeth, exaggerating each word. "You killed us, Timothy!"

His jaw hardened. "There *is* an us. If there wasn't, you wouldn't be so mad!"

"I'M NOT MAD!" she yelled.

Cleo sprang to her feet, barking furiously.

"Sit, girl!" Timothy commanded.

Cleo sat, hanging her head.

The gallery was so quiet Bonny could hear her own heart beating. And it was going wild, which made her even madder than she'd already denied she was. She wanted to smack Timothy silly, she was so mad—a thing she'd never done or even *thought* of doing to anyone in her life.

What she did instead was close her eyes and take a deep breath, and then another. *Starting a quarrel is like breaching a dam,* a proverb she didn't even know she knew came to her mind. *Drop the matter before a dispute breaks out.*

She opened her eyes. "Please, Timothy. This isn't the time or place."

"I know. That's why I want you to go out with me."

"I'm not ready."

She watched the struggle on his face, fascinated despite herself. Maybe she *should* go out with him. Just to see what he had to say for himself. Just to find out what was going on in that little pea brain of his.

"You're not being fair! All I want is a chance—"

"Fair?" She stared at him open-mouthed, any thought of giving in to him gone. "What has fair ever had to do with you and me?"

"I—"

"You said you loved me. We had a good life. The next thing I know you want a divorce. And now you pop back into my life expecting I'm going to say 'Welcome home'?"

"Not expecting. Hoping."

"Don't, Timothy. I'm moving on. You need to move on too."

"I can't move on without—"

"Get over it, Timothy. I have."

"What do you want me to do—take out an ad in the *Tillicum Weekly*?"

Ignoring his sarcasm—and Cleo's sudden mournful keening, which was even harder to do—Bonny smiled brightly. At least, she hoped it was brightly. She was certainly trying. "What a good idea," she said.

"Didn't go so well, huh?" Donnabelle asked, her voice sympathetic, when Timothy dropped by the pharmacy to pick up a bottle of ibuprofen. He had a massive headache.

"You could say that."

"Well, she does have reason—"

"I don't need to hear that, Mom! I know she has reason!"

Reese overheard the exchange. He poked his head out of the consultation window, frowning, his face red. "I won't have you using that tone of voice with your mother, Timothy." His own tone of voice said he wasn't kidding. "After all you've put her through—"

"It's all right, Reese," his mother soothed. "He didn't mean it."

"I'm sorry, Mom. He's right. I'm just so—*frustrated.*"

"Use it," Donnabelle said.

"Use it? My frustration? What do you mean?"

"Use it to put yourself in Bonny's shoes. To understand how she felt when she was trying to make your marriage work and you wouldn't talk to her."

"I *do* understand. I—"

He stopped. When he'd finally gotten his act together enough to know he couldn't *get* his act together without help, the counselor he'd talked to had helped him understand how Bonny must have felt when he stopped communicating—when, for all intents and purposes, he'd shut down.

But he'd understood it only in his head. Now he was starting to understand it in his gut. In his heart.

"All I want is a chance to tell her I'm sorry," he mumbled. "To try to explain."

"That's all you want? That's not what you've been broadcasting all over town since the minute you set foot in Pilchuck last weekend."

He closed his eyes and lifted his fingertips to massage his throbbing temples. Of course he wanted more than a chance to apologize. He wanted her back.

"You can't force Bonny to love you, Timothy," his mother said gently. "All you can do is love *her*."

His eyes flew open. "She won't let me love her!"

"She can't keep you from loving her. Respecting her feelings and her choices, for instance. When you can do that, dear, maybe she'll feel more inclined to respect yours."

"You're saying I should quit trying? Is that what you want me to do?"

"It isn't a matter of what I want, Timothy. Or even what you want. Would I like to see you and Bonny back together? Of course I would. I love her the way I love you. Do I think the good Lord would be pleased if you reconciled? I'm sure he would. He's the one who wrote, 'What God has joined together, let not man separate.'"

"So what's your point?"

"My point is that God doesn't move us around like pawns on a chessboard. He gives us free choice. And right now, you're not Bonny's choice. Not that you won't ever be—and not that you *will* be either. If you really love her, you'll give her the space she needs. And if anyone should understand the need for space…"

Timothy glanced quickly at his mother, startled at the insight of her final comment. He'd never really talked about his need for space with anyone except that counselor.

He set his chin. He was *going* to talk about it. With Bonny. He wasn't going to rest until he'd talked about it with Bonny. Until she understood.

16

The buzzer outside the stockroom door at the back of the gallery sounded at six-thirty, just as Bonny finished closing the till. She looked through the fisheye peephole before unlocking the door to Cait. She and Jack were right on schedule with their delivery.

Cait ducked in out of the rain, carrying a cardboard box with the flaps tucked in. Jack waved from the cab of his pickup, then took off down the alley.

"Where's he going? I thought he was bringing some furniture."

Cait shook the rain off her sou'wester. "He is. I forgot my purse, so he said he'd drop me off and go back for it so you and I could have some time to girl-talk. Isn't he sweet?"

Bonny was touched. With only six weeks of marriage behind them, Jack and Cait were still practically on their honeymoon. Even ten minutes probably felt like a sacrifice.

She lifted the box from Cait's arms and set it on a sturdy work-table. "Going somewhere after you leave here?" she asked.

"Just grocery shopping." Cait loosened the knot under her chin and took off her hat.

"Here—let me hang that for you. And your raincoat."

"Thanks." Cait slipped out of her jacket, shaking off the rain. "Man! What a night!"

"What a *day*," Bonny responded ruefully.

Cait grinned. "So I heard. Even though you never did get back to me about it."

Bonny's heart sank. So word had gotten around. No surprise, but she didn't like it. Not when she'd lost her temper the way she had. "Sorry about that. It's getting to be a habit, isn't it? Once again, things just went sort of crazy—"

"So I heard," Cait repeated.

Bonny sighed. "Okay, give me the dirt. What's the word on the street about Bonny Fairley's day?"

"Don't you want to see what I brought you first?" Cait asked, neatly avoiding the question. She opened her box and lifted out a rhinestone-studded velvet clutch. "I've got a dozen," she said, handing the evening bag to Bonny and reaching into the box for another, this one woven of satin ribbons in white and cream with a clasp in mother-of-pearl. "All different."

"They're beautiful, Cait. As usual." She ran her fingers over the soft velvet. Cait's elegant pieced-fabric evening bags were only a sideline to her dressmaking business, but they were some of Bonny's best sellers. "And you're trying to distract me. It's that bad?"

Cait sighed, as if resigned to her role as bearer of bad news. "Not too bad. But you know how this town talks."

"That's what worries me."

"Well...everybody knows about your date with Pete, of course."

"What are they saying?"

"Are you sure it's a good idea to meet your dates at the Kitsch 'n' Caboodle?" Cait asked instead of answering her question.

"I really didn't have a choice with Pete. He suggested it by answering machine, and I agreed by answering machine. And Norman and Charlie... It's the gallery, Cait. I just don't have time to be running all over the county."

"Charlie?"

"Breakfast tomorrow. I know nothing about him except his height and weight, his hair and eye color, and his age. After Pete, I made sure to check his age." Beyond the basics, Charlie said he preferred to talk in person. Bonny suspected he'd had a few no-chemistry disappointments like hers with Jules last night and didn't want to waste his time.

"And tomorrow night is Basso-Profundo Kendall, of course, and Friday night I have a date with Theo. The therapist."

Cait blinked. "Wow."

"I know. Well?"

"Well what?"

"You still haven't told me what people are saying about me and Pete."

"Oh. That." Cait placed the two handbags back in the box and retucked the flaps. "A few people think you ought to give Pete a chance…"

"Really!" That surprised her. "And the rest?"

"Most people think he's a nice guy, but not for you."

"Even if he wasn't twice my age," Bonny agreed.

"And the rest are divided. If you go out again, either Pete's a cradle robber or you're a gold digger."

"Good. I'm saving both our reputations. What else have you heard about my day?"

"Mrs. Schlichenmeier came into the Belle o' the Ball for her six-month perm while I was getting a trim this morning." Cait leaned back against the table. "Said she'd just come from the Blue Moon. Said Timothy came in, you had a short 'confab,' and he left without even looking around. Said he slammed the door so hard on his way out the timbers shook. She did say you didn't seem too upset about it though."

"I thought I handled it well."

"She was grateful. Her heart, you know."

"Who doesn't? Okay, what next?"

"Lonetta Yates dropped by the Kitsch 'n' Caboodle just as Cindy was finishing her shift. Right after she'd talked to you, apparently. Announced to the whole world Timothy was taking over her classes during her pregnancy leave."

"And was the whole world as shocked as I was?"

"So you were shocked? Lonetta said you were taken aback, but calm."

"'Taken aback' doesn't begin to describe it. The worst of it is, I think the main reason Timothy came by earlier was to prepare me. But would I listen?" Her tone was doleful.

"And the second time?" Cait eyed Bonny curiously. "I didn't get any details—just that he stayed awhile."

"Awhile? It wasn't *that* long."

"A good forty minutes is what I heard. Biddy called this afternoon looking for Cindy—something about a lost earring—and said Jonas Muncey saw Timothy pull up in front of the Blue Moon around two, and Harley Burns saw him leave a good forty minutes later. With a package and a 'jaunty air,' he said. That's awhile for a guy to be in a craft gallery, Bonny. I don't think Jack's ever spent that long in the Blue Moon, and he's your brother. And one of your artists!"

But Bonny was stuck back on Timothy's "jaunty air." What on earth had she done to encourage him to walk out of the store with a "jaunty air"?

"He was looking for a birthday gift for his mother," she told Cait primly. "These things take time."

"Mmm," Cait said. Whatever *that* meant.

"I suppose the twins told you he came back again—a *third* time, I mean. And brought that mutt of his right into the store again!"

"Oh, I wanted to tell you about the dog. Unless you've already heard?"

"Heard what?"

"Timothy had to kennel her yesterday. Turns out Donnabelle's deathly allergic to dogs. Thought she was coming down with a cold, but no, it was Timothy's dog. She could hardly breathe, poor thing. Too bad for Reese—I guess he was getting pretty attached."

"Really? I've never thought of Reese as a dog person. Of course I've never thought of Timothy as a dog person either," Bonny said thoughtfully. "And he adores that dog. It's written all over his face."

"Timothy's?" Cait sounded surprised. "That doesn't sound like your old cigar-store Indian."

A lot about Timothy didn't seem like her old cigar-store Indian...

She didn't want to think about it. "I'm sorry to hear about Cleo. A kennel's really no place for a family-member kind of dog."

"Timothy's looking for a dog-friendly apartment," Cait said, "but I guess they're not easy to come by. Anyhow, back to his bringing his dog in the store—"

"Whatever the twins said, take it with a grain of salt."

"Actually, I haven't talked to the twins since breakfast. They were here?"

"Saw the whole thing. *Heard* the whole thing."

"They weren't the only ones." Cait paused. "I told you I was making Camilla Thigpen's formal for the Spring Fling, didn't I?"

Bonny's heart sank. Camilla and her mother had been browsing in the gallery when Timothy dropped by with Cleo.

"She and her mom came by the house to drop off the fabric this afternoon," Cait added.

Bonny chewed nervously at her lower lip. "They heard our fight, didn't they?"

Cait hesitated.

Bonny groaned. "They did."

"I can't believe he walked into the store with that dog again, Bonny. I mean, really—"

"Cait," Bonny wailed. "What aren't you telling me?"

She sighed. "All right then. Camilla didn't say you had a fight. She said Timothy was just standing there minding his own business and you started screaming at him. Totally unprovoked. Though in my opinion—"

"Unprovoked! Why, that little snippet!" Camilla Thigpen was *not* one of Bonny's favorite teenagers. In fact, in Bonny's opinion, Camilla Thigpen was a disaster waiting to happen: fifteen-going-on-thirty when it suited her purposes, and a spoiled two-year-old otherwise. The worst of it was that she treated her mother like her personal slave. Lamentably, Mrs. Thigpen let her.

Bonny took a deep breath, trying to stay calm. "Surely you don't believe Camilla."

"Of course I don't. I mean, the man did bring his dog in the store…" She hesitated. "But I don't think it would take very much from Timothy to provoke you either, Bonny. Without him even knowing he was, I mean."

She sighed. "It didn't. He asked me out to dinner."

Cait's brow wrinkled. "You mean it wasn't about the dog?"

"I *like* the dog. I'd rather have the dog around than *Timothy.*"

"I wonder…"

But she didn't say what it was she wondered till Bonny asked. Even then she was hesitant:

"Maybe…if you gave him a chance to have his say…he'd leave you alone."

Bonny was too surprised to answer. Cait was actually giving her advice! Gentle advice to be sure, with that *maybe* attached to it—but advice nonetheless. It happened seldom enough that she wondered if she ought to pay attention.

"Or are you afraid your insides might go all soft and mooshy again if you hear him out?" Cait asked quietly.

The buzzer sounded at the back door. "Must be Jack," said Bonny, unwilling to answer Cait's question aloud.

Part of her *was* afraid, of course. But another part of her really did want to hear what Timothy had to say. Maybe if she finally understood what had happened between them…

Maybe what?

No. She didn't want to go there.

Jack had his truck backed up to the delivery door and had already started to untie the tarp that protected his load. "How about some help with this stuff?" he called over his shoulder.

"All you have to do is ask, Bro."

"I'm askin'!"

She could have kissed him for his timing. Unloading his "stuff"—beautifully crafted willow furniture—was a fine distraction from Pete Pickle, Camilla Thigpen, and especially Timothy Fairley. At least for a few minutes.

"What d' you think, Squirt?" Jack asked, absently using the nickname he'd called her since childhood, as he passed a chair down from the truck. "Does it pass muster?"

"You done good, Bro," she teased. "And to think I ever doubted you had it in you."

An aeronautics engineer who'd taken an early retirement, her brother was having the time of his life in his second career as a skilled artisan. He'd surprised her, she had to admit. Moving back to Pilchuck after twenty-odd years away, taking to his career change like a duck to water, falling in love with his old friend Cait...Jack had literally reinvented himself in the last nine months.

So it is possible...

She shook the thought away. Jack Van Hooten and Timothy Fairley had not a single, solitary thing in common.

The furniture—two chairs, a garden bench, and a porch swing like the one that hung from Bonny's front porch at home—was all stacked neatly at one end of the stockroom before Jack ruined their easy camaraderie by bringing up Timothy again.

"Heard you've had an interesting day, Squirt; I'm sure glad I'm not in your shoes. And I'm especially glad I'm not in Timothy's."

"What's *that* supposed to mean?" Bonny snapped.

"Are you kidding me?" he teased. "When you've practically declared war on the poor guy? You're one formidable adversary, Squirt. Timothy's got his work cut out for him."

"I'm not the one who's declared anything!"

Except "I do not need a good man," "Over my dead body," "Boyfriend, here I come," and "I'm not mad!" she reminded herself. "All I want is for Timothy Fairley to leave me alone," she said out loud.

"Hey—if that's what you want, that's what I want," Jack said. "Should I have a little talk with him? Tell him to back off? Rough him up a little?"

At least he knew how to make her smile. "Yeah, right. Like you'd ever lay a hand on anybody."

"Okay. But I want you to know—I don't care how the town goes, Sis. I'm totally on your side."

Her smile abruptly faded. "How the town goes? My side? You mean people are taking sides? Besides Camilla Thigpen, I mean?"

"Taking sides?" Jack hooted. "People are placing *bets* on—"

"Jack," Cait remonstrated.

Bonny's mouth dropped open as she stared from one to the other. She could tell from the looks on both their faces that what Jack had started to say was true. It wasn't just Pack Pruitt. The whole *town* was placing bets on whether or not she was going to go back to Timothy!

She groaned. "Don't tell me. They're giving me till the last daisy in that confounded bouquet withers away."

"You didn't think the town could leave Pack's challenge alone, did you, Squirt?"

Cait sighed. "You might as well know all of it, Bonny."

"There's more?"

"Pack Pruitt threw down the glove to Timothy, too."

Bonny frowned. "What d'you mean?"

"He said he didn't give Timothy as long as those gerbera daisies before you ran him out of town."

"But that's the opposite of what he told me!"

"Some folks just like to stir up trouble, and Pack's one of those." Cait hesitated. "He called Timothy a running fool, Bonny. And not in a complimentary way. In front of everyone. Biddy said the diner got quiet as a sepulcher, and for a second Timothy looked ready to crawl under a rock and die."

Bonny could hardly believe it, but she actually felt sorry for Timothy. He had a lot to live down in this town.

"It reminded me of your saying you'd be happy if Timothy crawled—"

"What a horrid little man," said Bonny.

Cait looked shocked. "I know you're angry with him, Bonny, but—"

"I don't mean Timothy, Cait. I mean Packard Pruitt!"

Feeling sorry for Timothy scared Bonny as much as anything had scared her so far. The thing was, it was hard to feel both sorry for someone and angry at the same time—and she needed to feel angry. She didn't even try to understand why. At the moment, she didn't *want* to understand why.

She understood only that feeling sorry for Timothy made her finding-a-boyfriend project even more urgent. And more serious.

So did the fact that Timothy was going to be around till at least the middle of June.

Four months! The one- or two-week fling she'd geared herself up for was one thing; a four-month fling was another. For two weeks, anyone who looked the part and was willing would have done. As long as there was a modicum of mutual interest and attraction, she could make *any* relationship fun for a couple of weeks.

If she was going to date someone a whole four months, on the other hand—or longer, if Timothy got it into his head to stick around—any potential boyfriend had better have a little more going for him than just looking the part and being willing. She might as well forget the whole thing if she wasn't going to enjoy herself. She could just as easily not enjoy herself fending off her ex-husband as fending off a stranger.

Until the last few days, the enticement of mere fun hadn't been nearly enough to convince her to dive into the shark-infested dating pool again, or even to tiptoe around the edges—let alone dip in a toe.

But with Timothy Fairley back in Pilchuck, Timothy bringing her pecan caramels and gerbera daisies and silver-furred teddy bears, Timothy melting her heart with his serenades and that feeling-heart mutt of his—

To fend off Timothy, Bonny was willing to dip an entire *set* of toes into the dating pool.

At eight o'clock, in fact, when she bumped into a pleasant-looking man wearing a well-cut navy overcoat outside the Kitsch 'n' Caboodle Café—and subsequently discovered he was her date for the evening— she decided she was willing to take a deep breath and jump right in.

17

His mother was right, Timothy told himself as he pulled a pan of golden cheese-and-chili cornbread from the oven and set it on the counter to cool. He couldn't force Bonny to love him. He couldn't even force her to listen to him.

But he couldn't just give up on her either. Giving up was what everyone expected him to do. Like old Pack Pruitt at the Kitsch 'n' Caboodle Café yesterday. No one had even challenged the ugly spirit of his comment to Timothy about being a running fool.

And why should they? Hadn't he proved it to them? Hadn't he run away from his responsibilities—his marriage, his job, his community—for no good reason?

No good reason that they'd been able to see, at least. No good reason that even he had been aware of. Except for his unhappiness, he reminded himself, lifting the lid of the pot on the stove to give his special-recipe four-pepper chili a stir.

"Reason? Try excuse, Timothy," he muttered as he settled the lid back over the chili.

His unhappiness had started small, more restlessness than anything else, really, when he and Bonny first moved back to Pilchuck. At that point they'd been married for one blissful year.

Their parents—both sets, thrilled to have them back in town— had made the down payment on the little working-class Victorian on Mulberry Street. Bonny had found plenty of work as a substitute teacher, and Timothy had taken his place at his father's side in the pharmacy, eager to finally do the work he'd been preparing for, certain he'd shed his restlessness as easily as a snake sheds its skin.

But he hadn't.

At first he'd told himself that he just needed time to get into the swing of things, that eventually he'd relax and settle into this job he'd been groomed for all his life. That he'd learn to enjoy being Pilchuck's junior health guru, giving advice to the endless parade of customers with runny noses and aching muscles and intestinal gas.

But he'd never really gotten into the swing of things. He'd hated working inside a little glass cage all day, trying to decipher doctors' scribbles, counting pills, issuing the same instructions over and over: "This-one-with-meals-that-one-on-an-empty-stomach-the-other-one-as-needed-but-no-more-than-four-times-a-day…"

He'd been as miserable as if he'd been lying in a hospital bed with both legs in traction. Or worse, with both legs cut off and no hope of ever running again…

He'd known where to go on the pharmacy's shelves for relief from the flu, an upset stomach, a muscle spasm—but where to go for a cure for his restlessness he hadn't had a clue.

Except to the open road.

Back then, as during his childhood and his days as a high-school champion, when someone called Timothy Fairley a running fool it had been with admiration—even awe. Not with Packard Pruitt's scorn.

Thank God for the annual eighty-mile Balder-to-Bellingrath relay. Thank God the entire town had expected him to participate every year. He'd always been in training for the big event, from the end of one run to the beginning of the next a year later. Such dedication! Such discipline!

At least that's what everyone in Pilchuck had thought. Even Bonny.

The truth was, training had little to do with it. Or dedication. Or discipline. The truth was, every time Timothy Fairley ran, it *was* the big event.

He didn't run to win; he never had. He ran for the love of running. He ran for the joy of it. He ran because when he was running, he was free. Free to be himself, free to please himself—and, on his return to Pilchuck as a "man with responsibilities," free to forget himself and his unhappiness.

Not that he'd ever been able to articulate that to anyone, least of all to himself. He didn't know if he'd ever have figured it out without the help of a wise and gifted counselor—the instrument of God's grace and healing when he finally humbled himself enough to look for help. And to admit that, in the end, he was the only person responsible for his happiness. Or lack thereof...

"Timothy! You've made dinner again? You sweet boy!"

He looked up, startled. He'd been so engrossed in his musings he hadn't even heard his parents come in. "Hey, Mom. Nothing fancy, but chili and cornbread sounded good on a rainy day."

"You shouldn't have to cook your own celebration dinner," she said.

"Celebration?"

"Yes, celebration! Didn't you get hired for a new job this morning? Or was that my other son?" she teased.

"Simon Wyatt dropped by," Reese said, coming in behind Donnabelle. "Says you were very impressive in your interview, son. Says he's looking forward to working with you."

Timothy looked at his father in surprise. Was that pride he heard in the other man's voice? "We had a good talk," he acknowledged carefully.

"Says he's getting a relay team together for the Balder-to-Bellingrath."

Timothy nodded. "Apparently his brother-in-law—Suzie Wyatt's husband—is a runner. And he's trying to talk Jack Van Hooten into it too. I'd be the fourth."

"Did you tell him yes?" his mother asked.

"He hadn't hired me yet—what do *you* think, Mom?" he teased.

"Oh, Timothy, don't be silly—he would have hired you whatever you said." She walked to the stove and lifted the lid on the chili. "My word, this smells delicious! When's supper?"

"Now. Have a seat and I'll serve you."

"How's your headache?" his father asked, pulling out a chair for Donnabelle and then taking a seat at the table himself.

"Much better, thanks." Timothy ladled chili into the bowls he'd warmed in the oven and sprinkled cheese and chopped onion over the top of each. "How was your day, Dad?"

"Busy. Colds and flus galore out there, and everybody looking for a cure-all. Can't do much for a virus except let it run its course…"

His father was in a surprisingly talkative mood all through dinner. He asked after Cleo, which Timothy appreciated, and even told a story or two about his own boyhood dog—Hambone, the one he'd never mentioned till Saturday night.

But he caught Timothy by surprise when he pushed his plate and bowl aside, cleared his throat, and asked without preamble, "How is it you settled on teaching, son?"

Timothy's palms started to sweat. It was the opening he'd been waiting for, but now he wasn't sure he was ready. With a quick prayer for guidance he plunged in: "Thanks for asking, Dad. It took me awhile…"

He told them how, after he'd left Pilchuck, he'd literally worked his way down Interstate 5, city to city: Seattle, Portland, San Francisco, L.A., finally San Diego. "Muscle jobs, mostly. Construction, warehousing, working the docks. The money was good, and I liked it well enough. For a while."

The truth was—though he didn't say it—he'd been exhilarated by the sense of freedom he'd felt outside the confines of the pharmacy: on the move, working his muscles, nobody crowding his space.

But it was an assistant track-and-field position at a San Diego high school that had finally given him focus. He hadn't gone looking for the job—he was already working long hours loading and unloading trucks in a grocery warehouse. "I ran on the beach every morning," he explained, "which is where I met the head track coach at the local high school. Another running fool. He was losing an assistant coach—and there I was."

He told them about the boy he'd worked with who could run like wild horses but was going to be off the team unless he pulled his grades up. "I made him my special project. And managed to get him through midterms, finals, and a research paper. It was kind of a shock when I realized how much I'd learned about myself in the process."

"Like what?" his mother prodded.

"Like the fact that I have a gift for hands-on teaching. And a knack for motivating kids." He stopped, thinking. "That kids believe in themselves when they have someone else who believes in them. That I'm one grownup who does believe in them."

"And you never considered teaching when you coached your way through college?"

"I was going to be a pharmacist," he said. "I never considered anything else. Especially after Pops died." He'd been a sophomore in high school then, he remembered. With his grandfather gone, his future had been clear: He'd work beside Reese in the pharmacy as Reese had worked beside Pops all those years.

"I wanted to work with you, Dad. I wanted to please you."

He looked at his father, who was rubbing his finger around the edge of his water glass and staring into it as if it were some kind of crystal ball. No one said anything for a moment. Finally Reese responded gruffly, "I know you did, son."

"Really?"

His father glanced at him briefly before once again focusing on his finger circling the edge of his glass. "To your own harm you wanted to please me."

Donnabelle nodded. "Like I told you earlier, Timothy, you were a dear, sweet boy who wanted to please everyone. But you didn't know how to please yourself. Except, I think, when you were running."

So they did understand! Perhaps had understood even before he'd understood himself...

"I'm sorry, Mom, Dad. For the way I left. Without telling you why. I hope..." He took a deep breath. "I hope you can forgive me."

His mother took his hand and squeezed it hard. "You know I have."

161

Some emotion flickered across Reese's face and then was gone. But he laid a hand on Timothy's arm and said, "It's covered, Son."

Timothy swallowed around the lump in his throat. "Thank you."

Bonny, meanwhile, was making a big splash with Norman. From the moment he first saw her and did a double take, Bonny knew she was making a splash. It felt good.

"You wouldn't happen to be my date, would you?" he'd asked hopefully, extending his hand. "Bonny Fairley?"

"I'm Bonny." She smiled as she took his hand. "You must be Norman."

"Norman Kipp. I'm pleased to meet you, Bonny." He had a nice handshake, she noticed, not too limp and not too aggressive.

He shook his head. "Wow. You weren't kidding around."

"Kidding around?"

"All-American beauty," he reminded her, his smile as nice as his handshake.

She didn't know if it was the compliment or Norman's assumption that she'd written her own self-aggrandizing ad, but she blushed like a tropical sunset. "Oh no! That wasn't me. That is, it's me, but I—the twins—"

Good grief, he must think she was a blubbering idiot! She took a deep breath. "My teenage clerks wrote the ad. I'm afraid they're a bit...theatrical."

"You have a hard time accepting compliments," he observed, his dark eyes meeting hers. He had nice eyes, with easy laugh lines at the corners. "No need to be embarrassed, Bonny. Now—tell me about the twins. Or shall we look at the menu first?"

You have a hard time accepting compliments. The comment left a funny little lump in her throat, and his easy dismissal of her embarrassment took it away again. What a very nice man! "Maybe the menu. Have you eaten here before?"

"First time. I don't have much reason to come to Pilchuck." He smiled again. "At least I haven't before."

Once Biddy had taken their order, Norman returned to the topic of the twins, and then went on to the Blue Moon, and her family, and growing up in Pilchuck, answering questions about his own life when she asked but always coming back to hers. It was interesting, talking about her life with a man who didn't already know it—the way Timothy had already known it, for instance, when she first started dating him.

"So how were things at the Blue Moon Gallery of Fine Crafts today?" he asked, slicing into his chicken almondine, Buster's dinner special.

She groaned and shook her head.

"That bad?"

"Not a day I'd wish on anyone."

"Want to talk about it?"

"Ex-husband stuff." She gritted her teeth at the thought of Timothy's telling her she wasn't being fair. *She*—not being fair to *him!* "You don't want to know."

"You sound angry. New divorce?"

"New complications."

"Ah."

Her divorce had come up in her conversation with Jules last night—as had Jules's. Typical first-date questions and answers—only the facts. Bonny certainly wasn't about to share any more than the bare bones with a stranger.

But for some reason, she did with Norman. Maybe because he didn't feel like a stranger. He was an excellent listener: He didn't judge, he didn't interrupt, he didn't give advice. He *did* understand, or at least he seemed to. At any rate she felt understood. He validated her feelings, naming them as she expressed herself, the way he had with her embarrassment and her anger: "Ouch. That must have hurt…" "You must have been so confused…" "No wonder you feel so resentful…"

It was comfortable talking to Norman, and at the same time odd. He listened the way a woman listened. No, it was a bit more detached than that. Maybe the way a therapist would listen.

She commented on it once, right in the middle of describing her final encounter with Timothy this afternoon. "How'd you get to be such a great listener?"

"Lots of practice," he said, smiling. Then, thoughtfully: "I wonder if some of that anger you're feeling is a cover for something else…"

"Like what?"

"This is only an idea." He smiled ruefully. "I'm afraid I'm a bit of an armchair analyst…"

"Really! I've been accused of armchair analysis in my time." Her smile was as rueful as Norman's. "I must own every self-help and pop psychology book published in the last five years."

"Oh? Ever read *Grieve Your Losses, Heal Your Heart*?"

"Hmm. Sounds familiar. Quackenbush?"

"De Priest. You're thinking of *Saying Good-Bye to Sadness*."

"Wow. You really know your stuff. So what does De Priest have to say?"

"Sometimes we use anger to keep from having to grieve our losses. Or to hide our fear of abandonment."

It felt peculiar, being on the receiving end of what she herself dished out so freely, but she was intrigued. How many guys could distinguish between Quackenbush and De Priest? Or had even heard of them?

"Does my anger strike you that way?"

"Possibly. It occurs to me you've had a number of losses over the last few years. Not just your husband's leaving, but your parents' moving out of town, your sister-in-law's death—even your cat's adopting the family down the street."

She'd mentioned Tabby just in passing when he'd told her he had a Siamese. Amazing. Could she learn some lessons about paying attention from this guy or what?

The better to listen to Timothy? her conscience niggled.

Yeah, right. As if old Wooden-Lips could actually express an honest emotion.

"Even having your best friend marry your brother could be seen as a loss," Norman added. "It must have changed your relationship with both of them when they started dating, right?"

Tears unexpectedly pricked at her eyes. She *had* struggled with Cait and Jack's relationship—not because she hadn't wanted them to be together, but because she'd felt so left out of their lives.

"I'm sorry—I've made you cry." Norman's voice was contrite.

Bonny attempted a laugh. "Hey—you think this is crying?" She wiped away the single tear that had somehow escaped down her cheek. "You should have seen me last night!"

"I'm sorry you're having such a hard time, Bonny."

She laughed self-consciously. "You must think I'm a basket case, using a stranger's shoulder to cry on."

"I think you're an honest, passionate woman who needs some tender loving care," he said, reaching across the table to take her hands between his. "And I don't think we're really strangers, do you?"

"It doesn't feel like it," she admitted. "But how much can you really know after one date?"

"Enough to know I want a second." He squeezed her hands. "How about dinner and a movie this weekend?"

She hesitated. She did like Norman—very much—even though she wasn't attracted to him the way she was to Timothy. They had a lot in common. There was certainly something between them. So why did she feel so uneasy?

Maybe because you just laid bare your heart to a perfect stranger?

She had, hadn't she? Not very circumspect, even if he did seem like a very nice person. Even if he *was* a very nice person, she amended. And a very perceptive one.

Oh, why not? It would give her a good excuse not to go to dinner with the Fairleys for Donnabelle's birthday. She'd already said yes, but that was a month ago, before any of them knew Timothy was coming home. They'd understand why she wouldn't want to be there.

"I'd like that," she said. "I'm open Saturday."

She didn't know quite how to say good-bye when he walked her to her car a few minutes later. A handshake didn't seem appropriate, but neither did a kiss.

Norman solved the problem by reaching an arm around her shoulders and pulling her to his side for a quick hug. It was a nice solution. Norman was a very nice man.

Cait called the minute Bonny turned on the kitchen light.

"You don't waste a minute, do you?" Bonny teased.

"Nope. So?"

"He's nice."

"Faint praise if I ever heard it."

"I don't mean it to be. He really is *nice*. He gave me some good stuff to think about."

"Such as?"

"Such as maybe I'm as sad and afraid as I am angry. About Timothy, I mean." She sighed. "I'm afraid I spilled my guts about Timothy."

"You did? To a perfect stranger?"

"Like I said—he's nice. But I do have other prospects, don't forget—Basso-Profundo Kendall, for instance."

"And Theo."

"And Charlie. I'm certainly having an adventure, aren't I, Cait?"

Cait paused thoughtfully for a moment before answering: "Mmm. No one can argue with that."

18

"Think those daisies are looking a little peaked, Biddy?" Bonny asked hopefully as Biddy seated her in the back corner booth at the Kitsch 'n' Caboodle Café the following morning.

"Fresh as they were the day Cindy brought 'em in," Biddy said proudly. "The secret's changin' out the water regular, feedin' 'em sugar and soda water, and snippin' just a bit off the stems every time."

"If I slipped you a fiver, d'you think you could ignore them for a couple of days?" she asked in a low voice, glancing over her shoulder at the counter. Packard Pruitt was sitting in his usual spot.

"Bonny Fairley! You afraid of those flowers lastin' longer'n you can hold out?" Biddy sounded pleased.

"No, I am *not*," Bonny whispered indignantly. "I just want to prove that horrid old farmer wrong, and the sooner the better!"

"Or maybe you just don't want 'em around remindin' you Timothy Fairley's out to win you back," Biddy suggested, eyeing her watchfully from behind her rhinestone-studded cat's-eye glasses.

Bonny sighed. "Maybe so, Biddy. But can you blame me? He isn't making my life any easier, you know."

"And you're not makin' his life easy either." Biddy shook her head. "Seems to me two perspicacious adults could work somethin' out if they'd just sit down and talk the situation over. I don't see any good comin' out of a sempiternal feud between the two of you."

Bonny didn't know if she could see any good coming out of a sempiternal feud or not, having no idea what Biddy was talking about. She was afraid to ask, so she ordered a cup of coffee and told

Biddy to be on the lookout for a good-looking blond/blue SWM, 35, 5'10", 165 lbs.

"Humph," sniffed Biddy. "We'll just see if Mr. Blue Blond brings you flowers and candy."

"There's more to a relationship than flowers and candy, Biddy."

"Darn tootin'—like a *relationship*."

Bonny sighed again. "The longest journey starts with a single step, Biddy."

"Next thing you're goin' to be tellin' me is you've got to kiss a lot o' frogs before you find your prince."

"That, too—or so I hear."

Biddy had just set down her coffee when the frog who started it all hopped in the door of the diner.

"Timothy!"

"Bonny!" There was a wild sort of look in Timothy's expression, Bonny noticed with a start. He was less a cigar-store Indian every time she saw him.

Before she could say anything—like "I'm expecting someone"— he slipped into the seat across from her. "I'm so glad you're here. I tried to call you at home but—"

"I'll get the coffee," said Biddy, and scurried away.

"It's Cleo."

Her heart jumped. "Cleo! What's wrong?"

He ran a hand haphazardly through his hair. Good grief, he looked as if he hadn't even combed it this morning. And he hadn't shaved either. She remembered suddenly how much she liked his face in the mornings before he shaved, how she liked to rub the back of her hand across his stubbly cheek, how she liked to rub her cheek against it...

"The kennel—they won't say how it happened—the dogs got loose, there was a free-for-all, blood and fur all over the place. Cleo—"

He stopped, as if he couldn't bear to go on.

Once again Bonny's heart jumped. "She's not—"

"No. But she looks about as bad as she did when I first found her.

Cuts and scratches and…" He stopped, swallowed, and went on, obviously fighting to stay calm. "A big chunk out of an ear. The vet says most of it's superficial wounds, she looks a lot worse than she is, but…" He stopped and swallowed again.

"Poor Cleo!"

Poor *Timothy.* He looked as if he was about to cry, for pity's sake. Bonny could hardly believe it—her cigar-store-Indian ex-husband Timothy on the verge of tears! And over a dog!

"Where is the poor thing now?"

"Outside. In the truck. I am *not* taking her back there."

"Should've taken her over to Critter Keepers Kennels in North Bellingrath, Timothy," Biddy said as she set a cup of coffee in front of him. "They've got the best reputability in the county."

"That's why I *took* her to Critter Keepers," Timothy moaned.

"That happened at Critter Keepers?" Bonny cried. "Oh no, Timothy!"

"Please, Bonny, I can't take her home, not with Mom's allergies…"

He wants me to take her in! she thought in dismay.

"I'm hardly home except to sleep, Timothy," she protested before he could even ask. "Especially this week. I have"—she almost said *dates,* but she really didn't want to rub it in, especially with Timothy in the state he was in—"appointments lined up every morning before work and every evening after. As much as I'd like to, I just can't take care of her."

"I wouldn't ask you to. And I know you're not home much. That's why I thought…" Again Timothy let his sentence trail off.

Bonny stared at him. "Oh no." He wanted her to take *him* in!

"I'll do everything—apply the antiseptic, change her dressings, give her the antibiotics. I can bring my laptop and work on my lesson plans for Lonetta's classes—so Clee would have company. And at night she'd have you there—she'd feel safe, it's the company more than anything, and having you there if she needs you…"

Timothy's dog in her house every night?

Timothy in her house? Every day? Even if Bonny wasn't around…

She'd be thinking about him being there, all day long while she was at the Blue Moon. And all night long when he wasn't there, she'd be thinking about his having been there. Sometimes he might even still *be* there when she came home—and there they'd be, together, in the house they'd bought together and fixed up together, the house where they'd laughed and loved and lived together...

The house where—Timothy seemed to have forgotten—their marriage had fallen apart.

He'd start to settle back into the house, and the house would like his being there, and he'd think he had a *right* to be there, and eventually the *house* would think he had a right to be there.

And then he'd leave again, and the house would feel so lonely...

And Cleo. Cleo hadn't been in one place more than two nights in a row since she and Timothy left San Diego, and who knew how many days she'd been on the road with him, poor thing, between the time they left and the time they landed in Pilchuck. If Cleo stayed at Bonny's house while she healed, she'd start to think it was her house, and the house would start to think of Cleo as the house's dog, and then Timothy would take her away again...

How could she?

An image of Cleo's homely but happy face flashed through her mind. And then an image of Cleo bloodied and torn, with part of one ear missing. Her heart sank.

How could she *not?*

"Only until I find a place to live," Timothy pleaded.

But finding a place to live in Pilchuck—a place that would let him keep Cleo—could take weeks. How could she?

Her eyes skittered nervously around the restaurant. She didn't want to see the expression on Timothy's face, the pleading, passionate, heartfelt emotion shimmering in his silver-blue eyes. She realized suddenly that her date last night had hit the nail exactly on the head with his armchair analysis. She was quite deathly afraid of what her ex-husband—especially this unexpected version of her ex-husband—might do to her heart if she let down her guard.

She took a deep breath. *Think. Think. Stay calm and think!*

The regular breakfast crew were all lined up along the counter, except for Otto Grummond, who was seated at a window booth this morning with his wife. Cindy's husband, Franklin, sat in Otto's spot, and Carl Peabody, editor of the *Pilchuck Post,* occupied the other stool. True Marie Weatherby and Nella Norland sat at a booth near the front window, sharing a pot of tea and a muffin. Lavinie Howell and her husband sat at another booth, Lavinie's postal uniform as crisply pressed as Richard's flannel shirt was rumpled.

Behind the counter, Cindy was pouring coffee and flirting with her husband, and Biddy was ringing up the Keeblers' bill. The colorful bouquet of gerbera daisies next to the register once again caught Bonny's eye. Timothy's gerbera daisies. *Her* gerbera daisies.

Loves me, loves me not...

A petal fell from one of the flowers, floating featherlike to the countertop, as if in response to Bonny's thought. Another week at the outside, and every petal would be gone, Bonny thought, Biddy's regimen notwithstanding.

"See those flowers?" she asked abruptly. She might as well get *some* use out of those daisies.

Timothy turned his head. "The ones I gave you Saturday. *Tried* to give you," he amended. "I don't care about the daisies, Bonny. Cleo—"

"I'll let Cleo stay till the last petal falls," she said. "No longer."

Timothy stared at her. "But what if—"

"And you are not to be in my house earlier than ten o'clock in the morning. Or after six at night."

"But what if—"

"And you are not to bother me in the store again. I have a business to run, and I can't do it with you there."

"But—"

"Those are my terms, Timothy. It's my house now. I'm the boss."

His jaw tensed noticeably. "Fine. I don't have time to argue. You have an extra key?"

She fumbled for the key ring in her purse and slipped off the back-door key, her heart in her throat. Was she really giving Timothy Fairley a key to her house? For Cleo, she told herself. How could she not?

"Excuse me," a sour voice came from over her shoulder. "Bonny Fairley? Did I get the wrong day?"

Bonny and Timothy turned their heads simultaneously.

And before their very eyes Bonny's good-looking, blond/blue, 5'10", 165 lb. SWM breakfast date turned into a wimpy, dishwater/mud-gray SWM, 5'8" tops, 165 lb.—if he'd been soaking wet and carrying a thirty-five pound backpack, *maybe*—breakfast disaster. He was wearing a brown polyester leisure suit and an open-neck polyester shirt. Not the new, miracle I-can't-believe-it's-not-rayon polyester either. The outfit must have been his father's thirty years ago.

He lifted his chin and looked down his nose at her. "Or did you decide to do *group* interviews this morning?"

Things went downhill from there. Timothy hurriedly excused himself, his expression the old unreadable one Bonny remembered so well. Charlie, on the other hand, looked as if he'd been sucking lemons and might still have a piece tucked in his cheek like a wad of tobacco.

"My ex-husband," she tried to explain.

Which didn't go over any better than the group interview.

Charlie didn't like the sound of anything on the menu, though he did finally take Cindy's suggestion and order Buster's eggs Benedict. He sent his coffee back twice because it wasn't hot enough, and when Cindy set his breakfast in front of him he sent it back because it had "yellow yuck spilled all over it." Buster, probably steaming, fixed him a whole new order without the hollandaise sauce.

He was miserable company over breakfast, carping and crabbing and generally making everybody within earshot miserable. Unfortunately, with his shrill voice, "everybody within earshot" was everyone in the restaurant.

When it finally came time to pay the bill, he pulled a calculator out of the pocket of his jacket, figured an eight-percent tip to the exact penny—"Eight percent is all they have to report to the government, and that's all I ever tip," he announced loudly—and divided the total by two, even though his eggs Benedict cost three times the price of her $1.99 breakfast special. Then he counted his half out—he had exact change—dumped it on the table, and told Bonny he had dates lined up through Saturday night, but he'd give her a call next week if he didn't meet anyone better.

She couldn't get out of there fast enough. But not before she added a ten-dollar bill to Cheap Charlie's pile and told Cindy to keep the change. "You deserve it," she murmured on her way out, her face burning like the neon sign in the window. "You deserve a gold medal!"

If he'd thought about it, Timothy wouldn't have gone near the Kitsch 'n' Caboodle Café for dinner that evening. Bonny had met three blind dates in a row at the diner. If he'd thought about it, he would have seen a pattern.

But as it happened, he'd had a very long day, beginning with his early morning drive to Critter Keepers to rescue his dog. He knew he ought to have been out combing the streets for a place to live, especially as Bonny had made clear the temporary nature of their arrangement for Cleo's care, but he hadn't had the heart—or the will—to leave his baby. So after setting up her bed in the living room next to the hearth of the gas fireplace—another of the improvements he'd made to the house when he and Bonny moved in—he'd stretched out on the sofa with the portable phone and spent all day apartment hunting that way. Unsuccessfully, as he'd feared.

His preference for dinner would have been ordering pizza delivered to Bonny's door and spending the evening with Cleo, if not with Bonny. But he'd promised to be out of the house by six, and he wasn't about to break a promise to Bonny. Ever again. His future with her depended on it. His future with her depended on her *believing* he would never break a promise to her again.

"I'll be back tomorrow morning, Clee. Not bright and early, but as soon as I'm allowed…"

Cleo's answering whimper was downright pitiful.

Reese and Donnabelle worked the late shift on Wednesdays. Timothy didn't feel like eating alone. That left only eating out as an option. And in Pilchuck, if one wanted dinner out, one ate at the Kitsch 'n' Caboodle Café.

As it turned out, he was in the men's room at the restaurant when Bonny arrived. When he returned to the dining room, there she sat with her back to him, the straight fall of her copper-penny hair unmistakable—and so beautiful he wanted to go up behind her and bury his hands in it, slide his fingers through it, lift it off her slender neck to rediscover that tender spot that had always made her shiver with pleasure when he kissed it…

He resisted, of course. He wasn't suicidal.

Only when he reseated himself at his table-for-one at the back of the diner did he notice Bonny's companion—and remember that tonight was the night she was meeting the professor with the voice like James Earl Jones.

He had a full-face view of the man, who was not at all what he'd expected. When he'd heard through the Kitsch 'n' Caboodle grapevine that his rival—this *particular* rival, that is—was a computer instructor at the local community college, he'd practically dismissed him out of hand as serious competition. A computer geek? Bonny didn't go for computer geeks, even ones who sounded like James Earl Jones. At least he didn't think she did.

She'd always been at least mildly anti-technology. He sincerely hoped she'd worked through her bias enough to recognize how extremely useful a computer could be for a small-business owner. But even if she had, even if she'd broken down and had a computer hidden away somewhere in her office at the gallery—if he knew Bonny, she probably wasn't using it to full capacity.

Which the man in question would be able to help her do, the thought suddenly occurred to him. Would probably *jump* to do. He was obviously attracted. It showed in the way he leaned toward her across the booth as he rumbled away, the way he tilted his head when Bonny was talking, the way he laughed in that low-throated sort of way men laugh when they're attracted.

On top of which, the guy was no computer geek. Every stereotype failed; he was stylish, smooth, almost too charming for words—and he had that voice going for him besides.

Timothy shifted uncomfortably in his chair. He didn't like the way Mr. Not-Even-Close-to-a-Geek was looking at his woman. The guy was practically salivating, for crying out loud!

"Sage-crusted lamb loin with angel-hair pancake and red onion–teardrop tomato salad," Biddy Barton announced as she set a plate in front of Timothy, blocking his view of Bonny's date in the process. She added sympathetically and sotto voce, "I'd of premonished you if I'd known they were comin' here, Timothy."

Warned him, she must mean. "Yeah," he mumbled, wondering if she was just being generally empathetic or if his feelings were written all over his face for everyone to see. He suspected the latter. If Bonny only *knew* how far this old cigar-store Indian had come!

"I figgered after this mornin' she'd be too mortified to set foot on the premises for a good long while. You got no competition there, Timothy."

"Yeah," he mumbled again.

But he did have competition here. The guy was perfect. Just a little too perfect, in Timothy's opinion. His hair was too black, his teeth too white, his shirt and blazer too crisp and unwrinkled to be possible. And he had this air about him...not quite arrogance, but more than confidence. He had the look of a man who knew women found him attractive—and took advantage of the fact.

A man could see right through a guy like that, but a woman—
Surely Bonny wouldn't be taken in!

Mr. Too-Good-to-Be-True chose that exact moment to reach across the table and take Bonny's hand. "I'm so looking forward to

getting to know you, Bonny," Timothy heard him say. He almost
oozed, he was so oily. Couldn't Bonny see it?

Apparently not. "Me, too," she said, sounding a whole lot more
sincere than Mr. Oily did. And far too breathless. And she didn't pull
her hand away.

It was excruciating, watching the guy pour on the charm and
watching Bonny respond to it. Timothy quietly scooted his chair
around to the other side of the table so he didn't have to watch the
date unfold. Which unfortunately put him in closer hearing range.

"Why did you decide to leave teaching?" Mr. Charm was asking
Bonny.

"I needed a change. I sort of…floundered, I guess you'd call it,
after my husband left me five years ago. I had some money from the
settlement—he was generous enough, I'll give him that—"

"But not much else," Mr. Oh-So-Amusing interrupted, a touch
of humor coloring his impossibly deep voice.

Timothy cringed. Bonny laughed. "But not much else," she
agreed.

Trying not to listen to them was like trying not to listen to a leaky
faucet on a sleepless night. Finally Timothy waved Biddy over and
handed her a credit card. He'd eaten hardly a thing on his plate, and
what he had eaten he hadn't tasted. But he couldn't stand being in the
same room with Bonny and Mr. Tongue-Hanging-Out-of-His-
Mouth a single minute longer.

"Is there some way you can get me out of here without Bonny
seeing?" he murmured.

"Down the hallway past the rest rooms," Biddy murmured back
sympathetically. "I'll meet you there with your charge slip and a
doggy bag. You'll want to be finishin' Buster's sage crusted lamb loin
once you're feelin' better."

Timothy didn't tell her he was afraid Buster's gourmet dinner was
going to be growing vast colonies of gray fuzz before he could even
imagine feeling better.

19

Kendall was almost too good to be true.

He was handsome. He was well-mannered. He was not only articulate; he said all the right things—and in that wonderful basso profundo voice of his too. Bonny was enthralled.

He peppered their conversation over dinner with words like *commitment, honesty,* and *old-fashioned values.* He talked about his students on the community-college campus in a way that told her he took a personal interest. He confessed that he still wanted children of his own, and he wasn't embarrassed to say so.

On top of all that, he listened to jazz, liked postimpressionist art and postmodern architecture, and subscribed to *Psychology for the New Century.*

And when he touched her hand, Bonny felt a zing like she hadn't felt in years—except when she'd come out of her faint in the Blue Moon on Saturday and Timothy Fairley was brushing her hair away from her face...

But she wasn't thinking about Timothy. She didn't want to think about Timothy. With Kendall sitting across the table from her, she didn't *have* to think about Timothy.

Chemistry. Definite chemistry.

Bonny couldn't believe her luck. If she'd had a man designed to her specifications, he couldn't have been more perfect than Kendall. Not a single red flag popped up. In fact, not even a *yellow* flag popped up. And after all the reading she'd done in the last five years on smart women making bad choices, she looked for red flags like a teacher looked for cheat sheets during finals.

He was attracted to her too, she could tell.

"Cranberry-walnut pie? A dish of apple betty?"

Bonny heard Biddy's voice as if from far away. She blinked. Who had removed their dinner plates? When?

"Coffee?" Biddy prompted.

And why was Biddy taking care of them instead of one of her waitresses? In fact, now that she thought about it, Biddy had taken care of her and Norman last night too. Was she being protective or just plain nosy? Bonny couldn't tell. And to be perfectly honest, at this point she was feeling too giddy to care.

"Bonny?" Kendall asked politely.

"Just coffee for me, Biddy, thanks. Decaf." Nerves and excitement had devastated her normally healthy appetite; she'd had only a cup of soup and a small green salad for dinner. "But, Kendall—if you're still hungry, I recommend Biddy's apple betty."

Maybe, she thought—her heart speeding up as her gaze met Kendall's across the table—maybe she was going to skip right over the frog-kissing stage. Maybe, against all odds, she'd met her prince already. Maybe she should go home and cancel the rest of her dates for the week. She'd managed to line up breakfasts and dinners through Saturday and even lunch on Friday and Saturday when both the twins would be in the store—but with a dream like Kendall about to come true, why bother to look any further? Norman, as nice as he was, paled in comparison.

"Coffee's fine," Kendall told Biddy, his deep voice rumbling. He smiled at Bonny—and my, did he have a heart-melting smile! "I'll try the apple betty next time."

Bonny's heartbeat quickened. Next time!

When Biddy returned with their coffee a few minutes later, Bonny didn't even glance up. Kendall was saying, gazing directly into her eyes, "Your ex was a fool to let you get away. You know that, don't you?"

She let the compliment wash over her, trying to ignore the fact that even though she of course wholeheartedly agreed with him, hearing Timothy called a fool felt...well, disquieting.

"What about you, Kendall? Was someone a fool to let you get away?"

"But of course," he answered lightly. He laughed, the sound rich and resonant. "Though I must admit my ex-wives probably have a different take on the matter."

Bonny, responding to his laughter with a shiver of pleasure, almost missed the comment.

Almost.

"Wives?" she asked, shaking her head. "As in more than one?"

"I've been married three times," Kendall said ruefully.

"Three times!" Bonny gulped as a red flag the size of Mount Balder popped up between them and started to wave. This was the man who'd been touting commitment and family values?

You believe in commitment and family values—and you're divorced. Not three times!

Give him a chance to explain...

"Third time wasn't a charm after all," Kendall added.

"So what went wrong?" Bonny asked, trying to keep her tone neutral. She didn't want him to think she was judgmental, for heaven's sake. Didn't the Good Book say, "Judge not, that you be not judged"?

"Bad choices," he said, rubbing his thumb along the back of her hand.

She murmured sympathetically. After all, she could relate to bad choices.

You think marrying Timothy was a bad choice?

Of course I do! Look how we turned out!

But remember how you were in the beginning...

Remembering how she and Timothy had been in the beginning was something she'd been avoiding for days. She wasn't about to start dredging up good memories now, not when just the lingering smell of his aftershave on that silly bear could reduce her to tears.

"I want to be totally honest and up-front with you, Bonny. I don't think a relationship can work without that, do you?"

Bonny started to relax again. "Honesty's very important to me too, Kendall." He was being very brave, really, to talk about his past marriages on a first date. And after all, didn't she want a man who wasn't afraid to open up? A man who was willing to talk to her?

"The first time should never have happened," Kendall said. "I was too young, for one thing—nineteen. She was only seventeen…and pregnant, unfortunately. I'm afraid her daddy had the barrel of a shotgun in my back all the way down the aisle, if you know what I mean." He sighed. "You know how fathers of young girls can be."

Bonny's eyes widened. He'd gotten his girlfriend pregnant…and married her only under duress?

It was a long time ago, Bonny. Everyone makes mistakes.

True. She'd been a high-school teacher. She knew a few teenagers who'd sown their share of wild oats before they'd settled down.

Nevertheless, she pulled her hand away from Kendall's and picked up her coffee cup, suddenly uncomfortable. "Didn't you say you don't have children?"

"I don't. She miscarried."

"Oh, I'm so sorry…"

Kendall looked appropriately pained—for about a second. Then he shrugged. "A blessing in disguise really. We weren't suited; there was no reason for us to stay together after the miscarriage. Besides, I wanted to go to college. I couldn't afford a wife."

Bonny stared at him in disbelief. A blessing in disguise? And he couldn't *afford* a wife? Red flags started popping up all over the place.

Judge not…

Maybe he didn't realize what he'd said. How it sounded.

"The second time…I hate to say it," Kendall went on sadly, "but my second wife went wacko on me."

"Wacko? You mean like crazy?"

He nodded. "She found some letters in my desk—where she had no right to be snooping, I might add—and decided I was having an affair. I came home from work to find the locks changed and all my clothes thrown out on the lawn. I never did get anything else from the house. Had plenty of money tied up in a state-of-the-art stereo system too. Never saw it again."

Pop, pop, pop, pop. Bonny could hardly see for the red flags unfurling. "Were you?" she asked cautiously. "Having an affair?"

"She blew it all out of proportion. You should have heard the way she screamed! Like I said, she went wacko."

As if that answered her question.

Maybe it does.

She was almost afraid to hear about the third wife, but she thought she'd better ask.

Kendall sighed tragically. "I should have known when I met her mother she wasn't going to work out."

"Her mother?"

"You know how women turn into their mothers?"

"Umm," Bonny answered, unwilling to commit herself.

Nothing—not even the sea of red flags waving—could have prepared her for the baldness of his next words: "Well, her mother was a fat cow."

Bonny gasped involuntarily, but Kendall appeared not to notice. "My wife was as slender as you are when we married, Bonny. But she started chunking up after the wedding, even though she knew fat totally turned me off."

"A metabolism problem maybe?" Bonny suggested cautiously.

Kendall shook his head. "It's all about discipline, Bonny. She simply had no self-discipline. I tried to help her—ordered her food for her when we went out, bought her diet books, gave her a membership to the gym—but she refused to take control of the problem. 'If you don't want to do it for you, do it for me,' I told her. 'How can you say you love me and not stay in shape?'" He sighed. "I guess she didn't, because she kept putting on the pounds."

"How much?" Bonny asked, still cautious.

"A good ten pounds in the four years we were married. I just stopped being attracted to her, Bonny."

Ten pounds? He'd made his wife's life miserable and stopped being attracted to her over ten pounds?

How could she have thought a mere ten minutes ago this guy was Mr. Wonderful? Forget *basso*-profundo. He was *wacko*-profundo—and beyond that had all the depth of a mud puddle! Timothy *Fairley* would be a better bet than this guy.

"Judge not," she muttered under her breath.

But another verse came suddenly to mind: *He who is spiritual judges all things.*

"I was pleased to hear you order soup and salad for dinner," Kendall said, smiling across the table at Bonny as if she were just the best little girl in the world, "and especially to hear you turn down dessert."

She shuddered. She should have ordered a Buster Burger—a third of a pound of meat with bacon, cheddar, and a fried egg on a toasted bun…or nachos dripping with melted cheese…or deep-fried halibut with chips. And topped it off with a humongous dish of Biddy's apple betty with Humphrey's extra-rich vanilla-bean ice cream.

She should have chewed with her mouth open, or licked her fingers, or eaten something off Mr. Wacko's plate.

Of course she hadn't *known* he was Mr. Wacko then…

What in the world was she doing with a guy who'd deserted one wife, cheated on a second, and utterly destroyed the confidence of a third over ten measly pounds? And actually *talked* about it on a first date!

"Your mother isn't a fatty, is she?" Kendall interrupted Bonny's thoughts. He sounded worried. Which turned on the light bulb in Bonny's brain.

"I prefer to call her Rubenesque," she answered sweetly.

"Rubenesque?"

"As in Peter Paul Rubens. The seventeenth-century Flemish painter who was famous for his oils of voluptuous women. I did tell you I minored in art history, didn't I?"

"Voluptuous?" Kendall repeated, ignoring her question.

"Daddy says Mom was slinky as a mink when they first got married. Now he calls her his little Pudge-Pot."

"Pudge-Pot?!"

"Of course, she didn't start putting on the pounds till she hit forty. I expect that's when I'll start to gain—although, the way I love mint–chocolate-chip ice cream, it could be sooner."

"Ice cream?"

The guy was sounding like an imbecile. How had she ever found him even remotely attractive? "Mm-*mmm*. I can eat a whole pint in one sitting," she added rapturously. "In fact, I did that just the other night."

Kendall raised his arm to make a show of looking at his watch. "Didn't you say you had choir practice?"

"You know, I really don't have to be there tonight. All this talk about food is making me hungry after that skimpy dinner. Why don't we go ahead and have a couple of dishes of apple betty after all? It's especially good with Humphrey's extra-rich vanilla-bean ice cream, Kendall."

Kendall stood abruptly and reached for the wallet in an inside pocket of his sports coat. "I'm afraid I can't stay." He pulled out a bill and dropped it on the table. "And Bonny—"

She looked up at him, her smile not the least bit forced. "Yes, Kendall?" she asked, sweet as honey.

"Just a little friendly advice. I suggest you see a psychiatrist before it's too late."

"A psychiatrist?"

"About your compulsive eating problem."

It was tough to keep from rolling her eyes, but somehow Bonny managed. And only the good Lord in his mercy, she told Cait later, kept the first thing that popped into her head from popping out of her mouth as well: *Oh really? And maybe you should see a surgeon about having that horrible growth on your neck removed. Oh! That's your head? Excuse me!*

Somehow she didn't think Wacko-Profundo Kendall would have appreciated the joke.

"Tell me your father does not call your mother Pudge-Pot," Biddy said a few minutes later when Bonny stopped at the cash register to pay the bill. At least Kendall had left enough money to pay his share.

"If my father called my mother Pudge-Pot, he would not be long for this world," Bonny said wryly.

Biddy, her brow knit with worry, handed Bonny her change. "You sure this personal-ad business is the best thing?"

Bonny sighed. "I'm not sure of anything—except if I see that man again in my *lifetime* it will be too soon."

"Course, you said that about your ex-husband, too, one time."

Bonny dropped her wallet into her shoulder bag. She sighed again. "I've got to say, Biddy, compared to my date tonight, Timothy Fairley's a veritable saint."

When she got home from choir practice almost two hours later and found Cleo curled up next to the fireplace, whimpering in her sleep, she was *especially* sorry she'd wasted her time with Kendall. She felt more than a little guilty, too; if Timothy had been gone since six, poor Cleo had been alone in the house for hours.

The house was better than a kennel, of course, but it was still a strange place.

She knelt next to Cleo's warm nest and laid a gentle hand on her back. The white dressing on the back of her neck glowed in the dim light. Poor baby. All alone.

"Timothy?" she said a few minutes later into the phone.

"Bonny! What's wrong? Is Cleo—"

"Cleo's sleeping," she soothed, picking up the silver-haired teddy bear from the corner of the sofa so she could settle into the cushions herself. She absently wrapped an arm around Bearley. "I just wanted to tell you I'll be out of the house by seven the next three mornings and probably not home till nine or ten at night. If you wanted to spend more time with her, I mean. And please—feel free to use the kitchen. There's not much in the fridge, but—"

"I'll bring groceries." Timothy sounded giddy with relief. "Thanks, Bonny. I've been worried about her. And—"

He stopped abruptly.

She couldn't resist. "What, Timothy?"

"I'm not sure you want to hear it."

"For pity's sake, Timothy, I *asked*. Haven't you been waiting for an opening?"

"I've been worried about *you*."

"Worried about me?" She couldn't have been more surprised.

"Just—just be careful with these guys from the personal ads, Bonny. You just don't know what a guy might really be like."

She should have been mad that Timothy was butting in where he didn't belong. She should have been offended that he thought she couldn't take care of herself. She should at least have been irritated that he thought he had the right to say anything at all about her personal life.

But she'd invited him to say it.

And strangely enough, it felt good to have Timothy worry about her—to know he was feeling protective.

Not that she was about to let him know. "I can take care of myself. I've been doing it for a long time now, Timothy."

Silence. Then a sigh. "I know you can. I know you've been. Good night, Bonny. Tell Cleo I miss her."

"I will."

After she hung up, Bonny made up a bed on her couch and spent the night in the living room three feet away from Cleo, just in case. Sometime during the night, Bearley found his way into her arms.

She woke in the morning to the faint smell of Timothy's aftershave and Cleo licking her face.

20

The best part of the day for Bonny on Thursday and Friday was coming home to Cleo. Especially after the likes of Supplement Sam, Double-Entendre Doug, Gloom-and-Doom David, Wolf-Man Tomm, and Badly-in-Need-of-a-Therapist Theo.

Sam, her Thursday breakfast date, had walked into the Kitsch 'n' Caboodle Café with a leather valise that later, in Biddy's retelling of the story, turned into a purse. Which technically it was, Bonny supposed, but Biddy's term was meant to belittle him.

Biddy and Buster didn't like Sam from the moment he ordered breakfast—oatmeal, plain, and half a grapefruit. When he pulled a collection of bottles out of his valise, lined them up on the table, and proceeded to ingest a series of capsules, tablets, and tinctures as if he might fall over in a dead faint if he didn't take them right that instant, Biddy was incensed.

"As if Buster's cookin' wasn't enough to keep the man healthy," she'd said indignantly. "As if Buster's cookin' was goin' to *harm* him some way if he didn't take his durned herbs before breakfast."

Bonny didn't mind Sam using herbs, but she did mind that he was so *public* about it; he announced to the whole wide world the purpose of each as he worked his way through them. Echinacea to keep cold germs at bay. St.-John's-wort to keep the blues away. Psyllium seed for constipation, pygeum for the prostate, valerian for anxiety. Gingko biloba as a memory enhancer; alfalfa as a breath freshener. And then there was the "carminative tincture" of nine different herbs and spices dissolved in eighty-proof vodka. Yes, vodka!

At seven o'clock in the morning! "For flatulence," Sam explained as Bonny blushed to her toenails.

It was mortifying, sitting across the table from Sam and his herbs and explanations. Why, Bonny asked Cait later, during her blow-by-blow of the morning, would a man even *mention* bad breath and flatulence on a first date?

"Maybe because he rarely gets to a second date," Cait suggested wryly.

She'd told him she didn't think it was going to work out.

After work that day there was dinner with Doug—the road construction guy with the two teenagers and the ponytail.

His teenagers were sullen. At least, the pictures he showed her made them look sullen.

His ponytail, she had to admit, was luxurious.

And his intentions with Bonny were abundantly clear. No question now what he'd meant by describing himself as "passionate and playful." The guy had narrow definitions...and one thing on his mind.

He seemed to think Bonny was equally interested too—how, she couldn't imagine, as she studiously ignored his not-so-hidden meanings.

When he grabbed her knee under the table at one point during dinner, it was pure reflex that her leg swung out and her foot caught him hard in the shin. At least that must have been his take on the matter, as it didn't stop his double entendres, and he looked shocked at the end of the evening when she told him she didn't think it was going to work out.

"You'd think no woman had ever said no to him before," Bonny reported to Cait from her living-room floor on Thursday night. She was leaning against the sofa with the portable phone to her ear and Cleo's head in her lap. Cleo was snoring contentedly.

"Oh well," Cait commiserated. "There's always tomorrow."

There was tomorrow all right. There was breakfast with Gloom-and-Doom David, who made Winnie-the-Pooh's friend Eeyore seem positively carefree. His large, sad eyes and hangdog expression advertised to the world that nothing in life had ever really worked out for him, and he didn't expect it to now. The worst that *could* happen probably *would* happen, if it hadn't happened already.

She was almost afraid to tell him she didn't think it was going to work out, for fear he'd jump off a bridge or something. But he seemed to take it in stride, with a morose "Why am I not surprised?"

Biddy, for her part, was pleased to be able to use two of her Word-a-Days for David: "Now that's one lugubrious prognosticator!"

Sometimes, Bonny reflected, Biddy really got it right.

Then there was lunch with Tomm, who was, he told Bonny—much to her consternation—"a wolf on the prowl for a woman to run with." *Wolf* seemed a good metaphor—there was something fierce and wild about him.

He was an elder in his men's group, he told her proudly. He chanted, he smudged, he drummed in the woods with his "wolf brothers" on a handmade deer-hide drum. He "embraced his masculinity" and rejected even the suggestion of "getting in touch with his feminine side," the whole idea of which was a feminist conspiracy against men being men. "Let women be women," he urged Bonny. "Let me be a man!"

The twins were wide-eyed when Bonny told them about it back in the gallery. "What did you say?" asked Rosie.

She sighed. "The usual: 'I don't think it's going to work out.'"

"What did he say?" asked Robin.

"That if I wanted a wimp instead of a real man, I was welcome."

The twins hooted in unison.

No one would have been surprised if by Friday dinner Bonny had lowered her expectations. But Friday dinner was her date with Therapist Theo, who surely must have his life together. He'd probably be an even better listener than Norman.

Therapist Theo, however, showed up for their date with a nervous tic and an elderly mother, who proceeded to cross-examine Bonny while Theo looked mutely on. At the end of her interview, Ma gave

Bonny thumbs-up, but Bonny had already given Theo thumbs-down.

"He's forty years old, he's never been married, and he lives with his mother," she reported to Cait on Friday night, this time from the comfort of her living-room sofa, where Cleo was draped across her lap, gurgling happily. "And no, I don't mean his mother lives with him."

"Timothy must be looking more appealing all the time."

"He is. It's a problem." Bonny reached absently under Cleo's chin to scratch her sweet spot. "Do you know," she said thoughtfully, "that in the last two days when Timothy's been here with Cleo he's put in a new light fixture, fixed a leaky faucet, built a handrail for the stairs to the basement, and cleaned the oven *and* the refrigerator?"

"Cleaned the oven? Really?"

"On top of which he cooked a beef stew yesterday—most of which is in my freezer—and baked a carrot cake tonight. It looks delicious. It even has cream-cheese frosting!"

"I didn't know Timothy cooked."

"I guess it's been cook or starve the last five years. I have to admit—I'm getting curiouser and curiouser to hear his story."

"You ready to give him a chance again?"

"No." The denial was quick. Almost too quick. "But I might be ready to *listen* to him."

"I wonder if you'd both feel better if you did."

"D'you think I can ever forgive him, Cait?"

"Not alone," Cait said gently.

"Even if I do…" Her voice trailed off into a sigh. "I'd still feel a whole lot better if I had a boyfriend, Cait."

"You really think so?"

"A whole lot *safer.*"

"Ahh."

"There's still tomorrow," Bonny said, forcing cheerfulness. "Al in the morning, and Howard at noon."

"I remember Al. But Howard?"

"He's the only one from my latest batch of calls I've gotten back to. Howard's in sales."

"What kind?"

"Don't know. Guess I'll find out tomorrow."

"And then it's dinner again with Norman?"

"Dinner and a movie. Norman's looking awfully good right now. *Awfully* good. A nice man. A *normal* man. Maybe he's my best bet, Cait."

"Maybe," said Cait, not committing herself.

By midafternoon on Saturday, when Cait dropped by the store for a birthday card and an update, Norman was looking even better.

"Hard-Sell Howard," said Bonny, "used our luncheon date to try to sell me natural cleaning products, prepaid legal services, and a time-share in Hawaii. Apparently he uses the personal ads for leads."

"No!"

"He had samples of the cleaning products, testimonials for the legal services, and a slick brochure on the time-share."

"At least he didn't weigh five hundred pounds and chew with his mouth open," Robin said.

Bonny winced.

"Not your breakfast date this morning!" Cait said. And at Bonny's nod, "Please tell me Robin's exaggerating."

"I wish I could. I had such high hopes for Al."

"The one whose message made you laugh."

Bonny nodded. "The one who couldn't believe he was doing the personal-ad thing again. I can't believe it either. You've got to give the guy credit for nerve."

Not to mention appetite. Al had ordered three breakfast specials, and when Bonny lost her own appetite watching him eat and couldn't finish her omelet, he'd polished that off too.

"He tucked his napkin into his shirt front—and spilled all over it. He talked with his mouth full. He drank his juice in a single gulp."

Cait clucked sympathetically. "How did you let him down?"

"The usual."

"'I don't think it's going to work out,'" Robin and Rosie chorused together.

"And how did he take it?"

"He looked resigned," said Bonny. "Like he'd heard it before."
She rubbed her finger across her nose. "I know it sounds superficial,
Cait—especially after the way I reacted to Kendall—but I just couldn't
get past his weight. Or his table manners."

"No comparison to Kendall," Cait assured her. "And your feelings are your feelings, after all. Besides, you've still got Norman.
Heard any more from him, by the way?"

Bonny brightened. "He called the store this morning to confirm
for tonight. You can't imagine how much I'm looking forward to a
nice, normal dinner-and-movie date with a nice, normal man."

"Oh I think I can. So what about next week? Any other dates
lined up?"

Bonny shook her head. "I think I need a breather before I start
answering any more calls. If I *answer* any more calls. To tell the truth,
I'm exhausted. And broke from all those Dutch-treat meals. And I
must've gained five pounds eating out so much this week. No, the
more I think about it, the more I think Norman's the guy for me."

"I don't think you should decide till you've met them all," said
Robin.

"She's had twenty-nine calls altogether now, Mom," said Rosie.
"Isn't that awesome?"

"Awesome," Cait said, grinning. "Just like her dates so far."

"It just doesn't seem right, Bonny not being here," Donnabelle said
sadly.

The three Fairleys were seated at a table overlooking the harbor
lights at the Inn at Lummi-Ah-Moo, enjoying chocolate-dipped
strawberries and coffee after an elegant meal. Dinner at Tillicum
County's four-star restaurant had been a birthday tradition for
Donnabelle as far back as Timothy could remember. And Bonny had
been part of that tradition for more than a dozen years, including the
last five—when Timothy had not.

"She came by the pharmacy with a gift and a card this afternoon," Donnabelle added. "But she didn't even stick around to watch me open them. I hope that's not the way it's going to be from now on."

Timothy hoped not too. "What did she get you?"

"I don't know. I thought I'd wait till I opened my presents from you and Reese, so she'd at least be there in spirit."

But Bonny wasn't going to be there in spirit, he thought miserably. At this very moment she was at the Kitsch 'n' Caboodle Café in body and spirit both, having dinner with some tax attorney. A second date.

The word on the street was that except for the tax attorney, Bonny's *Tillicum Weekly* dates thus far had been obnoxious, offensive, and otherwise objectionable—which suited Timothy just fine.

But all it takes is one...

"What did she say when she called to cancel?" he asked.

"Just that she didn't think it was going to work out this year," Donnabelle said.

His father traced a finger around the edge of his water glass. "I take it that means your campaign's not going so well, son."

"Not so well," Timothy soberly agreed. "It's a miracle she agreed to keep Cleo, even for a week—let alone have me in the house to look after her." In the last few days, he and Bonny hadn't talked about much except how Cleo had spent the day or night, but at least she'd stopped being openly hostile. "I'm sorry, Mom," he added. "I know how much you enjoy Bonny. Maybe if I'd stayed home—"

"Don't, Timothy. It wouldn't seem right without you here either."

"I called her back to see if I could change her mind," Reese said, "but she'd already made other plans."

"So I heard," Timothy said morosely.

Donnabelle reached for another strawberry. "No one's going to change Bonny's mind but the Almighty."

"I'm beginning to think you're right." Timothy wrapped his hands around his coffee cup. "Mom..."

"Hmm?"

"I've been thinking about what you said the other day. About giving up on Bonny."

"Oh, Timothy! Not giving up on her! Is that—"

"Hear me out, Mom. Because the thing is, I already gave up on her once. I gave up on everything: Bonny, our marriage, you and Fairley's Pharmacy, Pilchuck. *Everything.* It's how I got into this mess! How can giving up again do any good?"

His mother was shaking her head. "Timothy, I didn't mean you should give up on her. I meant that maybe you need to give her up. There's a world of difference! I never, ever gave up on you after you left. But I did finally have to give you up. Give you over to God, that is. Trust you to him."

"A hard lesson," Reese said gruffly.

"But hard as it was," Donnabelle went on, "we had to let you go. It was that or live our lives angry and miserable. We'd have had to anyhow, sometime—every parent does. But you forced our hand. And maybe Bonny's forcing yours now. Maybe the lesson you need to learn is the same one we had to learn with you: There's a time to hold on and a time to let go." Donnabelle placed a gentle hand on his arm. "Maybe it's time for you to let go."

Timothy was silent for a moment. His mother's words made more sense than he wanted to admit.

"I'm not sure I know how," he finally said.

"The same way we let go of you. By telling the Almighty, 'She's in your hands, God. Protect her, teach her, lead her—and if it suits your purposes someday, bring her back to us. If it doesn't—let her know she's loved.'"

It took Timothy the rest of the evening and half a sleepless night to pray that prayer for Bonny.

But finally he did.

21

Bonny also spent a sleepless night—searching her heart and not liking what she found.

It was Norman's fault—

No. It wasn't Norman's fault. It was her own fault.

Still, after all the times she'd said this week, "I don't think it's going to work out..."

To have it said to *her*—and by a perfectly nice, perfectly normal man like Norman, after a perfectly lovely evening—

His rejection had been a blow. And not a gentle one, as gentle as he tried to be.

He'd come by the store before closing to look around—which pleased her immensely—and waited patiently while she closed the till and tallied the day's sales on a deposit slip. After they dropped the money off in the night deposit box at the bank and left Bonny's car in her driveway, they drove into Bellingrath in his little red Miata for tempura at a new Japanese restaurant where they sat on the floor, bumping knees, and managed to make it through the entire meal without resorting to knives and forks.

She told Norman about Cleo's moving into her house and the terms she'd set with Timothy.

He seemed supportive.

She regaled him with tales of her personal-ad experiences since she'd seen him last—exaggerated only a little for comic effect.

He seemed amused.

"You're my knight in shining armor," she told him at the end of her recital. "Blessings on your head for coming to my rescue tonight!"

He seemed pleased.

They went to see a sweet romantic comedy, he drove her back to Pilchuck, she made so bold as to lean toward him for a good-night kiss—

And that's when he said it: "You're a nice person, Bonny, but I don't think it's going to work out."

"Don't think it's going to work out?! But…but didn't we just have a really nice time together?"

"I enjoyed myself."

"You don't find me…attractive?"

"I find you very attractive."

"Then what?"

He took her hand in his, gazed earnestly into her eyes, and told her, "Twice tonight you called me Timothy."

She stared at him in shock. Called him Timothy? When? How? *Why?*

"You aren't over him, Bonny—"

"I'm over him!"

"—and that's not fair to me."

And then he walked her to her door, kissed her lightly on the forehead, and told her he hoped, for her sake, she'd do whatever it was she needed to do to settle her heart.

She'd been numb when she walked in the door. Numb when she'd sunk to the sofa, pushing Bearley aside and not even noticing when he fell to the floor. Numb until Cleo plopped her head in her lap and made her funny little snort-snuffle sound.

She laid her hand on Cleo's head, and with the touch of fur and flesh and bone under her fingers, feeling returned. In spades. She slid sobbing to the floor, where Cleo tried at first to lap away the tears flooding down her cheeks and then simply lay across her lap, whining in sympathy.

Her Monday night crying jag was nothing compared to this.

The sobs stopped eventually, but the tears kept coming, along with a hiccup now and then. Bonny started to tell Cleo what was wrong three or four times, but couldn't get past "Norman says...Norman says..."

Finally, around her hiccups, she got out what Norman had said. And added, "He's right, Cleo. I'm not over Timothy. And it isn't fair to Norman. It isn't fair to anybody."

She hadn't been dating. She'd been interviewing prospects for a job. *Wanted: one reasonably presentable man to help me get over my ex-husband. Temporary position.*

"Here I've spent the last week finding every man I met wanting in some way—all except nice, normal Norman, who showed me *I'm* the one who's wanting. I used them, Cleo," she said sadly. "As if they were paper dolls and not real people with dreams and desires and hearts that could be wounded. Hearts that could be broken."

And then she wasn't talking to Cleo anymore. She was talking to God, pouring out her heart, confessing her pride and her fear and her lack of compassion, asking for grace to listen to Timothy, to let go of her anger and her fear—to forgive him, if such a thing was possible. "I can't bring myself to do anything more at the moment, God. To trust him again, I mean. To love him, even as your child. To open my heart the way I opened my heart in the past. But I trust you. I open my heart to you. Be my rock, my fortress, my present help, my guide..."

And lying on the floor next to Cleo, an afghan pulled over them both, just as the eastern sky began to lighten, she finally slept, peaceful as a newborn.

No one could have been more surprised than Timothy when Bonny invited him home for carrot cake and ice cream after church Sunday night. And as they sat in her kitchen eating it, nothing she might have said short of "I love you, I forgive you, let's get married again" could have surprised him more, after the week she'd spent fighting him off, than what she did say:

"I'm sorry I haven't given you a chance to have your say. Talk to me, Timothy. I promise to listen."

He stared at her across the kitchen table, dumbfounded. He'd known it was right for him to give Bonny up in the way his parents had encouraged him to do. Right for him and right for Bonny. But he hadn't expected the results to be quite so dramatic.

Hold on, he warned himself. *Just because she's willing to listen doesn't mean she's willing to forgive you, let alone invite you back into her life.* "Why now?" he asked, trying to rein in the hope galloping through his heart.

She hesitated, then shrugged. "I'm curious. And I'm...well, *tired,* frankly. And I think it would be good for both of us."

Hope slowed down to a trot. He would have preferred something like "I'm madly in love with you, and it's silly the way I've been denying it."

Yeah, right. When water runs uphill. "Good how?" he asked, trying to keep his tone neutral.

She sighed. "Look, Timothy, I really meant it earlier this week when I said it was time to move on."

Hope stumbled but regained itself when she added, "For both of us. My anger means I haven't done that yet."

Was she admitting she wasn't over him?

"Your...persistence, shall we call it," Bonny went on, "means you haven't moved on either—and won't be able to until I've given you a chance to say you're sorry."

Another stumble. It was that thing about moving on.

"Oh, Bonny, I—"

"But you do understand, don't you, that some things can't be fixed with 'I'm sorry'?" Her direct gaze impaled him. "Our relationship can never be the same again, Timothy. No matter what you have to say."

And another recovery, even with that look and the gravity of her tone. She'd actually used the word relationship!

I don't want it to be the same, his heart cried. *I want it to be better.*

Let it go, another voice whispered.

Bonny leaned back in her chair and crossed her arms, waiting. And suddenly, after more than a week of begging her to give him a chance to have his say, he didn't have the slightest idea how to begin.

Timothy looked absolutely petrified. And not cigar-store-Indian petrified either. Bonny felt so sorry for him she was tempted to ask him a question or give him some word of encouragement to get him started.

But she'd tried that with Timothy before—questioning, encouraging, wheedling, pouting, shouting, and just about anything else she could think of. And the outcome had not been good.

She sat back and held her tongue. It wasn't up to her. If he was going to talk, he was going to have to do it on his own.

He laughed nervously and ran his fingers through his hair. Bonny felt her heart soften again. "This is crazy," he said. "I must not really have believed you'd ever listen to me..."

When he finally did sort out what he wanted to say, he took her by surprise. For one thing, she'd sort of thought he'd grovel. In fact, she'd sort of been looking forward to his groveling. Hadn't she spent five years fantasizing about him bowing and scraping at her feet? He'd admit to all the ways he'd treated her badly. He'd say he was sorry. He'd say leaving her had been the biggest mistake of his life. He'd ask her for forgiveness, and if he said it just the right way, with just the right touch of remorse and shame—sackcloth and ashes preferred— she'd *consider* forgiving him.

She should have known Timothy wouldn't come cringing. But what on earth did the Balder-to-Bellingrath have to do with anything?

"Yes," she answered his question. "I remember how you were always in training for the big race. Everyone in Pilchuck knew. How could they not, when you were out there practically every day, in the dark all winter long, in the wind and rain and even the snow sometimes." She hated to compliment him, under the circumstances, but something made her say it anyhow: "Your discipline always amazed me."

"I know that's what you thought—you and everyone else. That I was disciplined. But I wasn't."

Bonny shook her head in bewilderment. "Nothing ever stopped you, even when you were working ten-hour shifts. How can you say you weren't disciplined?"

"Because I love to run. That's why I trained—not because I wanted to win some race," he said.

"Well, of course you did! Who'd work that hard for something they didn't love?"

An odd expression flickered across his face. "Never mind that now. What I'm trying to tell you is that it wasn't discipline. I *had* to run." He dragged his fingers through his hair once again. Why did that gesture tug at her heart every time he did it? Bonny wondered.

She shook her head. "I don't get it."

"I'm not doing this very well." He stopped, looked down, looked up again to meet her gaze. "I was so unhappy, Bonny. Running was the only thing that kept me sane."

She felt suddenly as if a giant hand had grabbed her lungs and was squeezing the life out of them. Another surprise—the intensity of her reaction to his simple statement. She took a deep breath, trying to loosen the grip.

"But Timothy—that's the part I don't get. What did you have to be unhappy about? I was good to you! We had a good life together! Then all of a sudden you…you just went *away.* You just weren't *there* anymore. And I don't mean the divorce."

"I know." He hesitated. "You know it wasn't about you, don't you? You were the best part of my life, Bonny."

The hand squeezed tighter. "Could have fooled me."

He looked pained. "I didn't know how to tell you, let alone tell you what was wrong. I hardly knew myself, and there you were, more and more in my face, trying to make me explain what I didn't know—"

"I can't believe it!" Her sudden anger broke the grip on her lungs, and the words tumbled out on a whoosh of air. "Are you blaming the divorce on *me?*"

"No! I'm just trying to tell you—I was so unhappy, so restless. I felt trapped—"

"What did I ever do to make you feel trapped?"

"No, no. You're not getting it—it wasn't *you!*" He sounded as frustrated as she felt. "No one was holding me against my will. No one was making me unhappy. I just *thought* they were."

"Why? How?"

He sighed. "I don't know, Bonny. I guess because I'd spent my whole life trying to make people happy, trying to please them, trying to figure out what they wanted from me. You know how I was—the good boy, the one who always did what was expected of me."

The giant hand again. "Like marry me, you mean."

Timothy shook his head. "No. I mean yes, the whole town did expect us to marry. But you were my choice too, Bonny. You and running—the two things I ever did that were both what I wanted and what everyone else wanted for me."

There was more: the expectations he'd lived with all his life as the third-generation Fairley of Fairley's Drug and Fountain, as the only child of Reese and Donnabelle and the only grandchild of the old man who'd started it all, as an academic star and a star athlete at Pilchuck High School, as the pride and joy of Pilchuck. And as the local boy come home after college to take his place in the community and at his father's side...

"You hated working at the pharmacy!"

She didn't have to hear him say it to know it was true; it was written all over his face. What in the world had happened to him in the last five years Bonny had no clue, but Timothy Fairley in his present incarnation was about as much like a cigar-store Indian as Bonny was like a wallflower.

"I can't believe it." She knew she must sound stunned; she certainly *felt* stunned. "I can't believe that we were married for seven years and I never knew you hated what you were doing! Why didn't you tell me?"

"I didn't know how. And…I wanted it not to be true."

"You didn't know how." She shook her head. "You sure know how now."

"Do I? I feel like I'm stumbling around in the dark."

"You're doing fine." She studied him for a moment across the table. He shifted uncomfortably but held her gaze. "How'd you figure out all this stuff anyhow?" she finally asked. "Let alone how to tell me?"

"A very wise counselor, a very thick journal, and a ton of prayer—my own and Mom's and, if I know her, probably Pastor Bob and half the congregation at Saints and Sinners."

Bonny wished she could tell him she'd been praying for him too. But she couldn't. She hadn't been. She'd been too angry. Maybe, it suddenly occurred to her, the fact that she hadn't been praying was part of the reason she'd stayed angry so long…

"But I haven't told you the most important thing yet, Bonny." Timothy's voice was resonant.

"And the most important thing is?"

"That I'm sorry."

That wasn't enough. Anyone could say "I'm sorry."

"For what?" she demanded, thinking fleetingly she might get to see him grovel yet.

But Timothy didn't grovel. He knew exactly what to say. "For running away from my unhappiness. For running away from you. For failing to keep my vow to love and honor you forever. For hurting you. I was wrong, Bonny. Can you forgive me?"

She sighed. "I don't know, Timothy. I honestly don't know. But I have asked God to help me."

"Am I an idiot to think you could ever love me again?"

She could hardly believe that he—her cigar-store-Indian ex-husband Timothy Fairley—would have either the inclination or the nerve to ask. Where had this stranger come from?

For a moment she rubbed vigorously at her nose with her index finger. Then, catching herself, she dropped her hand, lifted her chin, and frowned at him across the table. "Tell you what…let's try for forgiveness first. And then maybe trust—which I have to warn you, Timothy, could be a long time coming. As for love—"

She drew in a deep breath and let it out again. "Don't—push—your luck."

22

Biddy Barton insisted the daisies next to the register at the Kitsch 'n' Caboodle were still unwilted two weeks after delivery because of the diet she'd placed them on: sugar, soda water, and after the first week a single crushed aspirin every day. "That and snippin' the stems to keep the xylem and phloem functionin' expeditiously," the twins said Cindy said Biddy had told her.

"Gives new meaning to that old expression 'fresh as a daisy,'" Bonny said sardonically. "Biddy should think about marketing her formula."

It was Bonny's personal belief by this time that somebody—Biddy, old Pack Pruitt, maybe even Timothy—was replacing the worst of the daisies every day with new flowers straight from Buds 'n' Blossoms. In fact, she doubted there was a single original gerbera in the batch by now. She knew gerbera daisies. They didn't last that long.

Not that she was about to call anybody on it.

Sure, she would have liked to see mean old Packard Pruitt with egg on his face after those flowers were gone, with her not having begged for Timothy to come back to her and Timothy still in town. The sooner those daisies were gone, the sooner Pack got his come-uppance.

On the other hand...she'd given Timothy only as long as the daisies lasted to find another place for Cleo. And she was getting undeniably attached to the dog. *Extremely* attached.

Not having had a dog since childhood—or a husband since Tim-othy—she'd almost forgotten how wonderful it was to be awakened in the morning with a nuzzle to the neck and an affectionate kiss on the nose. Or to be greeted with unbounded enthusiasm and immoderate joy every time she walked in the door. Or just to enjoy the quiet companionship of another sentient being, sharing a room and a life with someone who wanted to be with her.

She would never admit it to Timothy, but she really hoped the dog would be around a little longer, even if that meant having Timothy around longer too.

She'd taken to leaving her ex-husband notes in the morning before she went to work—nothing personal, mostly updates on Cleo, who was mending nicely from her wounds. He'd taken to leaving her notes in the evening before he left for his parents' house—again nothing personal, mostly updates on his search for a place to live, which wasn't going well.

Unbelievably, her anger toward Timothy was gone. She didn't know if it came from her new understanding of what had been going on in his pea brain during those last few years of their marriage or if it was just an out-and-out, heaven-sent miracle, but anger simply wasn't a part of the mix of emotions she was feeling. She wasn't exactly sure what *did* make up the mix, but anger wasn't a part of it. She even started to think it might be possible they could be friends again…

But nothing more, she assured herself. Some things could never be undone.

"I've got to tell you," Timothy said to Biddy Barton one Saturday morning at breakfast exactly three weeks after he'd first come back to town. He'd been teaching Lonetta Yates's classes for two days now, Lonetta having delivered a healthy nine-pound baby girl on Thursday, and breakfast at the Kitsch 'n' Caboodle Café was his reward to himself for having endured the transition into her classroom. "I've never seen a bunch of gerbera daisies stay fresh so long. You've got the touch like nobody I know."

"Sugar, soda water, and aspirin," Biddy said modestly. "That and snippin' the stems. Anybody could replicate the outcome."

"If anybody could, why aren't they?" Timothy took out his wallet to pay for his meal. "I don't know, Biddy—maybe you ought to think about marketing your method."

Privately he was pretty sure Biddy was replacing the daisies one or two at a time with fresh ones, though he saw no reason to call her on it. The longer that bunch of gerberas lasted, the more time Cleo had to wriggle her way into Bonny's affections—and Timothy still had hopes of some of that affection slopping over onto him. Giving Bonny over to the Almighty didn't mean he'd given up hope. Not by a long shot.

Or maybe it was old Pack Pruitt filling in the daisies, Timothy told himself as he walked down Main Street toward Manny Mo's Variety a few minutes later, hunched against the wind and rain. The coming of March hadn't seen much change in the weather.

Pack might be hoping if the flowers held on long enough—or at least appeared to be holding on—he still had a chance of collecting on his bets. Or at least of saving face with his fellow Kitsch 'n' Caboodlers.

Maybe it was even *Bonny* who was keeping the bouquet fresh…
Yeah, right, he told himself. *When water runs uphill.*
And yet…

Bonny did seem to have lost the angry edge she'd had that first week he'd been back. And the word around town was that she hadn't dated any more guys from the personal ad, including that tax attorney she'd liked well enough to go out with a second time. She wasn't being *overly* friendly toward Timothy, but she'd taken to leaving him notes in the morning before she went to work. Nothing personal—mostly updates on Cleo. In fact, Timothy told himself sternly, Cleo was the *only* reason Bonny might consider slipping fresh flowers into Biddy's bouquet.

Then again…

One day this week she'd actually called him at the house to invite him to stick around and share the beef stew he'd made a couple of weeks earlier. To thank him for the little repairs and household chores he'd been doing while he was there, she said.

They'd had a pleasant if neutral conversation over dinner and had even taken Cleo for an after-dinner walk together.

He knew better than to read anything more than good manners and Christian charity into Bonny's change of disposition, but was he ever grateful for the change! Even if she never learned to love him again—in the way he *wanted* her to love him again, that is—at least she was willing to try to get along. At least she wasn't treating him like less than zero.

And he was being especially careful not to do anything or say anything or even to *look* at Bonny in any way that could be misconstrued as romantic in intention. Not after the way she'd ended that first real conversation. *Don't push your luck,* she'd said. He didn't intend to.

In fact, he'd come to the conclusion that if things were ever going to work out between them again—if he was ever going to inch above zero—slow and easy was going to be the way. Bonny had to be sure, as sure as he was. If they jumped the gun, they could spend the rest of their lives being miserable with each other. She wouldn't have learned to trust him, maybe, and she'd live in fear that he was going to disappear on her again. Or she wouldn't have forgiven him, and she'd keep bringing up his past mistakes, throwing them in his face. Or—

"Yoo-hoo! Timothy Fairley!"

He glanced up and groaned. It was True Marie Weatherby, waving at him from the doorway of the Belle o' the Ball Beauty Salon across the street. Platinum blond and curly-haired in her current incarnation, he noticed. True Marie advertised her salon services by changing the color and style of her hair on a regular basis.

"Don't rush off," the hairdresser called. "I'm between appointments. How about a nice hot cup of coffee to take the chill out of your bones?"

"Hey, True Marie." Timothy waved but stayed on his side of the street. If there was anyone in town he didn't want to talk to, it was

True Marie Weatherby. He could hardly believe he'd managed to stay out of her way an entire three weeks.

True Marie was a menace. Some people swore she was a mind reader. Somehow she could worm information out of a person that said person wouldn't have divulged to God himself, and the next thing said person knew, it was all over Pilchuck. There was enough buzz around town regarding Timothy Fairley without getting True Marie into the thick of things.

"Thanks for the invitation, but I'm in a bit of a rush," he called across the street without slowing his pace. "Maybe some other time." Under his breath, without thinking, he added, "When water runs uphill."

True Marie shouted something else across the street, but he was too far away now to catch it over the wind and rain. Something about somebody's daughter and a mill? That didn't make much sense, but then again—this was True Marie. When it came to gossip, sense didn't enter into the equation.

"…San Diego?" True Marie called.

San Diego what? Was she asking if he'd been living in San Diego? Surely she'd filed away that bit of information within hours of Timothy's arrival back in Pilchuck…

Oh, well. He wasn't about to stand out in the rain, puzzling over the hairdresser's eccentricities. "You got it," he called over his shoulder, waving as he ducked into Manny Mo's.

If he'd been aware of the clicking, grinding, and whirring in True Marie's brain at that very moment, he wouldn't have been so cavalier, of course. In fact, he'd have crossed the street and talked up a blue streak with her.

But how could he possibly have known?

Bonny was feeling the need for an evening devoted to self-nurturing. The day had been horribly hectic—unfortunately without the sales that normally made a hectic day worthwhile. The rain was beginning to wear on everybody, was Bonny's guess; she didn't remember when she'd had so many irascible customers in one day: "Why don't you carry *this?*" "Why do you carry *that?*" "When are you going to start carrying the *other* thing?" She was tired and tense, and her back and shoulders were killing her.

She'd been tempted several times that day to give Timothy a call, to invite him over after work for dinner and a video—mostly because Timothy knew exactly what to do to make her feel better when she was tired and tense and her back and shoulders were killing her.

And that, of course, was also the reason she'd resisted the temptation. It wasn't Timothy's place to take care of her that way anymore. It wasn't her place to ask him—not when she'd made her position as to their places in each other's lives so abundantly clear. On top of which...

It was odd really, after Timothy's vow to crawl over broken glass to get her back, after the pecan caramels and the gerbera daisies, after the moonlight serenade and Leggett Lee and Bearley, after multiple visits to the Blue Moon and an invitation to a candlelit dinner, and especially after the introduction to Cleo the feeling-heart dog...Timothy's efforts to woo her had stopped. Completely. After five days of everything, there had been two weeks—more than two weeks—of nothing.

Isn't that what you wanted?

Well yes...

Isn't that what you asked for?

It was. He was being extremely accommodating.

Or had he just lost interest?

So what if he has? she asked herself irritably. Frankly, Timothy's losing interest would make life easier all around. Was already making life easier all around.

That settled, she dropped by Rainy Day Videos for copies of *What About Bob?* and *Groundhog Day* and *The Man Who Knew Too Little*—her funny bone needing some tickling—and then drove over to the Apple Basket Market to see what she could find in the deli all ready to pop in the oven. A nice hot bath, a nice hot meal, an evening of funny movies, and she was bound to feel better.

It wasn't the same as Timothy's fingers massaging the tension out of her scalp or his strong hands working the knots out of her shoulders or his arms enfolding her as they sat on the floor in front of the television—he propped against the sofa, she propped against his chest—but it would do in a pinch. It would *have* to.

"Yoo-hoo! Bonny Fairley!"

Oh, no. True Marie Weatherby, radar engaged.

Pretending not to hear, Bonny grabbed a basket from the stack by the door and ducked around a corner and down the aisle toward the delicatessen.

True Marie was waiting for her. "You must not have heard me when you came in. Preoccupied by the news, no doubt. Poor dear, it's quite understandable. Timothy Fairley's just full of surprises, isn't he?"

The news? Timothy full of surprises? What was she talking about?

True Marie patted Bonny's arm. "Of course, it stands to reason. If you're not interested—and I can certainly understand why, after what he did to you, dear—then there's nothing for him to do but look elsewhere, is there?" She peered at Bonny. "You *aren't* interested, are you, dear?"

Bonny stared dumbly at True Marie. What was she saying? That Timothy had backed off in his pursuit of her because he was pursuing another woman? That he'd decided she was never going to come around? That he was giving *up* on her?

"One has to wonder though, doesn't one?" True Marie persisted. "About this—*Gwen*, I believe he said her name was. One has to wonder about *Timothy.* Did he bother to tell Gwen that he had an ex-wife as well as a job opportunity back in Pilchuck, Washington? Did he bother to tell her he was going to try to cozy up to his ex-wife? And if so—and now that his ex-wife has turned him down—will she be willing to take him back again?"

Bonny was too shocked at True Marie's words to hide it. She could literally feel the blood drain out of her face. In fact, she felt precariously close to fainting. *Breathe!* she commanded her lungs as she reached for the deli counter. *In, out, in, out, slowly...*

By sheer force of will she stayed on her feet, but there wasn't a thing she could do about her expression. She knew without having to see her reflection that she looked stunned.

It hadn't occurred to her—not even once since Timothy first walked into the Blue Moon—that he might have another woman in his life. A girlfriend! Even an *ex*-girlfriend, who might or might not someday—maybe soon—be an *ex-ex*-girlfriend.

How could she have been so totally boneheaded? When Robin and Rosie and all the female customers who'd been in the Blue Moon that Saturday morning had practically swooned at the sight of him walking in the door with a box of candy and a bunch of gerbera daisies—and without the reasons she'd had to swoon?

"Oh, my dear!" True Marie gasped, her hand fluttering to her chest. "You didn't know! I thought surely by now—but perhaps I'm wrong." Once again she patted Bonny's arm. "Perhaps this—perhaps she's only a friend. I just thought—well, I don't think he meant me to hear, and then when I asked him about her, he was in such a hurry to get away—"

"What exactly did he say about her?" Bonny demanded before she could stop herself.

"She runs a mill, he said. In San Diego. Or maybe it's her daughter who runs the mill."

Bonny wrinkled her brow. "A mill? In San Diego? What kind of mill?"

"I didn't catch the details. He was in an awfully big hurry. But I'm pretty sure he did say it was the daughter who ran the mill. If her daughter runs a mill, she must be quite a bit older than Timothy, mustn't she?" True Marie asked thoughtfully. "Maybe it isn't Gwen. Maybe it's the daughter…"

"For all I care, it could be Gwen's grandmother," Bonny said darkly, though the beauty wearing the hard hat in her imagination was far from the grandmotherly type. Well, Timothy could have her! And she could *certainly* have him. The jerk. The cad. The beast! Announcing to the whole world that he'd crawl over broken glass if that's what it took to get her back—when all the while he was hedging his bets with some female industrial tycoon back in San Diego!

She lifted her chin. "I'm sorry, True Marie, but you'll have to excuse me. I have a lot to do this evening." And she marched straight to the freezer section, where she snatched a pint of mint–chocolate-chip ice cream off the shelf and dropped it in her basket. If she'd had a spoon in her pocket, she would have dug in right then and there.

23

Timothy knew he was in some kind of trouble the minute he opened the front door to the insistent knock. And when he found out what kind of trouble a few minutes later, he felt as if he'd been hit upside the head with a two-by-four, taken a punch to the stomach, and had the rug pulled out from under his feet—all at the same time.

Jack Van Hooten was on the doorstep.

And he didn't look happy.

Big and solid, with thick dark hair and blue eyes, Jack looked as little like his sister as a grizzly bear looked like a tiger—except, at the moment, for the fire in his eyes and the determined set of his chin, which Timothy recognized in a flash as distinctively Van Hooten.

"Got a minute?"

"Uh—sure. Come on in."

"I don't think so." It wasn't a gracious turndown. "This won't take long."

Timothy felt the hair on the back of his neck stand on end. Jack looked about ready to deck him. "What's your problem, Van Hooten?"

"You, Fairley."

"Me!"

"I swear, if you hurt my sister again—"

"Jack. I am not going to hurt Bonny." He tried to keep his voice calm. Getting upset himself wasn't going to help matters—or help him get to the bottom of Jack's fury either. "I've come back to Pilchuck to set things right again, man," he soothed. "Not to hurt anybody."

"Oh yeah? You call getting my sister's hopes up 'setting things right'?"

Getting her hopes up? Did that mean Bonny was softening toward him? "I—"

"You call stringing two women along at the same time 'setting things right'?"

Timothy blinked. "Stringing two women—"

"Because *I* call it unconscionable."

"Wha—"

"Who's going to 'set things right' when you go back to your girl-friend in San Diego, Fairley?"

Timothy's mouth dropped open. "My girlfriend!"

"Who's 'setting things right' for your *girlfriend,* for that matter, while you're 'setting things right' with Bonny?"

"My girlfriend!" Timothy repeated. "What are you talking about?"

"Come on, Fairley. You're not going to try to deny it."

"I most certainly am!"

The look of disgust Jack flashed him was enough to make Timothy's blood boil—and curl his hands into fists. If the guy wasn't Bonny's brother—

"Pilchuck isn't the place for secrets like that, Fairley. You ought to have known someone would find you out."

Timothy deliberately unclenched his fists. The guy *was* Bonny's brother. And there had to be some reason for the outlandish things he was saying. "Jack, listen to me. I don't know what you're talking about. *I don't have a girlfriend*—in San Diego or anywhere else."

"No? Then who's the woman who runs the mill?"

"The woman who runs the mill!" Timothy felt suddenly as if he'd slipped into the *Twilight Zone.* "What mill?"

"You tell me."

Timothy's hands involuntarily curled into fists again. "Look, I don't care what you've heard. *I don't have a girlfriend!*"

"So you lied about this woman? 'Gwen' is just a figment of your sick imagination? What—to make Bonny jealous? You think that's how you're going to get her back?" Jack sounded outraged.

Timothy closed his eyes, took a deep breath, and counted to ten. "Jack, listen to me," he repeated when he opened his eyes again. He had to force himself to stay calm. "I honestly don't know what you're talking about. It probably sounds pathetic for a man of thirty-seven, but Bonny's the only real girlfriend I've ever had. I don't know how or where the girlfriend rumor got started, but that's all it is—a rumor. *A totally false rumor.*"

For the first time, Jack looked unsure. "Bonny said True Marie told her you told her yourself."

Bonny! Oh no. If Bonny thought he had a girlfriend—

He couldn't think about that now. "Look, I haven't spoken to True Marie since I got into town, except to say—"

He stopped. He'd been about to say "except to say hello," but he suddenly remembered the half-heard comment the hairdresser had called across the blustery street earlier today. Maybe she'd said something about a mill after all. And he'd definitely heard her say "San Diego"...

But a *girlfriend* in San Diego? "Gwen"? And what on earth did this crazy *mill* have to do with anything?!

"Jack..." Timothy took a deep breath and said once again, "Listen to me. Who in their right mind would tell True Marie Weatherby anything they wanted to keep a secret? Think about what you're saying, man!"

Jack lifted a hand to massage the back of his neck. He looked even more unsure. "You've got a point there." He dropped his hand and shook his head. "But why would she just invent something like that? Out of thin air?"

"God only knows," Timothy snapped, finally losing his temper. "Maybe it was just a slow news day!"

Jack glared at him. "Weak, Fairley. And the burden of proof's on you, man. If the girlfriend is nothing more than a fabrication, I suggest you straighten it out with True Marie as soon as possible.

Otherwise, you might as well tuck your tail between your legs and run back to San Diego. Before you get run out of town."

Once she'd blown off her steam to Jack and Cait, who'd just happened to be pulling into their driveway the same time she was pulling into hers, Bonny's anger hadn't lasted through even a single scoop of ice cream. For one thing, it was hard to stay mad with a happy soul like Cleo burrowing under her arm as if she couldn't get close enough, gurgling away like a percolator.

There was something wonderful about having a dog around the house, she thought. *This* dog. She was sleeping next to Bonny's bed by now, instead of in the living room. She snored once in a while, but not so much it kept Bonny awake.

Bearley, of course, didn't snore at all—a good thing because Bearley had not only, like Cleo, moved from the living room into Bonny's bedroom, but was sleeping in Bonny's bed. Not that there was any significance to the fact...

She smoothed a hand down Cleo's back, careful to avoid the still-tender spot where the hair was growing back over her stitches. "You know what else, Clee? It's hard to stay mad when there's so much else going on inside me."

She recognized her anger following True Marie's announcement as the same defensive strategy she'd used the entire first week Timothy had been back in town. The double-whammy defense, she told herself wryly: anger and mint–chocolate-chip ice cream.

But alongside the anger this time—or maybe beneath it, if Norman's armchair analysis was as on the money as she thought it was—there lay a slew of other emotions. A *turmoil* of emotions, in fact. Anxiety, tension, nervousness. And excitement, surprisingly—the same little rush of anticipation she'd felt those first few times she'd listened to her personal-ad voice mail.

And then, of all things, jealousy! She never would have guessed it.

"What if he does have a girlfriend, Clee? What if there's someone waiting for him in San Diego?" For a moment, she actually felt sick to her stomach at the thought.

Cleo burrowed farther under Bonny's arm and made the noise she always made when she had something in particular to say—a sort of combination snort-snuffle that ended in a high-pitched whine.

"No, you're right. Timothy wouldn't have made that vow to win me back if he had a commitment to someone else." The sick feeling in the pit of her stomach eased. "I know Timothy. I don't care what True Marie thinks she knows."

"Aaroo," Cleo agreed.

Timothy wouldn't *do* that to her, Bonny told herself. He wouldn't do that to a *girlfriend*. Even during his cigar-store Indian days—even when he'd been so closed she hadn't been able to get a smile out of him—she'd had only a fleeting thought that there might be another woman. There hadn't been. She was certain then, and she was certain now. Infidelity wasn't in his nature.

What in the name of sense and sanity do I know about what's in Timothy's nature? she asked herself, the blood rushing back to her face, her anger rising again along with it. *It wasn't in his nature to leave me either—or so I thought. I don't know a thing about Timothy's nature!*

But once again her anger quickly dissipated. The truth was, as little as Timothy had shared with her those last years of their marriage, she did know him well enough to know he would never string two women along, even to hedge his bets. If he'd been seriously dating Gwen in San Diego, he wouldn't have come back to Pilchuck for Bonny.

She dug her hand in Cleo's fur and absently massaged the loose skin on her back. "It's funny how I know that, Clee, but I do…"

The fundamental things about Timothy's character she *did* know. The things one found out growing up in the same town with a person, going to the same school and the same church. The things one knew from living with a person, whether he talked a lot or not.

"But I'd like to hear what he has to say about Gwen in person. Just who is she? What does she mean to him? What *could* she mean to him if he gave himself a chance with her?"

She'd be a fool to think Timothy had been a hermit the last five years. And as far as having a good friend in San Diego in whom he might or might not be otherwise interested, especially now that he knew Bonny was a practically hopeless case—

"Why wouldn't he?" she asked Cleo, rubbing vigorously at her nose. "Why *shouldn't* he? I don't have any claim on him. Not when I told him he shouldn't expect I'd be able to trust him anytime soon, let alone love him again."

And yet here she was, trusting him over True Marie's evidence to the contrary. Where had that trust come from? Another heaven-sent miracle?

Cleo nudged Bonny's arm, whining sympathetically. Bonny couldn't help but smile. She ran her hands over the dog's long ears and cooed. "Such a sweet thing!" She didn't even try to stop Cleo from lapping at her face. Dog kisses were better than none.

"What am I going to do without you, Clee? When Timothy finds a place to live and takes you away from me?"

"Aaroo," Cleo howled, as mournful as Bonny. Then, unexpectedly, she did her snort-snuffle-whine routine.

Bonny jumped. "Well yes, it's big enough for all three of us…" Her heartbeat quickened. "But it's not so easy as you might think, Clee."

Cleo perked her ears—as much as such a long, limp pair of ears could perk—and repeated her snort-snuffle-whine.

"Because he's not my husband anymore, that's why."

But Cleo wasn't satisfied. She whined again.

Bonny shook her head. "It's not that easy," she said again. "I mean, *I'm* feeling all of a sudden—I don't know why—as if I'd like to…explore the possibilities, shall we say. But *Timothy*…" She sighed. "To tell the truth, I think I've run him off, girl. I think he took me seriously when I told him it was time for both of us to move on. I'm afraid I didn't leave him much room for hope."

"Arf!" said Cleo, pawing the floor.

Again Bonny jumped. She stared at the dog, her heart beating like crazy. "Cleo, the very idea scares the living daylights out of me! But I think you're right. How else is he going to know? How else will he ever give me the same chance he'd give to Gwen? Or anyone else?"

She reached for the phone.

Timothy didn't even bother with dinner. As soon as Jack left, he changed into his running clothes, left a brief note for his parents that dinner was in the pot on the stove, and headed down the driveway. The rain had stopped earlier in the afternoon, but there were plenty of puddles to splash through.

He missed Cleo, but Cleo wasn't completely up to snuff yet. She probably wasn't ready for the kind of run he needed tonight. Besides, he couldn't bear the thought of dropping by Bonny's house to pick up the dog. As mad as Jack was, he couldn't be half as furious as Bonny must be. Where on earth had True Marie come up with her story about a girlfriend in San Diego? She was a notorious gossip, and she did get the facts skewed once in a while, but he didn't remember her ever just making a story up, slow news day or not.

Straighten things out with True Marie, Jack had said. As if he had any control over what anybody thought, let alone said, about him. As if anyone had any control over True Marie. How was he going to straighten it out with True Marie when he didn't know what had set her sideways in the first place?

He ran all the way out to the Pruitt farm and back, stretching his legs out over the road, tuning in to his heartbeat and the air flowing through his lungs and the muscles working, letting go of everything else. His running tonight felt like a prayer. Like the letting-go prayer he'd offered two weeks before, the giving-Bonny-up prayer. Only this time he didn't need words. He just ran. Remarkably, he felt as if the God of the universe was running right along beside him.

By the time he got back to the house, his parents had already gone to bed. His mother had left a note taped to the refrigerator door: *Bonny called. Four times. See you in the morning.*

He slept like the dead. But when he woke up, he was thinking about Bonny, True Marie, and Gwen in San Diego. He was still thinking about them as he followed his nose to the kitchen a half-hour later, drawn irresistibly by the smell of fresh coffee and bacon.

"Morning, Son." Reese greeted him from the table where he sat with a pencil and an open magazine, working out one of his ubiquitous logic puzzles while he waited for breakfast.

"Did you have any dinner last night?" Donnabelle asked from the stove with a touch of motherly worry.

"Hey, Dad. Mom. I had some soup when I came in," he answered his mother's question. "Turned out good, huh?"

"Delicious. But are you all right, dear?"

Timothy poured himself a cup of coffee from the pot on the counter and joined his father at the table. "All right?"

"Well…all the calls from Bonny. And that was a long run last night, Timothy."

"How did she sound?"

"Bonny? I don't know. Anxious to talk to you. Maybe you should give her a call before church."

"Maybe I'll just wait till I see her at church," he said. There was less chance she'd blow up all over him in church, he told himself.

"You need to give Priscilla Wyatt a call sometime today too, by the way," his mother added. "She came by the store yesterday to say her dad's house on Hokanvander Street is going to be available. Pris manages it for him. And she and Simon are dog people—maybe they wouldn't mind Cleo."

"Really?" He brightened. The Cornwell house was only a block off Main Street, right next to Saints and Sinners, and close to the high school. He could walk to work if he wanted to…

"You know you can stay here as long as you want," said Donnabelle.

"I know. Thanks, Mom. But a grown man needs a place of his own."

"Especially if he's planning on courtin' a woman," Reese drawled, glancing up from his puzzle with a twinkle in his eye that surprised Timothy all the way to his bones.

"Speaking of which…" His mother eyed him speculatively. "Who's Gwen?"

Timothy groaned. "Not you, too! Mom, I swear, I have no idea where the whole *idea* of Gwen came from. She doesn't exist. I just don't get it."

He told his parents about his conversation with Jack Van Hooten the night before. "He claims that True Marie Weatherby claims that *I'm* the one who told her I have a girlfriend named Gwen who either runs a mill or has a daughter who runs a mill in San Diego, which is ridiculous on the face of it. A mill? In San Diego? What kind of mill? But the most ridiculous thing is that I've barely said more than hello-and-how-are-you to the big blabbermouth since I got into town!"

"Now, Timothy," Donnabelle gently reproved. "You needn't be unkind. True Marie just likes to feel involved in things, is all. I'm sure she'd feel awful if she knew she was causing anyone hard feelings."

"Ha!" said Reese, once again surprising Timothy. "True Marie Weatherby feel bad about dishing dirt? When water runs uphill," he said cynically.

Timothy jumped. *When water runs uphill…*

It was Reese's saying, and Timothy's Grandfather Fairley's saying before that, and who knew how many generations before *that*.

Now it was Timothy's saying: *Yeah, right. When water runs uphill…*

"Did I say that to True Marie?" he mused aloud.

His mother set a plate of pancakes on the table. "What, dear?"

"I did! I mean, I didn't, not to her face, but…"

When water runs uphill. Hill, mill. Water, daughter. When…

"No."

Donnabelle drew up a chair to the table. "*What*, dear?"

"When, Gwen! When water runs uphill… *Gwen's daughter runs a mill!*"

Reese scratched his head. Donnabelle frowned.

"I can't believe—True Marie—" Timothy sputtered.

"*What?*" his mother demanded.

He shook his head in wonder. "The woman doesn't read minds after all—she reads lips!" No wonder she knew everything in town—everything and then some.

"In San Diego?" she'd called across the street.

"You got it!" he'd replied. And there she had it. Right from the horse's mouth. Reese, once Timothy explained, thought it was the funniest thing he'd ever heard in all his life. He howled. He laughed so hard the tears streamed down his face.

Timothy would have thoroughly enjoyed his father's unaccustomed hilarity if he hadn't been so worried. How in the world was he going to set Pilchuck straight on the matter? Because there wasn't a question in his mind that the entire town had heard about 'Gwen' by now.

And if Pilchuck thought Timothy had a girlfriend in San Diego, Pilchuck was not going to let him get near Bonny. Not after last time. All that warming up to him the Kitsch 'n' Caboodlers had been doing over the last few weeks would be for nothing if they thought he was two-timing Bonny. He wouldn't even get a chance to set the record straight with her.

"True Marie's the one you have to set straight." Donnabelle echoed Jack's advice from the night before, though in a much friendlier tone. "She'll take care of the rest of the town. But I'd suggest you tread lightly, Timothy. She prides herself on the accuracy of her intelligence.

"Intelligence?" Reese guffawed. "Belle, I know you don't like to be negative—but *intelligence!*" And he was off on another gale of laughter.

As funny as the whole thing might have been to Reese, Timothy couldn't get into the spirit. "What if True Marie thinks I deliberately misled her? Knowing she'd tell Bonny?" he fretted. "What if she thinks the same thing Jack does—that I made up Gwen to make

Bonny jealous?" He dropped his head in his hands, groaning. "I'm *toast* in this town."

"Of course you're not, dear," his mother soothed. "Although if True Marie *does* think you deliberately misled her…"

She didn't finish the thought. She didn't have to.

"Wait." Reese, his laughter finally under control, swiped at his eyes with his napkin. "I have an idea…"

It was a good one too. At least Timothy thought it was; he could only hope that True Marie was as gullible as his father believed she was.

24

After her four failed attempts to reach Timothy on Saturday night, Bonny finally got through to him Sunday morning. Cleo had suggested not only that she talk to Timothy about wanting to "explore the possibilities" of a renewed relationship, but that she do it in style. A home-cooked meal: meatloaf, mashed potatoes and gravy, green bean casserole—not very elegant, but all of Timothy's favorites. Cole Porter in the background and tulips on the table—Timothy's favorites again. Candlelight. He'd always loved the way she looked in candlelight.

"You want me to come to dinner?" Timothy asked. He didn't sound just surprised; he sounded astonished.

"Tomorrow at six." She didn't give him the details, of course. Wouldn't he be floored! For once she'd take the whole day off, or at least the afternoon. She'd make sure everything was perfect—the house, the meal, herself...

She had that orchid-colored angora sweater she'd bought at an after-Christmas sale at Strawbridge & Fitz in Seattle and hadn't yet had a chance to wear. It had cost her a small fortune even at forty percent off. But Timothy had always loved her in that color—not that she'd been thinking about Timothy when she bought it.

He liked her in snug jeans, too. The sweater would look great with blue jeans. And maybe she'd even take the time to paint her nails.

"Well, yeah," Timothy said. "I'd like that. But Bonny..."

"Hmm?"

"There wasn't...anything you wanted to ask me? Like about—Gwen?"

"We'll talk about Gwen tomorrow," she said. If they ever got around to it. If Gwen even came to Timothy's mind while he was sitting across the table from Bonny Fidelia Van Hooten Fairley illuminated by candlelight.

The twins called right after she hung up with Timothy—both of them, on different phones at the same time—to invite her over for a breakfast of waffles with blueberries and whipped cream.

"We heard about Timothy's girlfriend," Robin sympathized.

"Whoever would have believed it?" Rosie added. "Maybe you should check out those *Tillicum Weekly* guys you never got to, Bon-Bon."

"At least Jack gave it to him *but good* last night. Or so he says."

"Gave it to him but good? Timothy? What's that supposed to mean?"

"Come on over and ask him yourself, Boss-Lady. Eight o'clock sharp."

"Earlier if you can," Rosie added. "Coffee's already on."

Bonny was ready in record time; she wanted to hear about Jack giving it to Timothy *but good*. Could Jack be the reason Timothy had seemed so hesitant about accepting her dinner invitation?

"Oh, Jack! You didn't!" she told her brother when he related the story of last night's encounter with Timothy.

Jack looked surprised. "What's wrong? You were so upset about Gwen last night, I figured somebody should deal with him."

"But five minutes after I talked to you I realized Timothy would never have done that to me. Two-timed me, I mean. Or anyone else."

"Well you didn't tell me," Jack grumped. "I was just trying to do something nice for you."

"Poor guy," Bonny mused. "No wonder he went out on a three-hour run last night."

"People do call him a running fool," Cait said mildly. "So you believe him, Bonny? That there isn't a Gwen, I mean?"

"If Timothy says it, I believe it."

Cait raised her eyebrows. "This is a change."

"I know. Weird, isn't it? But I just have the strongest sense about him, Cait. He's a good man. He always was. He made some mistakes—but who hasn't?"

"Wow," said Robin. "I can hardly believe it's you!"

"Maybe it's not," said Rosie. "Maybe an alien's taken over her body."

"Very funny," said Bonny. But the buoyancy she was feeling was certainly alien—at least to her experience in recent years.

There wasn't a Gwen! She was sure of it.

And after tomorrow night, there wouldn't be anyone but Bonny.

Donnabelle was the one who got True Marie into the fountain at Fairley's later that afternoon—called her up at home and told her she'd won a Fairley's Famous Banana Fudge Royale in the weekly business card drawing, but she had to redeem it this afternoon. Could she come in?

"I don't remember entering any drawing," True Marie said as she slid onto a stool at the counter not half an hour after Donnabelle's call, "but I'm not about to turn down a free Banana Fudge Royale. Bring it on, Donnabelle!"

Timothy, meanwhile, sat at the other end of the counter with a pad of paper and a pen, alternately studying his notes with a concentrated frown and writing furiously.

"Miriam's mother sells cars," he muttered. "Julia has red hair. Jan lives in Albuquerque."

"Timothy! I didn't see you sitting there! What's this about Albuquerque?" True Marie called down the counter.

"The favorite food of the daughter of the woman who lives in Seattle is lasagna," he continued to mutter, pretending he hadn't heard the hairdresser. "Gwen lives in San Diego, and her daughter runs a mill—"

"Timothy," his mother interrupted, "True Marie's speaking to you, dear."

"Oh!" He looked up from his notes with what he hoped was a startled expression. "Good afternoon, True Marie. I'm sorry—I get so involved in these logic problems I forget myself."

"Logic problems?"

He slid his notebook down the counter, where it landed right in front of True Marie, and changed stools to sit next to her.

"I've been working on this one since yesterday morning," he said. "Found it in one of dad's puzzle magazines."

True Marie picked up the notebook and squinted at it. She needed reading glasses but—everyone said—she was too vain to wear them. "Gwen, Jan, Susan, Miriam, Julia, Natasha," she read the list of names aloud.

"Three mothers," Timothy explained. "Three daughters. Each one lives in a different city, has a different color of hair and a different favorite food, and works at a different job."

"Lasagna," True Marie read. "Chocolate cake, T-bone steak, gardenburgers. Cobb salad. Corn on the cob."

"You get a certain number of clues," Timothy went on. "Supposedly enough to figure out what daughter belongs to which mother, where they all live, who has what job, who likes what kind of food."

"And who has what color hair," True Marie reminded him.

"Right."

Donnabelle set a large banana split in front of the hairdresser. "Timothy? Anything more for you?"

"Thanks, Mom—just a refill on the coffee."

True Marie took a big bite of vanilla ice cream with strawberry sauce.

"Gwen lives in San Diego," Timothy pointed out, just to emphasize the information he most wanted to pass on to True Marie. "So I put a star here on the grid where Gwen and San Diego intersect, and I crossed off San Diego for all the other women."

"Mmm," said True Marie—whether in response to his explanation, the mention of Gwen, or the Banana Fudge Royale Timothy couldn't tell.

"Same for Jan and Albuquerque," Timothy added.

"And Julia and red hair," said True Marie, reaching for another bite.

"It gets a little trickier when you get into things like Gwen's daughter running a mill," said Timothy. "Who *is* Gwen's daughter?"

"Not the woman whose favorite food is lasagna," True Marie said, frowning at the notebook. "Her mother lives in Seattle."

"Exactly!" Timothy said.

"The woman who sells cars has a daughter who's a waitress." True Marie read one of the clues over his shoulder before popping another spoonful of ice cream into her mouth.

"So Miriam is a waitress," Timothy pointed out, "which means she can't be Gwen's daughter, and I can cross her off my list...*here*." And he drew a large *X* through one of the boxes.

By the time True Marie was finished with her banana split, every box on Timothy's grid had been filled in either with an *X* or a star— and True Marie was convinced she had a gift for logic.

"I should have known Julia was Natasha's mother," she said triumphantly as she filled in the final block with a star. Timothy had long since relinquished the pencil.

"Oh?" he asked, his interest entirely unfeigned. True Marie truly did have a fascinating mind. "Why's that?"

"She's a redhead," the hairdresser said, as if that explained everything. Timothy's expression must have been blank. His mind certainly was.

"A redhead would name her daughter something dramatic like Natasha," she explained patiently. "Can you imagine a redhead naming her daughter Miriam?"

"I get your point," said Timothy.

He only hoped True Marie got his.

Bonny stared across the counter at Cait in disbelief. "You mean Gwen was just a name in a logic problem?"

Cait grinned. "I mean to tell you! Gwen and her daughter and that mill in San Diego. True Marie's been trumpeting the story all over town—and not even minding the razzing everyone's giving her for getting the story wrong in the first place. She thinks she's the cat's pajamas, Bonny—she has a gift for logic!"

Bonny heard the whole story over dinner the following evening. Gwen hadn't been *just* a logic problem after all. She laughed till the tears ran down her cheeks at Timothy's story of True Marie's lipreading. And my, did it feel good to laugh!

"You can't tell a soul," Timothy warned her. "If True Marie ever found out…"

"Not even Cait?"

"Not a *soul.*"

"My lips are sealed," she vowed. To tell the truth, she liked the idea of sharing a secret with Timothy. He'd had so many secrets he'd kept to himself in the past that sharing this little one, the first in many years, felt especially significant. "Gwen and her daughter and the mill in San Diego go with me to the grave."

They laughed a lot over dinner. She couldn't have said about what—they just did. Laughed and talked and even quoted poetry once—a three-liner Bonny had written in college and Timothy still remembered:

> *General Botany*
> *has won the war—*
> *I surrender.*

Cleo, who spent the evening lying on the floor between their chairs, her eyes hopping back and forth between them, seemed to find the lines especially amusing. Bonny swore sometimes her gurgle sounded exactly like a giggle.

It was a magical evening all around. Even without Bonny's string of disappointing *Tillicum Weekly* dates in February to compare it to, it would have felt magical. There was all the comfort, she told herself at one point as she refilled Timothy's glass with sparkling cider, of being with someone she knew like she knew her own heart—along with all the anticipation and excitement and newness of getting to know a stranger. A very attractive stranger. As she already knew, she and Timothy had chemistry in spades.

He was so appreciative of the efforts she'd made to please him too, from the food to the flowers and music to her appearance. "I've always remembered the way you glow by candlelight," he told her, raising his glass in salute. "Like you're lit up from inside…"

She wiggled her stockinged toes under Cleo's tummy, grinning. "He used to call me his little jack-o'-lantern, Clee."

Timothy laughed. "Not for long, I didn't. You got all riled up about it. Jack-o'-lanterns were short and squat, you said."

"And associated with witches."

"And associated with witches," he agreed. "Which had nothing to do with anything…"

The past came up often in their conversation, although not the last few years of their marriage, not the divorce—they seemed to have made a tacit agreement to keep things light tonight. Instead they resurrected older memories—good-time memories.

And they had so many to choose from! So many good times, so much laughter, so much love…

"Think how much more fun we could have had with a dog," said Timothy.

"Arf!" Cleo agreed.

Bonny shook her head. "I tried to tell you…"

"I know, I know. All I could see was more responsibility."

"As if fun and responsibility were mutually exclusive."

"For me they were." He sighed. "I could have learned from you they didn't have to be. But did I?"

"We can only learn what we're ready to learn," Bonny philosophized. But then she narrowed her eyes at him. "So what took you so long to get ready?!"

Now it was Timothy wriggling his stockinged toes under Cleo's tummy. "Does she talk to you this way too, girl?" he asked, pretending injury.

"Aaroo!"

"Clee's a wonderful audience, isn't she?" Bonny said later, leaning against the sofa in the living room with a cup of Evening Delight herbal tea. Cleo was curled on the floor between her and Timothy, one front leg crossed over the other, her chin resting on it, her eyes once again hopping between them as they talked.

"The best." Timothy ruffled the fur between her ears. "I don't know how I can thank you enough for keeping her for me, Bonny. I know it wouldn't have been your first choice, under the circumstances."

"She's been *such* a burden."

"Yeah? Well, you'll be happy to know she'll be out of your hair in less than two weeks. Think you can put up with her that much longer?"

Bonny's heart jumped. "Two weeks? Timothy, I was teasing about her being a burden. You're kidding, right?"

"Nope. But we'll be close. The old Cornwell place on Hokanvander. You can come visit us anytime you like."

Bonny looked down at Cleo. Cleo looked up at Bonny, raised her head, and snort-snuffle-whined—reminding her of their conversation on Saturday.

"Timothy…" Bonny laid her hand on Cleo's back for fortification, took a deep breath, and plunged in. "I've been thinking…"

"Now there's a concept," he teased. "What about?"

Her heart must have been beating a hundred miles a minute. Why did this feel like the scariest thing she'd ever done in her entire life?

After all, she knew Timothy wanted her back. She knew that's why he'd come home to Pilchuck—not for Lonetta's job, not because he missed the rain, not for the Balder-to-Bellingrath. For Bonny.

All she had to say—just as she'd told Cleo—was, "I'd really like to explore the possibilities between us, Timothy…"

"Bonny?"

She looked in his eyes. She took a deep breath.

"Let's get married again."

She gasped.

It wasn't Timothy who'd said the words. She'd said them herself.

It was the hardest thing Timothy had ever done in his entire life—turning down his ex-wife's proposal of marriage.

Maybe if she hadn't looked so stunned when she realized what she'd said, he wouldn't have been able to tell her no. Or maybe if Cleo hadn't leaped up between them at just that moment with a loud bark, breaking the mood...

But he did say no. He had to.

"I love you, Bonny. But just two weeks ago you told me you hadn't forgiven me, you didn't know if you could ever trust me again, you doubted you could love me. I can't say yes to marriage until I know you want it as much as I do.

"I can't say yes until I know that you forgive me. And trust me. And most of all—that you love me with all your heart."

25

The twins breezed into the Blue Moon early the following afternoon to report that Bonny's marriage proposal was the talk of the Kitsch 'n' Caboodle—which really was no surprise, as Biddy Barton was Cindy Fitz's boss, and Cindy was Cait Van Hooten's daughter, and Cait was Bonny's best friend and sister-in-law. And Bonny hadn't specifically *told* Cait not to pass the information along.

"Cindy says old Pack Pruitt was gloating all over the place to hear you'd begged Timothy back just like he said you would," Robin told Bonny.

"Till Biddy pointed out, number one," Rosie said, "that a marriage proposal is solemn, dignified, and nothing *like* begging—"

"—and number two," Robin took over, "even if the proposal could be construed as begging, old Pack's wager wasn't just that you'd beg Timothy back, but that you'd beg him back before the last bloom on his bouquet of flowers gave up the ghost."

"Those daisies haven't drooped in practically a month," Bonny said glumly. "So I guess the old man had reason to gloat after all."

"Nope. The daisies were dead, Bon-Bon!"

"Dead!"

"When just last night they were fresh as the day Timothy Fairley walked in here with 'em!"

"We know that for a fact," added Robin. "Last night we took Narcissa by for a bowl of Biddy's apple betty for her birthday. We saw them."

"But Biddy says you can reinvigorate cut flowers only so long," said Rosie, "no matter what kind of diet you put 'em on. And they'd just overnight happened to reach their 'so long.' Old Pack was mad as a hornet, Cindy said."

Good for Biddy! Bonny thought, feeling more cheerful than she had since Timothy'd turned her down. So it was Biddy all along, replacing the daisies in the bouquet in order to give her and Cleo— and Timothy—more time. And saving the dead ones just to make sure Packard Pruitt got his comeuppance...

Unfortunately, Pack's comeuppance was the only bright spot in the whole affair. Timothy didn't believe she really loved him—didn't believe *she* loved *him*, of all things!—and in two weeks' time she was losing Cleo.

She sighed. Wasn't this just exactly the reason she'd balked at taking Cleo in—knowing she'd eventually have to say good-bye? But she'd gone and let herself get attached to the mutt, and now Cleo was leaving, and the house was going to feel as empty as it had ever felt before.

Or at least as empty as it had felt since Timothy Fairley left town.

Timothy, for his part, when he got the news about the sudden demise of Biddy's seemingly invincible daisies—he was in the checkout line at the Apple Basket Market at the time—hustled right over to Buds 'n' Blossoms, where he discovered that yes, Biddy Barton had been buying gerberas two and three at a time every day for the last three weeks or so, and yes, they did have in a fresh supply...

He ordered another large bouquet, which he delivered personally to the Kitsch 'n' Caboodle Café. "Thank you," he told Biddy fervently as he handed them across the counter.

"Don't know what you've got to be thankin' me for, but I do thank you, Timothy Fairley. Gives me another chance to work on the reinvigoratin' formula." She leaned toward him, adjusting her cat's-eye glasses, and said confidentially, "I'm thinkin' of addin' a little bleach to the solution. Hear it keeps the bacteria at bay."

Timothy grinned. "I think you missed your calling, Biddy. You've got the makings of a fine research scientist."

Biddy liked that almost as much as True Marie Weatherby had liked finding out she had a gift for logic.

"Oh, and by the way"—she leaned even closer—"I think you're handlin' Bonny just right. You make her want you, Timothy. Women been doin' that for years."

"Biddy! I'm not trying to manipulate—"

"Did I say anything about manipulate?" she interrupted, her voice suddenly fierce. "You implyin' that's what women do?"

"Never," he soothed, thinking better of trying to explain himself. Some battles a man couldn't win.

He'd given his parents the scoop on Bonny last night after he'd come home, figuring they'd be better off hearing it from him than through the Pilchuck pipeline. They were both as shocked as Timothy himself was that he'd turned Bonny down. Or at least his mother was. You could never tell with Reese.

"It isn't time," he'd said to Donnabelle. "She isn't ready—any more than I was ready to come home until I did."

"Let's hope she's a little quicker on the uptake than you were, dear. Your father and I would like a grandchild or two before we get too old to enjoy them."

She had a point. Reese and Donnabelle were both close to sixty, Timothy was going to be thirty-eight this year, and Bonny was only two years younger.

"I want it to be right this time, Mom. For both of us. In every way."

"I know you do. I'm proud of you, dear. So…when are you seeing her again?"

"Maybe Sunday."

"Sunday!"

"I'm a busy man, Mom," he defended himself. "Lessons to plan, papers to grade, experiments to set up…"

But Bonny didn't let him forget her—as if he could have.

Wednesday, during his second-period chemistry lab—much to

his embarrassment and his students' delight—he got a delivery of fresh tulips.

Thursday, when he checked his mailbox in the teacher's lounge, he found a can of Almond Roca wrapped in sixteenth-century blue moons.

Friday, late at night after he'd gone to bed, he got a serenade. Bonny and Cleo in two-part harmony—if you could call it that: "Won't you come home, Tim Fairley? Won't you come home?"

Saturday, in the mail, he got a Polaroid snapshot of Bearley propped up against the pillows on Bonny's bed. The note that came with the photo read:

Bearley has a home. So does your heart. Please give "us" a chance.

Sunday morning and Sunday evening, he and Bonny sat together in church—he wasn't even sure whose idea it was or how it happened. After the evening service she invited him home for coffee. He preferred the Kitsch 'n' Caboodle, he said. She acquiesced.

He walked her home in the moonlight. She lifted her face for a kiss. He swallowed, took a deep breath, and pressed his lips against her forehead.

It took her another two weeks—after he'd moved out of his parents' house and into the Cornwell place with Cleo—to convince him that he really should try out her lips.

That kiss was almost his undoing.

And it took her another two weeks to convince him they ought to start dating "officially"—though he didn't know how much more official they could get than being the talk of the Kitsch 'n' Caboodle Café.

But in the end, it took Bonny crawling over broken glass to convince Timothy she really, truly loved him with all her heart.

Patience had never been one of Bonny's strong points. Yes, the two months she and Timothy had been officially dating had flown by in some ways; "time flies when you're having fun" was more than just an old saw. The times they were *together* flew, anyhow.

The times she and Timothy were apart, on the other hand—especially the hours that stretched between the time the gallery closed in the early evening and reopened the following day—dragged like the night before Christmas dragged for a kid. Bearley, sweet and soft as he was, just didn't do the trick. Cleo would have helped, but Cleo was currently on the other side of town. Timothy, who was helping out with both the track-and-field and cross-country teams at the high school, was out of town for meets more weeknights than not.

The only way they were ever going to see more of each other—let alone enjoy each other in all the ways they'd enjoyed each other as husband and wife in the past—was to live together. In the same house. Her house. *Their* house. Married, of course. Neither she nor Timothy would have it any other way.

It was ridiculous, Bonny told herself irritably as she pulled into the parking lot at Pilchuck High. Timothy playing coy with her when he knew she knew he loved her and he knew she loved him—

He had to know by now, didn't he? What more could she do to prove it to him?

Nothing.

She sighed. She and Cait had had this very conversation just last night. Cait hadn't given her advice, exactly, but she had suggested that really, when it came right down to it, other people's responses were entirely outside one's control. "Look at your change of heart regarding Timothy," her friend had reminded her. "One day you're kicking the poor guy out of your store, the next you're asking him to marry you. Now where do you think *that* came from?"

"You're right, Cait. My change of heart was an out-and-out miracle."

Bonny closed her eyes and briefly bowed her head over the steering wheel. *Okay, God. All I can do is love him. You do the rest.*

I will.

She climbed the stairs to the front entrance of the old brick high school building with a spring to her step that hadn't been there when she'd walked to her car that morning. Amazing how quickly a few words with the Almighty could adjust an attitude.

She'd taken to dropping by Timothy's classroom for a few minutes before school every day just to say hello. Most days it was the only time she saw him. Besides, she liked to see him in his "native environment." And remind him, if he should need reminding—and sometimes after a particularly harrowing day or a late night grading papers, he did need reminding—that teaching really was the work he wanted to pour his life into.

The building was quiet, though she did pass a couple of students at their lockers and greeted several teachers as she made her way down the hall, around the corner, out the double doors to a breezeway, and through another set of doors into a concrete building that had always been known affectionately as the Boonies. The ag and science classes had been in the Boonies as far back as she could remember, the chemistry lab downstairs in the basement. "Back of beyond," Lonetta had told Timothy, "so we don't stink up the entire school with our malodorous experiments."

The door to the lab was closed, but Bonny could see through the wire-reinforced safety glass of the window that Timothy wasn't alone this morning. Two boys straddled stools at one of the tables, their backs to her, engrossed in something. Doing a makeup lab, probably. School didn't start for another forty-five minutes, but as a teacher Bonny had often arranged for students to come in for makeup work in the mornings while she graded papers or did last-minute prepping.

Timothy sat on a stool at the demonstration table at the front of the room, pen in hand, his head bent over a stack of papers. It was nearing the end of the school year, when papers tended to stack up. Bonny felt a rush of tenderness as he lifted a hand and ran it through his hair in that unconscious gesture she found so oddly endearing.

She pushed the heavy door open, then closed it quietly behind her so as not to disturb the boys working at the table. Timothy looked up at the soft click of the latch, his mouth lifting in a crooked smile when he saw her. Bonny knew from experience the image would warm her the rest of the day.

Then, suddenly, the room exploded. Or at least it seemed to explode. A crash, the sound of breaking glass, a huge billow of purple smoke—

"Timothy!"

"Bonny! Get out of here!" he bellowed. Another crash, and so much nose-stinging, eye-watering purple smoke she couldn't even see across the room.

Out of there? As if!

She plunged into the acrid fog without another thought, automatically dropping to her hands and knees where the air was still clear as the smoke alarm started shrieking. Timothy! Where was he? Where had those boys been sitting? That's where Timothy would be—he'd have jumped immediately to his students' rescue, not even thinking about his own safety—

He was going to die.

No. He couldn't die!

She saw him just then, through the legs of the stools and tables, on his hands and knees as she was and, just as she'd known, scrambling straight toward the source of the purple smoke instead of away from it.

Her heart constricted. If she couldn't save him, *she* was going to die—

Either from trying, or from the broken heart he'd leave behind.

"Timothy!" she thundered, crawling around a table toward him. "Don't you dare leave me again!"

At which point—only seconds after the explosion, though it seemed an eternity—the automatic sprinklers in the ceiling came to life, raining water over the classroom. At the same time Bonny's hand came down hard on something sharp.

"Ow!"

She jerked her hand off the floor and found a shard of glass jabbing into the heel of her hand, blood trickling from the wound. Through the water streaming off her head she saw that pieces of broken glass were strewn across the floor in front of her.

"Bonny, get out of here!" Timothy shouted again.

The next few minutes were a complete confusion in her mind. By the time it was over, the room looked as if a hurricane had blown through it. And the four of them—Bonny, Timothy, and the two boys Timothy should never have left on their own even though they were among his best and brightest students—looked and sounded like coughing, wheezing, half-drowned rats, though otherwise they'd all escaped relatively unscathed.

Fortunately, the "explosion" turned out to be more purple smoke than anything else. The crash Bonny had heard was stools overturning as the boys leaped away from their experiment-gone-bad, the breaking glass was a tray of beakers one of them had accidentally swept to the floor, and the second crash was Timothy tripping over furniture as he leaped to the rescue, not knowing exactly what his budding scientists had wrought.

As a swarm of volunteer firemen took over in the chem lab, Timothy discovered the gash on Bonny's hand. And practically went into hysterics over it, for pity's sake.

"It's no big deal, Timothy—"

"Medic!"

There wasn't a medic, of course, but Timothy managed to rustle up a first-aid kit and bandaged her hand so thoroughly she looked as if she'd broken her wrist instead of having suffered a minor cut.

"What on earth were you thinking, Bonny?" he groaned. "Didn't you hear me yell for you to get out of there?"

"And leave you to suffocate? Or burn to death? Or drown?"

"It could have been something a whole lot worse than it was—"

"Precisely. And who would have been there to rescue you after you rescued those boys? No one, that's who. Just me."

"But you could have been hurt. You could have been killed!"
Bonny thrust out her chin. "So could you. And I wasn't about to
let you get away with it!"

Timothy couldn't help but laugh. Wasn't that just like Bonny? Stubborn, prickly, and as hotheaded as redheads came. Or was that tenacious, courageous, and passionate?

He wrapped his arms around her and held her as if he'd never let
her go. But it wasn't till an hour later, after they'd both been interviewed by the police chief and the fire chief and the superintendent
of schools and the editor of the *Pilchuck Post*, that he took her bandaged hand in his, gazed tenderly into her eyes, and said with as
much sincerity as he'd ever said anything:

"Bonny—sweetheart—I've always wanted a woman who would
crawl over broken glass for me. What d'you say we get married sometime soon?"

It was just like her to faint on him. *Then.* After having just committed the single bravest act of her life thus far—unless one counted
her own marriage proposal. That, she told him later, had been just as
instinctive as plunging into the purple fog to rescue him—and even
scarier.

The last Saturday in June, Timothy, Jack, Simon, and Harrison Hunt
won the Balder-to-Bellingrath, Timothy having done his personal
best on the mountain leg of the cross-country relay. Cleo had run the
whole way with him.

The last *Sunday* in June, Bonny closed the Blue Moon Gallery of
Fine Crafts for the day and left a note on the door inviting anyone she
might have inadvertently missed to the nuptials at the gazebo in historic Homesteader Park, where, for the second time in a dozen years,
Pastor Montgomery Bob performed the ceremony uniting Bonny
Fidelia Van Hooten and Timothy Reese Fairley in holy matrimony.

Bonny, wearing a tea-length gown of ivory chiffon over orchid-colored taffeta—a Cindy Fitz and Cait Van Hooten original—carried a bouquet of rainbow-hued gerbera daisies. The very same bouquet, in fact, that Timothy had personally delivered to Biddy at the Kitsch 'n' Caboodle Café more than three months earlier. Or at least Biddy claimed it was the same bouquet. Adding bleach to her reinvigorating solution had done the trick, she said.

Cait Van Hooten was Bonny's maid of honor, of course, and Jack Van Hooten stood in as Timothy's best man. And Cleo, with a daisy chain of gerberas around her neck, made a huge splash as flower dog. Especially when she raced through the fountain pool during the picnic reception in pursuit of Gordie Wyatt and his mutt, Woof, whom Gordie had sneaked to the wedding in the back of the family minivan.

Mickey and Hubbard Van Hooten were back in Pilchuck for the second time in six months to see the second of their two children married for the second time—and just as pleased to see Bonny back with Timothy as they'd been to see Jack marry his childhood friend Cait Anderson.

Donnabelle Fairley, typically, cried buckets.

Reese Fairley, untypically, beamed.

Near the end of the celebration, when Bonny tossed the bridal bouquet over her shoulder, it landed neatly in an astonished Olga Pfefferkuchen's lap—despite the twins' attempts to nab it. While Carl Peabody and Nella Norland of the *Pilchuck Post* were concentrating on Olga—snapping photos and garnering quotes—Timothy quietly pulled from behind his back the white daisy that had earlier been at the bouquet's center.

"This one's for you, sweetheart."

Bonny stared at the flower in his hand and rubbed nervously at her nose, knowing what he wanted her to do. But plucking a daisy's petals seemed a risky business on her wedding day. What if the loves-me-loves-me-nots came out wrong? Ending up on a loves-me-not wouldn't exactly be an auspicious sign. Not after all they'd been through already.

"Go on," Timothy urged her.

Reluctantly, she took the flower and pulled off a petal, watching as it drifted to the ground. "He loves me." Another. "He loves me not." She took a deep breath and began plucking petals with abandon. "He loves me, he loves me not, he loves me, he loves me not…"

And as she pulled the last one from the daisy, triumphantly, "He loves me!"

Timothy wrapped his arms around her and pulled her so close she thought she was going to melt right into his skin. "He most certainly does," he murmured against her ear. "Always. Forever. Amen."

"Seal it with a kiss?" Bonny invited, flirting outrageously.

He didn't need any other encouragement.

Neither did Carl Peabody and Nella Norland. The caption under the picture in the following week's edition of the *Pilchuck Post* read, *Love Is Always Sweeter the Second Time Around.*

Postscript

And so, Gentle Reader, an old, dusty, once-upon-a-time romance was by the grace of Almighty God resurrected. Renewed. In Biddy Barton's lexicon, *reinvigorated*. And except for the complications occasioned by Cleo's undying belief that she was human, little Natasha's explosive temper, and little Leggett's propensity for running away...

THEY LIVED HAPPILY EVER AFTER!

If you enjoyed *LOVES ME, LOVES ME NOT*,
be sure to ask for, or order, Barbara Jean Hicks's
An Unlikely Prince and *All That Glitters*
at your local bookstore.

∽

AN UNLIKELY PRINCE

Suzie Wyatt's dream of running her own day-care center comes true.
But her neighbors—handsome Harrison Hunt and crotchety Mrs.
Pfefferkuchen—are horrified by the prospect of having seven children around. Suzie and her charges endear themselves to Harrison,
who captures Suzie's heart. But when she discovers he's joined forces
with Mrs. Pfefferkuchen to close her doors, can she forgive her
Unlikely Prince? (ISBN 1-57856-122-1; Available now)

ALL THAT GLITTERS

After seven years of waiting tables in tiny Pilchuck, Washington,
aspiring apparel designer Cindy Reilly is starting to despair that she'll
ever see a line of evening dresses with her name on them. And when
her longtime boyfriend falls for a classy big city society girl, her future
looks even bleaker. Cindy embarks on a campaign to win back her
boyfriend, and Franklin Cameron Fitz III—a department store
heir—reluctantly agrees to help. But when both "princes" fall at
Cindy's feet, will she choose the right one? (ISBN 1-57856-123-X;
Available now)

Also ask for Barbara Jean Hicks's novella,
"Twice in a Blue Moon" in the best-selling
PORCH SWINGS & PICKET FENCES!
(ISBN 1-57856-226-0; Available now)

Printed in the United States
by Baker & Taylor Publisher Services